The Last Heir of Re'Vall

KAREN THROWER

This is a work of fiction. Names, characters, places, and incidents are products of the author's imagination or are used fictitiously and are not to be construed as real. Any resemblance to actual events, locations, organizations, or persons, living or dead, is entirely coincidental.

World Castle Publishing, LLC
Pensacola, Florida
Copyright © 2025 Karen Thrower
Hardback ISBN: 9798310941540
Paperback ISBN: 9798891263505
eBook ISBN: 9798891263512
First Edition World Castle Publishing, LLC, March 11, 2025
http://www.worldcastlepublishing.com

Licensing Notes

Cover: Cover Designs by Karen
Editor: Karen Fuller

To my friends, this wouldn't be possible without you.

CHAPTER 1
L.G.R. AND FRIENDS

When the carriage pulled up to the palace in the capital city of Ardenry, Mother Lily Marcel saw several people waiting for her on the grand marble steps. An older gentleman in a nice, black tunic quickly opened the door, and a young woman with short dark hair walked up to the carriage, all business. She was wearing a long, black skirt with a white apron and matching shirt.

"Mother Lily Marcel?" She managed a smile at hearing her late husband's surname and nodded her head.

"Yes."

"I'm Jas. The prince has given me the task of taking care of you while you're here in the palace. The pages should take care of the rest of your things." Lily held up her worn travel bag. She supposed she could have gotten a new one, but this one held a lot of memories and, more importantly, had no holes.

"This is it." Jas's eyes widened in confusion, and Lily noticed her head tilt and peeked into the carriage.

"Really?"

She chuckled, "I don't need much. Otto provides what I can't carry myself."

The young woman nodded and looked impressed. "All right then. If you'll follow me, I'll show you to your room."

"Thank you, Jas." She followed the girl up the grand steps and into the palace. It looked the same as it did the other day when she met with Prince Max, if not a few more people walking quickly from one room to another. The large tapestries were just as grand as the first time she saw them. Battles and beautiful landscapes with flowers and forests hung along the large walls, no doubt covering up boring wood paneling or plain stone walls.

She could smell the fresh flowers that had recently been put out and the remnants of breakfast, waffles, and sausage. There were men up on high ladders next to the ceiling. It looked like they were washing the white columns that dotted the entryway. *What a scary job,* she thought as they turned a corner into the hallway.

"So, is Jas short for something?" Even though she was only staying here a few days, she felt she should get to know the girl.

Jas cleared her throat as she turned down another long corridor. "Jasmine."

Lily smiled, "That's a beautiful name." Jas turned and kept up her diligent pace as she started walking backwards.

"Thank you?" Lily could see her face had that confused look on it once again and couldn't help but chuckle.

"Was that a question?"

"No, no, it's just," Jas turned back around and stopped before a big wooden door. "The first thing out of most people's mouths is, 'you don't look like a Jasmine.'"

Lily nodded as the girl opened the door. "Of course you look like a Jasmine. That's your name." They walked inside, and Lily took a minute to look around. It was warm and well-furnished. A large bed with curtains was the focus of the room. Matching blue tapestries hung from the high vaulted ceiling, and the window was open, letting in a morning breeze. There was a bowl of rose petals in water on the table next to the bed, giving off a lovely scent. "Thank you, Jasmine, the room is perfect." Lily put her bag on the bed and turned to see the young woman wringing her hands together. It was clear that curiosity was just eeking from her.

"You're welcome, Mother. You will be dining with the prince tonight, so I'll come get you when it's time. You should find some appropriate attire in the wardrobe. Just let me know if you need help with getting dressed."

She noted the wardrobe across the room and nodded. "Thank you, and please call me Lily."

Jasmine nodded and turned to leave but stopped before

she got to the door. "Lily, is it true you and your husband found over a thousand missing people?" she asked quickly, her hands hugging the door's frame.

Lily nodded and looked over at her. "Sounds about right." Over the years she and Henri had used their connections and money to create a well-oiled organization that traveled all over the world and found countless people over the years. Those stolen, those who ran, anyone who was lost was found. That's how Prince Max heard of her and wanted her for this sensitive mission.

She could see pity forming on the girl's face. "I'm sorry about your husband."

Lily sat down on the bed while giving some thought to her words. "Thank you, Jasmine, he is missed." It had been just over two years since the wasting disease took her love from her. They had only been married six years. So little time, she often thought to herself. But no matter how much Otto resided in her heart or how powerful her healing spells were, there was nothing that she could do for him. She had never felt so helpless in her life. Those who contracted this disease couldn't be healed by prayer like a broken bone could. It was the body attacking itself. But Lily still prayed to Otto in case it was different. It wasn't. But she kept up the business, knowing there were always those who would need her to find them, and it helped to keep him close.

Jasmine gave her a little curtsey and bowed her head. "I'll be back for you later." She shut the door, leaving Lily alone to her own devices. She sighed and walked over to the window that looked out on the expansive garden behind the castle. There were rows and rows of flowers of all colors, and the trees were finally getting their spring leaves. It was a shame she'd have to leave so soon, or she would have loved to take a walk among them. But the prince had summoned her to be part of a covert group to recover an orc named Sobrei Re'vall. The rightful ruler of the kingdom of Dal En Val, and that mission was more important than a walk through a garden.

Everyone knew Sobrei had been kidnapped five years ago, the same night his father died. So far, no one had been able to find him, and many feared him dead. Prince Max said he had a lead and wanted the group to find the orc and bring him to Ardenry, where he would be a political prisoner. Most likely treated better than his current captors, but a prisoner, nonetheless. Prince Max wanted to use Sobrei as a bargaining chip to get the ever-encroaching orcs and cultists who worshiped the human on Sobrei's throne out of his territory. He was sure that when they learned the true ruler was found, Dal En Val would rally to him and want him back on the throne. But first, they had to find him.

Lily had heard the rumors of the old orc rulers of Dal En Val, how its citizens worshiped them like gods. It was ridiculous, really, but after Sobrei was taken and a human supplanted on his throne, a new breed of cultists popped up, who now worshipped the human. Lily loved and trusted her god, Otto, with every fiber of her being, but what they did in Dal En Val was plain idolatry.

Her eyes slowly took in the wooden wardrobe across from her. It was huge, ten feet tall, and about eight feet wide, with intricate carvings of flowers on the front. When she opened it, she couldn't help but let out a quiet gasp at all the colorful, delicate gowns hanging in front of her. After Henri died, she went back to mostly wearing her white clerical robe throughout the day instead of the beautiful dresses he bought for her. She smiled at the thought of Henri's fingers gently touching each one before he found one he liked. She found a dark green silk dress with dark jewels sewn into a corseted bodice and held it against her body.

"I hope this one fits," she whispered to herself. She didn't often buy new dresses for herself, especially these last two years. Only if they required it of her for a ball to make more connections, so this was a rare treat. She reached up and laid her hand on their wedding rings that hung on the gold chain around her neck. "We're going to find the ultimate lost man," she said, "Hopefully, we'll be as successful as you and I were, my love."

Just as the sun went down, there was a knock on her door. "Lily, it's Jasmine. May I come in?"

"Yes, come in!" Lily was standing in front of a big floor-length mirror, wearing the dark green dress she had picked out earlier. Green clothes always made her eyes pop, and tonight was no exception. Half of her long, blonde hair was pinned up around her head like a wreath, and the rest flowed in soft ringlets down her back. Her two necklaces completed the ensemble, one with her blessed seashell, the other their wedding rings. If anyone didn't know her, they might think she was a high-born lady, not just a priestess from Fairwinds.

The door creaked open, and she heard Jasmine giggle. "Well, I'd say you found the gowns all right." She walked up and stood behind Lily. "You look beautiful. Dare I say you will turn heads." Lily turned and slipped her feet into the delicate, black slippers she found under all the gowns.

"I don't need to turn heads. I just wanted to look nice. Do you know if anyone else is dining with us tonight?" *Please let there be others,* she thought to herself. Despite being used to visiting dignitaries in her own home, the prince was another beast altogether and dining alone with him would be panic attack inducing.

Jasmine nodded. "Yes, there's Lord Giles from Raventree and his squire Leo and," Her eyes squinted as she tried to remember, but clearly it was futile, "others I know, but I can't seem to remember their names. A tall man who doesn't seem to wear much," Lily could see a blush creep over her cheeks, and she held back a giggle, "and a loud dwarf."

"Don't think I've met a quiet one," she turned and gave herself another quick once over, "I guess I'm ready."

"Then, if you'll follow me." They walked from the room and Lily was surprised to see a man standing guard outside her door.

"Was he there all day?" She asked as soon as they were out of the man's earshot.

"Yes, the prince said your safety was of the highest priority and assigned a guard to your door. Does that bother you?"

"No, no, I'm just surprised," she said as she glanced back at her guard. As they walked to dinner, she thought about the one guest she knew would be there, the Lord of Raventree. She had never been to Raventree. It was an old kingdom that had barely survived the last war against the Shackled One, but she knew nothing of its royal line. Mountains and dead cities separated it from most of the world. It was easy to get there from Salthole, but it could still be a dangerous trip.

"Oh!" Jasmine turned, "I just remembered, the other man dining with you is one of your Seekers. He's been in your employ for several years."

Lily smiled at the news. "Oh! How fortuitous, I take it you don't remember his name either?"

"No, I'm hopeless when it comes to names of those I'm not looking after." She looked apologetic, but Lily didn't mind. She'd met them all eventually. She mostly communicated with her employees through letters or magical messages, so she hadn't formally met a great number of them. She assumed this man wouldn't be any different. It lifted her heart, knowing that someone she already had a connection to would be coming as well. Jasmine led her to the same room where she met the prince just a few short days ago. The fire was still going, and she saw appetizers and wine waiting for her on a silver serving tray.

"Guess I was a little early in getting you, I apologize."

"That's all right, I prefer being early." She slowly walked around the large oak table, her stomach fluttering with nerves. "I don't know how I'm supposed to eat tonight. I'm so nervous."

Jasmine smiled. "I don't blame you. I think I would be, too. If you'll excuse me, I'll start warming some water for your bath." And left the room before Lily could protest. She wasn't used to being waited on so diligently and admitted it felt a little silly. Even when Henri insisted she get a lady's maid, she refused, preferring to do most things herself.

She walked around the expansive room to try and settle her nerves when she saw a large painting on the far wall. It was one of the biggest paintings she had ever seen in her life, around twenty feet tall and wider than that. A great battle was taking place in the background, but in the foreground, there was a giant red demon trying to steal a young priestess from her friends. Lily heard the door open and turned to see Prince Maximilian walk in. He was dressed in a fine orange tunic, an intricate lion stitched onto the front, and dark pants. She noticed another man walk in next to the prince and assumed this was Lord Giles. He looked to be about Lily's age with short, graying hair. The symbol on his black tunic was a big spindly tree covered in birds, ravens, she suspected. Behind them was a tall, blonde-haired young man who couldn't yet be eighteen, wearing the same livery as Giles. They were talking quietly amongst themselves when the prince suddenly looked up.

"Priestess, is that you?" He asked with an appreciative smile.

She suddenly felt very shy and clasped her hands in front of her as she bowed. "Yes, it's me, Your Highness." Max and the other two men walked over, and to her surprise, the stranger gave her a little bow.

"Priestess, it's an honor to meet one of such power and conviction. I am Lord Giles Raventree. This is my squire and adopted son, Leo." Giles's accent was interesting, almost a drawl if there was a word she knew to describe it.

"It's a pleasure to meet you, my Lord," she leaned over a little and saw Leo still standing quietly behind his father/Lord, his eyes roaming around the expansive room. "And you, Leo, how fare you this evening?"

His eyes snapped to hers, and he gave her a nod. "Well Mother, and yourself?" He was a handsome-looking kid, and she had a feeling he'd break a few hearts in his life.

"I'm well, but I must admit I feel a bit out of place." She stood straight as the Lord of Raventree smiled at her.

"Well, you look like you fit right in, Mother," Giles said. A few servants came in and started handing out the wine and appetizers. Lily took a glass and sipped while she listened to Giles and the prince speak about the mission at hand.

"It can take a while to ride to Cyranar, Your Highness. Perhaps we could take a boat from Fairwinds to Salthole? From there, we could go north through my town to get to Cyranar," Giles suggested. She held back the choke she felt when she heard him say Cyranar. The long-dead cursed city that no one willingly traveled to. Was that where the orc heir was being held? If so, it was a damn good hiding place. Despite the horror of their destination, Giles' plan sounded good to her. She'd love to at least say hello to her father in Fairwinds before leaving again, but to her surprise, the prince shook his head.

"Normally, I would agree with you, Giles, but I recently learned that two orc legions are camping between Raventree and Salthole. Making that route impossible."

Lily saw Giles' eyes go wide as he almost spit out his wine. "What! When did you hear this?"

"This morning," he laid a hand on Giles's shoulder, "I know it's an awful thing to learn, but I'm sending a legion of my own to aid your people in case the orcs decide to get violent." Giles set the goblet down and ran a shaky hand through his hair. "My wife and young son are still there." Lily could hear the worry in his voice as Leo laid a hand on his father's shoulder. Giles reached up and gave it a pat.

"All the more reason to get this mission underway." Max looked between the three of them. "The sooner Sobrei's in our custody, the sooner the orcs will withdraw from our land, and we'll be left in peace."

"What exactly are we to do with Sobrei once we have him?" Lily asked. "I doubt he'll just come willingly."

"No, I doubt he would either," Max shook his head. "Subdue him to the best of your ability. Spells or, gods forbid, a hit to the head. I have a teleport scroll for your group. It'll take you directly to a room here in the castle where he won't be able to leave. When he's here, I'll let Dal En Val know their rightful king is alive and well, in our custody, and we're willing to give him back with some concessions." Max crossed his arms over his chest. "Once they know Sobrei is free, they'll have to recognize his sovereignty."

Lily sighed, "No offense, Your Majesty, but they don't." He was about to respond when the door to the room opened, and two more men walked inside. One was a tall, lithe man with short-cropped dark hair and tan skin. He was wearing a loose pair of pants and a saffron-colored shift of fabric across his chest. Lily was shocked at his complete disregard for formality in the prince's presence. But Max didn't seem to be bothered by it and abandoned whatever he was going to say to her and walked over to the newcomers.

The other man was a few inches taller than herself and looked a bit younger. He had half of his shoulder length, dark hair tied behind his head while the rest lay down his neck. But even across the room, she noticed his eyes. They were dark blue, like glittering sapphires. As she studied him, she felt a sense of peace surrounding him. She forgot herself and put her hand on her chest, surprised at the feeling this man radiated. She wasn't sure any of the others in her employ were priests, but she wouldn't be surprised if this man was.

Max stopped in front of them and extend a hand to the men. "Koizumi, William, welcome, please have some wine." *William,* she thought. He must have been a Seeker who only used his initials. Unfortunately, there were several seekers whose names started with W, so she still wasn't sure which one he was.

Kozumi gave a polite smile and held up his hand. "Thank you, but I must abstain." His accent was also different. He emphasized parts of words in a way she had never heard before, making them sound completely foreign to her.

"As you like," Max turned to William and shook his hand. "William, I'm glad you could join us. We were about to start dinner."

"Thank you, Your Majesty. It's an honor to be part of this endeavor." He took a glass of champagne, and Max motioned for Lily and Giles to join them at the table. Lily took a breath and lowered her hand, remembering herself. The servants began placing fancy-looking plates on the table and clearing away the appetizers. Leo walked next to Lily and held out his arm for her to take.

"Thank you, young man." He gave her a happy smile and led her to the table, where he pulled out a chair for her. "Such fancy manners," she chuckled a little, and he sat down next to her.

"A Knight is more than a man with a sword and a house," Giles said. "He has manners and cares about those in his charge."

"Well-spoken, my Lord." She looked over as William took the other seat next to her.

"Mother Lily, it's an honor to finally meet you," he held out his hand for her to shake, "I'm one of your Seekers, William Voltain." She couldn't hide the smile on her face if she wanted to. She took his hand, and that peaceful feeling flowed over her. As he said his full name recognition blossomed in her mind.

"W. V.," she said, and he nodded with a smile. She covered his hand with her free one so she could hold his hand in both of hers. "I know you, I'm so glad you could join us." He was indeed one of the men who searched for her. In fact, he was unrivaled in his successful trips compared to the rest of them. It was like he was meant for the life of finding the lost.

"I am as well. Honestly, I couldn't turn Prince Max down when I heard you were one of our number."

"Oh?" She took her hands back and put them in her lap.

He chuckled, "To work with you directly, how could I say no?" She fought to keep the blush from rising on her cheeks.

"Well, I thank you for your dedication to our cause." He gave her a little bow, his blue eyes sparkling in the candlelight. It had been a long time since she couldn't take her eyes off a man.

The prince's voice got her attention, and she turned as he sat down at the table. "It seems we're still missing one of our number, but I'm sure he'll be along. He'd never miss this meal," he teased. When everyone was seated Leo quickly stuffed some bread in his mouth. She knew young men had voracious appetites and managed to keep her giggles to herself.

"Mother, this is Koizumi," Giles said, "he will be joining us on this mission, Koizumi this is Mother Lily Marcel, Priestess of Otto."

"It's a pleasure, Koizumi."

He nodded, "Mother."

A large hunk of meat was wheeled in and placed next to the prince. "Ahh, smells wonderful!" Max got to his feet and took the knives from the carver. "I think I shall serve my guests tonight." He began cutting large slices off the side of the bird. Lily smiled at that. A prince who was willing to serve his own guests truly knew their worth. The door banged open, making Lily jump as a large, stocky dwarf walked in and sat next to Koizumi. From the corner of her eye, she could see William holding back laughs. The dwarf's brown beard was decorated with braids and beads, and his boots were worn.

"Not late, I see," he said, grabbing the nearest goblet and draining it quickly.

"Mother, this is Krag. He's the last of your party," the prince said as he placed a thick slab of meat on her plate.

"His specialty is not letting the enemy through," Giles said proudly.

"They try, they die," Krag said as he looked up and practically sneered at her. "A woman? Have you ever traveled like this before, Mother?" The last word was rather unfriendly, and she crossed her arms over her stomach.

"Officially, no, but—"

"Bah!" He threw his hand up in the air, "Max, it's bad enough you got a woman, but a green one at that!"

Lily scoffed, "Has anyone ever told you it's not nice to

speak ill of your healers?" All the men chuckled at her words.

Krag picked up a roll and took a big bite. "Nope, but I don't plan on getting hurt." Lily rolled her eyes as Leo sniggered softly next to her.

"Krag, this is Lily Marcel, and I suggest you play nice because she's right about that making fun of healer's thing," The prince said as he put some meat on the dwarf's plate. Lily saw his eyes go wide, and she realized he had heard of her. But instead of acknowledging that fact he just cleared his throat and stuffed his mouth full of meat. She snuck a glance at William, wondering what he made of the exchange. The corner of his mouth was tilted in a little smile as he gave her a wink. She turned back to her plate, a little smile on her own lips.

The dinner was excellent, juicy beef and fluffy mashed potatoes with plenty of butter, greens, and fresh rolls with honey on top. Lily heard William make an appreciative noise as he ate a roll.

Lily chuckled, "Good?"

"Perfect amount of honey," he said around the heavenly bread. He looked to be a few years younger than herself and wondered how many years he had been working for them instead of living a normal life. Most of their seekers were older, retired guild members or people who had no family. There weren't many young people who were willing to set their life aside to search for others.

"Now that our plates are full, I say we talk of more pleasant things and get to know each other," the prince said as he sat down. "Giles, how about you first?"

The regal man finished his bite and wiped his mouth. "Well, my family has been the ruling body of Raventree since before we can remember."

"I hear your cavalry is unparalleled," Koizumi said.

Giles nodded, "Yes, our most devastating force is our mounted cavalry. The only thing that keeps the orc threat at bay is the fact that they don't know our numbers aren't nearly what are needed to take them on." He sighed, "But we're supposed to be talking of happy things, so I digress. I have a wife, Siddah, and a son, Giles Jr., and of course Leo." The young man gave the table a closed-lip smile as his mouth was full of food. "They are the only family I have since my father passed away."

"How old is Giles Jr.?" Lily asked.

She watched the Lord smile as he thought of the boy. "Two, he climbs all over everything. I swear he'll give his mother a heart attack one day."

Lily smiled, "Two's a fun age."

Giles picked up his goblet and took a sip. "What about you, Mother? Tell us about yourself." Lily cleared her throat and sat back. "I'm from Fairwinds originally. When my husband and I got married, we settled here in Ardenry and started our little rescue operation. Which William was a big part of." She motioned to him, and he bowed his head a little.

Everyone but Koizumi nodded, and Giles turned to him. "Mother Lily and her husband started a sort of business to counteract the trafficking of peoples. They saved a lot of lives."

The strange young man turned back to her. "He does not mind you leaving home for this?"

Lily shook her head, "No," she chose her words carefully. "He died two years ago. I've kept up the business, mostly to keep him close." She touched the rings hanging from her neck.

"Shouldn't you be home with your kids?" the dwarf asked. Tact was clearly something beyond him.

"We didn't have any children," she could see the conversation getting too personal and quickly changed the topic, "My father is alive and lives in Fairwinds. I hope that when this is all over, there might be more good in the world." She looked back at the young man named Koizumi, "So what about you? Where are you from?"

He swallowed the bite he was eating and cleared his throat. "I am from The Pillars of Heaven." The very mention of the name made her ears twitch. "The Pillars, really? Henri lived there for a few years when he was a boy. How do you find life under the clouds?" She asked with a big smile on her face. The Pillars of Heaven was far to the north. It wasn't really pillars, just mountains that were so tall you couldn't see the tops from under the clouds. It was a popular destination for those wishing to challenge their mental and physical abilities.

Koizumi tilted his head and gave it some thought. "It's different. It's much quieter among the clouds than your cities. It's bright, and many of our monks attain inner peace in our mountains. I think it would be hard to do so here among the dark and noise."

"I agree," burped the dwarf. Lily sighed and continued eating while Leo told his little tale. He was the son of one of Giles' best banner men. His mother died bringing him into the world, and when his father died, Giles adopted him when he was ten. Lily could tell the young man was grateful to be taken in by him, and it spoke highly of Giles that he had done so. Most Lords would just give the boy some money and try to find other family members to raise them or pay the church to take them in. What Giles did was the sign of a good man with a good heart who cared immensely for his people.

Krag didn't talk much, but, he was also one of Giles' men and said he would follow his Lord wherever there was a fight, and this seemed like a good one.

"What about you, William?" Max asked, motioning to him with a glass of champagne.

"Oh, not a lot to tell. I grew up in Raventree," he motioned to Giles, "We moved when I was five to a farm about a week from The Citadel. It was just me and my parents. My father died a few years ago. My mother is still on the farm." He looked over at Lily, and she couldn't help but smile a little. "A few years ago, I got in contact with Henri and became a Seeker for him."

"One of the best Seekers we've ever had." She had to brag about him.

He chuckled, "You're too kind. It was a fulfilling life, but when Max contacted me about this job, I knew I had to go." She was glad he answered the call.

"Could you see any dragons from where you lived?" Leo managed to keep his mouth empty of food long enough to ask.

"Only when they flew overhead heading somewhere else. I'm afraid a week is a bit too far to gaze at dragons flying every day." He smiled at the young man.

"I'd like to be a dragon rider," Leo stuffed half a roll into his mouth, "gotta be a knight first, though," he said around the roll.

"That's a worthy aspiration, young man." Lily laid a hand on his shoulder and hoped he'd make it through this mission to fulfill that dream.

———

When dinner was over, another servant pushed in a cart with so many desserts on it that Lily's eyes couldn't make sense of them all. Puff pastries and pies, several flavored puddings, and frosted cookies covered the plates, and like Lily figured, Leo was the first to pick something out.

"Eat well now, boy," Giles teased, "when we're on the road, we'll be lucky if we don't half starve."

Leo looked up, his eyes wide, a bit of cream still on his lip. "What?"

Lily chuckled and laid a hand on the young boy's shoulder. "Don't worry about that," she looked over at Giles, "none of us will starve. Unless I die, then you'll be suffering," she said with a wink.

"More than I realize, I'm afraid," Giles said as he turned back to the prince. Koizumi and Krag were sitting across from each other, playing chess while the other men talked amongst themselves. Lily found herself unoccupied and walked back to that unusual painting.

Obviously, nothing about it had changed, but the closer she got to it, the more depth she saw on the canvas. At first, it looked as if the demon was trying to take the young priestess.

But now that she had time to study it, she realized the priestess was being held back by her friends, and she seemed almost desperate to get to the demon who looked rather distraught that he couldn't touch the woman.

"Creepy picture." She looked over and saw Leo standing next to her, eating his second vanilla cupcake, staring at the painting.

"You think it's creepy?"

He nodded. "Well, yeah. That demon wants that girl. Not much creepier than that." She looked back at the painting and wasn't surprised the young man couldn't see the emotion in the faces of the two most prominent figures.

"Do you like it, Mother?" Her ear twitched as she heard the prince walk up behind her.

"It's... interesting."

He walked closer and pointed to the name in the corner. "The artist made it as an experiment, to see how different people would react to it. What does it make you think of Mother?"

She sighed and looked at the demon. "He looks like he's in pain, like he wants to be with that young girl, but her friends are keeping her from him. She looks the same. She looks heartbroken that she can't be with him."

Krag scoffed from the chess table. "Romantic drivel, that's all that is. Demons don't love, they can't, and you know it, Mother."

"I know that, but in this painting, he does." She pointed at the demon.

Giles walked next to Leo as he held his bearded chin. "Well, I don't know about 'romantic drivel,' but it looks to me that the girls' friends are just trying to keep her safe from heartbreak." Lily sighed and agreed with Giles. As much as it may hurt to be separated from her love, it was dangerous being with something like that, and she knew it was for the best to keep them apart.

Leo was staring wide-eyed at the painting. "So much pain and death in the background," he said quietly.

Lily looked at the bloody battle taking place and held back a shudder. Dead bodies littered the ground, soldiers with bloody swords gave no quarter to their enemies, and she swore she could hear the sounds of armored feet stomping on bloody ground.

"I hope I never see a battle like that," she whispered.

Leo turned to her, swallowing the rest of his cupcake. "I bet most priests say that."

She nodded. "We do. Seeing life violently taken from those who didn't deserve it is heart-wrenching."

"But if they're not on your side, then they're your enemy, right? Enemies deserve to die." *He sounds so young,* she thought.

"Everyone has a right to defend their life and their home," she said and turned to him, "but taking a life is something that weighs heavily on the mind and soul of the ones who take it. It changes a person, and depending on how they deal with it, is the kind of person they will turn out to be. There are those who atone with their god and can deal with the lives they've taken. And then there are those who can't process what they've done, and they take those bad feelings and let them spill into their lives, where feelings like that don't belong."

Leo stared at her wide-eyed. "Like… why some men beat their kids?" he asked shyly, and she noticed Giles laid a hand on the boy's arm.

She nodded. "Some, yes. There's a price for taking life."

He slowly gazed back up to the painting, crossing his arms across his chest. "I never thought about it that way."

"That's why I felt Mother Lily would be a good addition to the group." Lily forgot that the prince was standing behind them. Talking with Leo felt a little like a sermon, and she often lost herself while speaking to an audience. "Not only is she a talented healer but after hearing her interpretation of that painting, I'm confident she will bring a unique perspective for the group on how you'll delegate things," the prince said.

"Thank you for your confidence, Your Highness."

Giles turned and whispered in Max's ear while he nodded.

"Leopold, my boy," Max slapped the young man's shoulders and began leading him away, "let me show you my first set of armor." Leo stumbled on the carpet a little from the sudden jostling but recovered quickly and followed the prince out of the room.

"Subtle, my Lord," Lily said with a smile.

He chuckled, "I thought so." Giles sipped on his amber drink while Lily watched him study the painting a little more. "What you said to Leo was wise, Mother. I don't think I would have spoken to him like that till after he killed a man."

"I didn't mean to curb your teachings, my Lord."

He shook his head. "No, no, you didn't," He sighed and turned to her, "I think, if anything, you've made him a little wiser."

She smiled. "Well, it's nice to be appreciated."

Giles chuckled a little and swirled the dark liquid in his glass. "Oh, you'll be most appreciated when we need you to heal our wounds."

"I'd like to be appreciated for more than just my healing skills. I want to be someone who the others feel comfortable to talk to and help with their problems that don't involve bleeding."

"I have no doubt you will," he said with a smile. "So, you like being a priestess?"

Lily nodded, the smile still on her face. "Oh yes, there's nothing better than helping people in Otto's name." While her situation was a little different than most priestesses in Ardenry, she still gave sermons and spent time in the temple helping the people. Most lived and worked full-time in the temple, but when the Pontiff heard what she and Henri wanted to do, he gave her permission to live in the city proper. Not that he would stop her since they were married, but it was good to have his permission. She was glad he didn't insist she move into the temple after he died.

William walked over to her and handed her an oatmeal raisin cookie, the corner of her mouth tilted in a smile. "My favorite." She took a bite, it was sweet, the raisins were big, and the cookie was chewy and warm.

William cleared his throat. "Priestess, I wanted to give my condolences on the loss of your husband. He made a dramatic difference in the world, and that's more than a lot of us can say we did."

She bowed her head a little. "Thank you, and please call me Lily. Did you ever meet him?"

William looked up at the picture and nodded. "Once, four years ago, I think? He wanted to thank me for finding a young girl who had been taken from her farm." As he said that, the memory of that particular case came to mind. It was a difficult case where the kidnappers moved her around every few weeks.

"I remember that one. We had sent three other Seekers before you found her." It really did seem like a miracle that William found the young girl.

"Can I ask Lily, how did he die?" Giles asked softly.

She took another bite of the cookie as she nodded. "You can ask me anything, no worries. It was a wasting sickness, happened so fast, and there was nothing anyone could do but keep him comfortable." The waves of grief she felt over her husband were few and far between now. Mostly, the happy memories gave her peace, and she was glad for that.

"I remember hearing that he passed, and I couldn't believe it," William said, "I wanted to report to Ardenry and see if there was anything I could do, but then I got another letter with another person to find. I remember being so grateful that you were keeping the business going."

Lily licked her fingers as she finished her cookie. "It was important to him, to us. I felt it was the best way to keep his memory alive."

"Indeed." Giles toasted her.

"So, William," while she didn't mind the questions, she wanted off the topic of Henri, "what do you think of the picture?"

"Hmm," he took a bite of his own cookie, "there's a lot of layers to it." He pointed at the demon with his cookie, "The demon is trying to keep his love, and her friends are begging her to let go, but she doesn't want to let go either. Maybe she wishes they could all get along despite their differences."

Lily looked over at him, his eyes taking in the painting. "Makes sense." William was a handsome man with a sharp jawline and muscular. She wondered if he had a love stashed somewhere safe. The prince walked back in, holding Leo's attention with a thrilling story as they walked back over to them.

"When my dragon finally got up, I saw that everyone around me was dead," he said with a sweep of his arm.

Leo's eyes were wide as he listened to the story. "Whoa."

Lily couldn't help but giggle at the young boy's enthusiasm. "So, when are we leaving Your Highness?" she asked him.

"Tomorrow morning, I'm anxious for this to be over, and I know you all are too." *Tomorrow,* she thought, her stomach flipped from the fear of unknown dangers they might face. "Since we are doing this dangerous task for you, My Prince, will you be giving us something to aid us, weapons or armor perhaps?" Not that she needed weapons or armor, but she knew the others would.

"Of course," he said with a smile. "In the morning, you will find what you need in your room before you head west. You will be given swift horses to aid in your travel since I know no mage who would willingly teleport anyone to Cyranar." He sounded disappointed, Lily was too. If he found a mage that would teleport them, their job wouldn't take nearly as long.

"I'm glad to hear it. I think I will get an early start on some sleep. I have a feeling it won't come easy once we're on the road."

Giles and the Prince gave her a little bow. "It will be an honor fighting with you, Mother," Giles said.

"Thank you, I will pray for us all tonight. Hopefully, Otto will bless us with success." She saw Leo going for one of the frosted cookies. "Goodnight, Leo." He turned and took a big bite of the cookie as he waved goodbye. She giggled and hoped her morning spell could satisfy the young man's appetite.

"Good night, Lily." She gave William a little nod, their

eyes locked, and again, she couldn't help but stare at his beautiful sapphire eyes. That feeling of peace once again filled her heart.

"Good night, William."

"Do you…need an escort to your room?" She could hear the hope in his voice and gave him a little smile and held out her arm. He quickly took it, and they started for the door.

"Good night, Mother," Koizumi said as he knocked over a piece on Krag's side of the chess board.

"Bah, blasted monk, again!" The dwarf started setting up the pieces as Lily chuckled and walked into the hall, William on her arm. To her surprise, Jasmine was already waiting for her, her dainty hands clasped in front of her, and it seemed the smile had never left her face.

"Did you have a good dinner, Lily?"

"I did it was…" she gave William a little glance, "informative and interesting. You haven't been standing out here all night, have you?"

"No, no, just after dinner was over. I didn't think you could remember the way back to your room."

"Most likely not, thank you. Shall we?" She looked up at William who gave her a nod, a little smile on his face. As they walked, she could feel the muscles in his arm under her fingers. He was strong, and she could feel how warm he was as they walked. She had forgotten what that was like, to feel the warmth of someone next to you, and didn't realize how much she missed it.

The same guard was standing outside of her room when they got back, Lily stopped in front of him as his eyes moved to her. "Hello, I'm Lily, what's your name?"

"Lux, ma'am." He gave her a quick bow before returning to his position.

"Lux, I thank you for your time." She turned to William and withdrew her arm, "Thank you for the escort."

"You're most welcome." She was about to turn towards the door when she felt him take her hand. Lily stopped and looked up at him as he gave her hand a squeeze. "I want you to know that I'll protect you with the best of my ability while we're out there."

"We'll protect each other." She noticed a seashell peeking from underneath his collar. "You follow Otto?" Lily reached up and gently touched the grey shell and the familiar power of their god surrounded them.

"I do."

She nodded. "I will pray for all of us tonight. It was lovely meeting you."

He slid his hand from hers and walked a few steps before turning. "You are more than I could have ever hoped for, Lily. Good night." She felt heat on her cheeks as he turned and walked down the hall. Jasmine opened the door for her, and Lily could tell she was trying not to smile.

"Well, isn't he nice," she whispered. Lily snickered and walked into her room and saw a big brass tub just under the window. Jasmine must have had someone bring it in during dinner. There was steam floating off the water, and her muscles relaxed just looking at it. "I'm not used to people doing such things for me, Jasmine, but thank you for drawing the bath." The dark-haired girl laid a big, fluffy robe on the handle that was attached to the end of the tub.

"Give it no thought, it's my job, and I'm happy to do it. I'll lay out a comfortable nightgown for you."

"Thank you." She gave Lily a little bow and turned to the chest of drawers and began digging through the piles of clothing. Lily put her hand in the water, it was perfectly warm, and an unexpected smile spread across her face as she thought about how warm William felt next to her.

When Jasmine left the room Lily undressed and relaxed in the warm water. She could see the moon shining through the window and smiled at the thought of her father looking up at it at the same moment. *Tomorrow morning, I am facing an unknown foe, possibly more dangerous than anything I've ever faced,* she thought to herself. She thought back on these virtual strangers from dinner, these men she had to take care of while in battle, and hoped she wouldn't let them down.

Lily got to her knees in the water and looked up at the moon. "Blessed Otto, please keep me and my companions in your good graces while we face unparalleled dangers. Lead us down the path of righteousness so that our deeds reflect on the world in a positive light. Keep their swords sharp and accurate, keep their aim true and their minds sober from the horrors that I cannot keep from them. I ask you, great God of the sea, to keep us alive so that we all may join our loved ones again and rejoice in your name, for you have made it so. May you bless us and keep us from all evil and bring us to everlasting life, Blessed Otto."

———————

William walked back into the dining room, his hands in his pockets, and a smile on his face that he couldn't hide for the life of him. He walked over to Giles and Max, discussing strategy for when they had custody of the orc prince. But he wasn't listening. His thoughts were for Lily. He had heard of her beauty, but to see it and feel the peace that radiated from her was something he was unprepared for. Her green eyes reminded him of the forest surrounding his mother's farm, and her hair looked so soft he fought not to play with one of the ringlets as it lay on her shoulder throughout dinner. Her voice was lovely, and every time she said his name, he felt his heart speed up.

"William?" He heard his name and turned. Giles and Max were staring at him.

"Yes? Sorry, I was miles away."

Max chuckled, "She's a beauty, isn't she?"

William sighed, "I feel like I've been run over by a carriage." He admitted to the men, who laughed.

"Well, I already told Leo it's his job to protect her, so you'll have to fight him for that honor." Giles patted his arm.

William laughed, "That's all right. The more, the better." He gave the painting one more glance and prayed to Otto that they'd all make it back. "I think I'll head to bed," he shook Giles's hand and gave Max a bow, "early morning and all that."

"Night," Giles called out, and Max nodded his head. As he walked back to his room, he wondered if he'd even be able to sleep with the Priestess on his mind.

CHAPTER 2
OFF THE BEATEN PATH

The sun was barely up, and Lily was already dressed for the day. As the prince promised, there was a big box waiting for her by the door. Inside was a light, silver suit made of chain mail for her and a dagger with the crest of Ardenry stamped into the blade. Lily was never much for weapons. She hated causing others pain, but a dagger was an important survival tool that could be used for much more than just stabbing people, and she would happily put it at her hip.

She wore her suit of armor under her white robes; luckily, it didn't show much, and it looked like she wasn't wearing any protective gear. She had never worn so much armor before and didn't want to feel hampered by it. But this armor must be magical to feel like there was almost nothing under her robes.

There was a brief knock on the door, and Jasmine walked in with some food. "Thought you might be hungry," she said with a smile. She set the tray by the fireplace and set to getting the fire blazing again. "I didn't think your stay in the palace would be so short."

Lily sighed and walked over to the food. "Me either, but the sooner this is over, the sooner we can all get back to our lives." She lifted the silver lid, and the smell of bacon and biscuits filled the air. "Smells wonderful, Jasmine, thank you." Lily picked up a piece of bacon and was about to take a bite when she heard Jasmine sniffing. The young woman was still kneeling by the fire like she wanted to hide her face. "Are you all right?"

Jasmine rubbed her nose and nodded. "I'm fine, how's your breakfast?" But Lily could hear the tears in her voice and walked up behind her.

"Jasmine, what's wrong?" She laid a hand on her back, and the girl turned, her teary eyes red from the effort of hiding.

"Is it true you're going to Cyranar?"

Lily's eyes widened. "What? Where did you hear that?"

She shrugged and shyly looked at the floor. "You know, servants talk." She looked up and took Lily's hands. "Please don't go there, Lily. There's all manner of devils and evil there!" Everyone knew the story of Cyranar, which was why most sane people stayed away. The once great city was where the fall of The Shackled One took place almost a thousand years ago. The resulting holy explosion leveled the city and killed everyone within a five-hundred-mile radius. Raventree was barely spared. Now, it was said the city was cursed by the people who died and that the explosion opened a rift directly into the abyss. People said that devils and demons claimed the city for their own. Since the only people who went there were treasure hunters, most of whom didn't come back, no one argued the rumors.

She took Jasmine's hands, trying to comfort her. "They're just rumors, Jasmine, besides we're not going to Cyranar." Lily knew servants talked, but maybe if she told the girl they weren't going, that rumor would spread, and they might be spared an awful surprise down the line.

Her squinted, teary face relaxed a bit. "You're not?"

"No." She wiped the tears from her cheeks, "So be at peace. We're not doing something as insane as going to the fallen city."

Jasmine took a deep breath and sighed. "Good. I'd hate to think of you in that awful place." *Me too*, Lily thought to herself.

"Why don't you leave the fire alone and join me for breakfast. There's no way I can eat all of it myself."

Jasmine smiled. "Thank you." She led the jittery girl over to the tray and handed her a biscuit. "You know, I wish I could wait on you full-time, Lily. No one's ever treated me half as good."

Lily chuckled, "I've hardly seen you."

"That's just it," she took a bite of biscuit, "most people

have me running around all day, do this, do that, wash this, wash that. It's been wonderful serving you. I've actually had time for myself."

Lily nodded. "I understand, but I don't need a servant. I am one."

———

When every bit of breakfast was gone, Jasmine showed Lily the way to the stables, where she found Lord Giles and Leo saddling up some horses.

She turned and gave the sweet girl a hug and a blessing before she left. "May Otto bless you, Jasmine."

"Thank you, Lily. Stay safe." She gave her one last smile and walked back to the palace.

Lily moved over to Giles as he put a bag into his black horse's saddle. "Good morning, my Lord, Leo. Did you have a good night?"

The young man popped up from the other side of the horse he was working on. "I slept like a log. That bed had to be the softest thing I've ever slept on," he said with a smile.

Giles chuckled and bowed a little to her. "Good morning, Mother."

"Please call me Lily."

"I will if you call me Giles," he said with a smile.

Lily nodded her head. "All right then, Giles." She stared at his horse, a big black brute that stood proud and still. "He's amazing, what's his name?"

"This is Malice," he patted the horse's nose, "Malice, this is Lily, say hi." To her surprise, the horse dipped his head in greeting. "He can get protective, but I've never had a better horse." She could hear in the lord's voice just how much he loved the black stallion.

"Nice to meet you, Malice. So, which horse is mine?" She craned her neck and looked into the stable. It was full of fine-looking horses that one would expect a prince to own. Down the corridor she saw Max walking with a stable hand who was leading a lithe white horse down to them.

"Good morning, Mother!" The prince called out when he saw her approaching.

"Good morning, Your Highness." She bowed her head and when she looked back up, he was handing her the reins of the beautiful animal.

"This is your horse. Her name is Calliope. I hope you find her satisfactory." Lily walked closer and laid a hand on the mare's strong neck. She nickered and rubbed Lily's cheek with her nose.

Lily laughed, "She's wonderful. Thank you, Your Highness." The sound of a horse slowing down got her attention, and she looked up as William rode up to them on a beautiful brown horse.

His handsome face looked happy to see her. "Good morning, Lily."

"William." He was wearing dark leather armor and had a sword at his side. His hair was still half up behind his head.

"Did you not get any armor?" He jumped from his horse and walked over to her. "Even I got some, and I didn't need any." He laid his hand on her elbow and seemed to startle for just a moment. "You did." Lily smiled and lifted her sleeve to show him the chainmail underneath. "That's incredible." His fingers ran along the silver mail, up to her shoulder and back down to her elbow. "It's so light."

"It is, and thank Otto, too, because I am not used to wearing this much armor." She chuckled and put her sleeve down. She also thanked Otto for the armor covering the goosebumps she got after he touched her arm like that.

Krag's dulcet voice rang loudly in the stables. "If you think I'm getting on one of those beasts, you're dead wrong." They both turned as Krag and Koizumi walked in. Lily snickered and walked her horse over to Giles and Leo.

"Would you like a pony instead?" The prince asked him as the others laughed.

Krag grumbled and leaned against one of the closed gates.

"I'll give you a pony." Lily thought she heard him mumble. Another sleek horse, this one all black was led out and the reins handed to Koizumi, but the strange man just shook his head.

"I will not be needing a horse, Your Majesty. I can keep up just fine."

Lily's eyes widened. "How will you keep up?"

"I move much quicker than a normal man. I would hate to tire out a beast with something I can do myself." Lily looked around at the others, but they didn't seem phased by what he said as they continued to saddle their horses. She looked up as a large, stout horse was brought out and she couldn't help but gasp at the height of the creature, its head towered over hers.

"Master dwarf, perhaps you'll find this animal more to your liking?" Krag looked up at Max's words, and Lily watched as his head slowly looked up to the height of the beast, which towered over the price.

"By the mountain, now that is a horse!" He laughed and made his way over and inspected it. "You've been holding back, Max!" It was fitted with a special saddle that easily let the dwarf get on the horse's back. "Ha! I've never been so tall without being on a hill!" Giles and Leo laughed at the dwarf while he took his horse for a little 'get to know you' trot around the coral outside. William stepped up next to her and helped her up into the saddle before getting back onto his own.

"Do you find your armor satisfactory, Mother?" the prince asked, patting her horse's flanks.

"I do, thank you, Your Highness. I'm sure it'll come in handy." She walked her horse near Giles, as did William.

"Morning, Malice," he called out. The black stallion stomped his hoof, clearly annoyed that the man deigned to speak to him.

"Oh, now cut that out, boy," Giles warned him, and Malice turned so he wasn't looking at William.

Lily chuckled, "You weren't kidding." Giles sighed, shaking his head as he gave his horse a big pat on his back. The prince walked over to Giles and handed him a scroll case as he and Leo mounted their horses.

"Here's the map, with a few extra tips about Cyranar and that teleport scroll I was telling you about."

Giles took the case and slipped it into his saddle bag. "Thank you, Max."

"May the gods bless you on your journey."

"May they indeed," He turned to the dwarf, "Krag!" With a gentle kick, Malice began trotting away from the palace. Leo fell in behind his Lord and Lily behind him then William. She heard Krag's horse give a loud, powerful neigh as he left the coral and joined them. Worried about Koizumi, she turned and saw he was running next to her! She could hardly believe it and laughed as the group left the castle grounds and entered the wilderness.

———

That first night, they camped by a little lake about twelve hours south of Ardenry. Leo and Koizumi had fished for their dinner. Well, Leo fished. Koizumi stood in the water and plucked the fish out like a bird of prey. It was incredibly entertaining. William tried it but only succeeded in falling in the water, saying his future as a Monk was doomed. As they sat eating their meal Giles studied the map while Lily looked over his shoulder, eating her own fish.

"I guess we're heading west tomorrow?"

Giles speared a little bit of fish and blew on it before popping it into his mouth. "Nope, we're going to keep going south."

Her eyes widened. "South? Why south, Cyranar is west."

Giles put down his plate and rolled the map back up. "The prince is wise in choosing us for this mission, but he's sorely mistaken if we don't need more help. There is a man living to the south who used to work for my father. He's a mage. A powerful one at that, and I know if I asked him to join us, he would. So, we're taking a little detour first." *A mage,* she thought, *how fortuitous* it was the one thing they were lacking.

"Well, that sounds like a good idea. How far south is he?" She took a big bite of her fish. It was hot and the freshest fish she had ever eaten, which was surprising since she grew up by the ocean. Giles cleared his throat and handed the case to Leo, who put it back in his saddle bag.

"About another day."

Lily gave it some thought before her jaw slowly dropped. "Another day? That would put us in the middle of The Shade."

William looked up at that. Clearly, he wasn't privy to the Lord's plan either. "Wait The Shade?"

Giles nodded and sucked at his teeth. "Yep."

She stared at him for a moment. He had to be kidding. "You're taking us to the Shade?"

"Yes, Mother, I am. We need Artimus for this." Lily sat down and put her plate on the ground, *what have I gotten myself into.* The Shade was a cursed wood, filled with werewolves, undead, and all manner of undocumented monsters. Truthfully, she might be the one asset they had to make it through the woods until they found this Artimus. But that didn't mean it didn't scare her.

"What's the matter Mother, a few undead got your knickers in a twist?" Krag laughed.

"Krag," William scolded him, but it didn't hit his target.

Slowly, Lily looked up. "Have you ever been surrounded by undead, dwarf? Have you ever been so close to them that you can smell their flesh rotting and hear their skin slough off their bones? Have you ever felt their dry, dead hands on you and wished you could run, but if you did, you knew they'd rip your arm out of its socket? Because I have, and I have no desire to experience any of that again." Krag stared at her for a moment. She thought he looked a little more subdued and hoped he'd get the hint. The healthy fire crackling in front of them was the only sound for a few moments.

"Were you really surrounded?" Leo's voice piped up first. It didn't really surprise her. He seemed like a curious lad.

She nodded. "I was."

"What happened?" Lily ran her hands through her hair while she thought back on that horrible day.

"My husband and a friend and I were heading to Fairwinds when we came across a small town. We thought we could rest, but it was a trap. A worshipper of the Shackled One had turned the entire town into mindless zombies. We walked right in the middle of it." Everyone's eyes went wide as they listened.

Krag cleared his throat. "I guess you made it out okay since you're sittin' in front of us."

She shrugged. "From the initial attack, yes, we made it out. He tried to sacrifice me," she laid a hand on her stomach where his blade went deep, "but my friend Taren was dead by the end of the day. The cultist killed him as we were making our escape."

"I'm so sorry, Mother." She looked up at Giles and could see he really meant it. William laid a hand on her shoulder as his own apology.

"Thank you," she reached up and laid her hand on Williams, "it was a long time ago I've come to terms with what happened. But I hope you can understand my hesitation in going into the Shade." She took her hand off Williams, though she didn't really want to.

Giles nodded. "I do, Mother, and I apologize, but I'm afraid it's a necessity."

"Lily," she reminded him, "I understand, and I will not balk at my responsibility. Just know that the things in those woods are infinitely worse than some mindless zombie that a cultist created. Creatures breed in those woods and there are things that would make a lesser man insane at just the mere sight of it." Giles cleared his throat and subtly jerked his chin over at Leo. When Lily's eyes landed on the poor boy, she could tell he was white as a ghost.

She clicked her tongue sympathetically and touched his knee. "I said 'lesser man' Leo, we'll be fine. I just want everyone to be prepared for what can come at us."

His eyes lingered on her hand before meeting hers as he swallowed loudly. "Don't worry, Mother. I will protect you with my life as my Lord has commanded."

Her head whipped over to Giles. "What?"

"Leo's job is to protect you, Mother, uh, Lily," Giles said, "I know you can probably take care of yourself, but I'd feel better knowing he was guarding you as well." She looked back at the young boy, barely seventeen, and felt her heart sink at the thought of him getting hurt while protecting her. She glanced at William who gave her a little nod, confirming what Giles said was true.

She made sure Leo was looking into her eyes as she spoke. "You will guard me, and I will guard you, Leo. We'll be fine, I promise."

The boy managed a brave smile. "I believe you, Mother."

"Good." She turned back to Giles, "I suppose I should turn in, tomorrow morning I'll make us a good breakfast that will hopefully lift our spirits some."

Krag clapped his hands together once. "Mmm, already drooling, Mother."

She snickered as she got out her bedroll and kneeled on it. "Blessed Otto, thank you for this day, and I pray that you will be with us tomorrow as we enter the Shade and protect us from the unknown." She laid down, her back to the fire. "Good night, all."

"Night, Mother." Leo piped up. Lily closed her eyes and kept praying silently before sleep took her, she had never been somewhere so evil as The Shade and hoped her resolve wouldn't let her down.

———

The warm sun woke her as it fell across her cheek. Lily opened her eyes and instantly remembered where they were going that day. *The Shade*, she thought to herself and tried to put on a brave face. She sat up and saw Koizumi was already awake. He was probably the last watch of the night, and he smiled at her when he saw she was up.

"Good morning, Lily."

"Koizumi, I take it the night was quiet?"

He nodded. "Indeed. Do you need help with the breakfast you said you were going to make? I am an excellent cook if I may say so." She smiled and crawled out of her bedroll, careful not to wake Leo, who was already taking his guard duty to her seriously and had moved his roll next to hers. William had moved his bedroll so his head was near hers. She assumed he wanted to guard her as well but didn't want to step on Leo's toes.

"I don't need help making it, just eating it." She walked a few feet from the camp and held her hands up to the sky. "Blessed Otto, my friends and I are in need of nourishment to break our fast." She prayed and watched as several kinds of piping hot meat, bread, fruits, jams, rice, eggs, and three kinds of juice, along with all manner of hot cakes, appeared on a table before them. It looked like there was enough food for at least twenty people.

Koizumi got to his feet and walked over. "That is amazing, Mother!"

Lily laughed as he stared at the bountiful meal. "Otto's amazing. He just works through me. Now, how about that help?"

Koizumi smiled. "Don't mind if I do." They each picked out a nice, hearty meal. Lily got hotcakes and sausage with a big bowl of fruit while Koizumi ate some rice, eggs, and ham. Soon the camp started stirring and were amazed at the feast they saw.

"Wow, Mother, how did you manage all this?" Giles asked as he poured himself some juice and pulled a breakfast steak on a plate.

"We can eat like this every morning if I pray to Otto. The food will disappear after an hour or so, but not from our bellies."

William sat next to her, covering his plate with eggs, sausage, and hot cakes. "I was hoping this is what you meant," he gave her a little wink, "I love this spell." Lily chuckled and ran her fingers through William's impressive bedhead, trying to tame his hair.

"It's a lot of people's favorite," she said, taking her hands back.

Leo laughed as he saw the spread and sat down, piling eggs on his plate. "I'll make sure and guard you extra well if you're going to feed us like this every day." Lily laughed at his enthusiasm and finished her meal as Krag joined them.

"Nice spread, Mother." She watched as the dwarf's plate almost beat Leo's.

As the group finished their meal and got to their feet, Leo suddenly stopped. "Huh, I feel different."

"Just a blessing the food gives us. Hopefully, it'll come in handy today," Lily explained.

Giles got to his feet and walked over to her. "When Max told us you were coming on the mission, I felt lucky. Now, I feel blessed that such a wonderful, powerful priestess is with us. Thank you, Mother."

She felt her cheeks blush. "You're welcome, my Lord. Now, I guess we better pack up. The Shade awaits us." William put what she assumed was supposed to be a comforting hand on her back, but nothing would comfort her before going into that cursed place.

The group quickly got their things together and packed up the horses. Leo took his place riding beside Lily. He started talking about his life and friends back home. She didn't mind the chatter. It helped her relax.

A few hours later, Giles yelled back. "Leopold, you are going to talk Lily's ear off if you keep it up!"

Lily saw the boy's cheeks blush a little. "That's okay, my Lord, I like the company."

Leo looked up and smiled nervously at her. "I'll stop talking if you really want me to."

She giggled. "No, please keep telling me about your home, I know almost nothing of Raventree." Leo smiled and was about to continue when Krag's dulcet voice floated in the air back to them.

"As much as I like hearing about the tree that got a splinter

in his arse when he was nine, I think we should be quiet now."
Lily was about to chastise the dwarf but stopped when she saw
what was looming in front of them. The trees of The Shade crept
over the horizon, and Lily's arms broke out in goosebumps as
she felt the evil radiating from the forest in front of them. She
couldn't stop herself from reaching up and holding her holy
symbol tightly in her hand.

"Blessed Otto, please be with us."

"Just looks like a forest." She heard Leo say.

"Maybe we'll get lucky, and that's all it'll be." It was more
for Leo's sake than hers that she said that. As they rode closer,
she concentrated on the forest, trying to pinpoint where the evil
was in hopes of avoiding it. But the more she concentrated, it was
clear to her that there was one pure being in the forest. It was
moving quickly to and fro like it was searching for something,
and she smiled at the thought of running into whatever it was.

The closer they got to the forest, the more nervous the
horses got, except Malice. He looked like one of the war horses
that Giles talked about, and Lily knew he wouldn't misbehave
no matter what was chasing them. She patted her horse's neck
and whispered calmly to it as they entered the dark woods. The
sun was shining brightly that day, but the instant they crossed
into the forest, the sun was cut off. The long-twisted branches of
the immense trees choked off most of the sunlight before it could
reach the forest floor. It shone in little streams every so often,
definitely not enough to light much of their surroundings.

"So, where does this friend of yours live, Giles?" Lily
asked quietly.

"Just this side of the big creek that runs through the
woods. We should be able to get there before midnight." Lily
nodded and accepted their fate as she silently prayed to Otto for
safe passage through the woods.

No one spoke while they traveled. At first, the only sound
anybody heard was the horses' hooves crunching on dead leaves.
Then the noises started. All forests have noises, little animals

skittering on the floor, birds flying through the trees, but the noises in the Shade were far different than any the group had heard before. A groaning sound flew past them, and all the horses, save Malice, reared up in fright.

Lily swallowed a scream as Krag's huge beast of a horse nearly kicked Calliope in the head. She heard William's frantic yell as her stomach bottomed out, and she and her horse hit the ground hard. A sharp pain in her hip stole her breath, and just as quickly as it happened, the horse got up and ran blindly into the woods.

"Calliope!" Lily got to her feet as fast as her hip let her and watched as the beautiful horse ran deeper and deeper into her woods.

"Mother, are you all right?" Leo jumped off his horse and brushed some dirt off her robe.

"I'm fine," she sighed, disappointed at the loss and annoyed at the pain in her hip.

Giles cantered over and dismounted. "Calliope was a gentle horse. Max should have chosen something better for you."

William jumped down and picked up the pack that fell off her horse. "You can ride with me, Warden is a strong horse. A lady shouldn't walk if there's a horse available."

"Thank you, William." She put her foot in the stirrup, and it took everything she had to push herself up. Her hip was screaming at her the entire time. But she didn't want to waste any healing on herself, not yet, not in the Shade. William helped her get into the saddle and settled behind her.

"Are you hurt?" His hand went to her shoulder, "Not a lot of people walk away from having a horse fall on them."

She took a cleansing breath and gave his hand a pat. "I'm all right."

"If you say so." He gave her shoulder a squeeze, and she held onto the horn of the saddle while he put an arm around her waist. She might have let herself settle against him and relax if they weren't surrounded by things that could kill them.

Giles gave Lily a nod and they started deeper into the woods. Soon, the noises started again. Loud howls behind them made everyone feel trapped. In the distance, a scream made everyone stop, but Lily quickly realized what it was.

"It's one of the banshees," she said, "It knows we're here, and it's trying to lure us from our path. Don't listen." The screaming got worse before it went away. Leo covered his ears, and Koizumi shook his head, trying to clear whatever it made him think of. When it reached Lily's ears, she gasped and knew why the men were so affected. To her, the screams sounded like Henri.

"Are you all right?" William whispered to her.

She turned a little, her heart beating wildly in her chest. "It's been two years since I've heard Henri's voice, and this is how I hear it, in agony, screaming for help," she whispered back to him. Banshees could change their scream to sound like something or someone the intended victim loved. They were cowardly creatures by nature and tended to lure their victims to them with their voices rather than attack outright. It was a good strategy that few could resist. It was hard listening to her husband's voice in such agony and do nothing.

"I'm so sorry." He hugged her with that arm around her waist.

"I don't know whether to cover my ears or be thankful." She closed her eyes, hoping tears wouldn't fall from them. William laid his head on the back of her neck and held her tight. As the screams slowly faded, he loosened his grip around her waist. She was glad he was there. If she were still on Calliope, she didn't know if she would have been able to stay with the group. They barely had time to be thankful that the Banshee's scream was over before a loud, menacing roar pierced the air. Lily shook in the saddle. She swore she felt William shake, too.

Everyone stopped and listened. "It's far away," Giles said, "but it's big, whatever it is."

"Otto, keep it from our path," Lily said aloud.

The group rode all day until they reached a good-sized creek. "We'll stop here and start again after some rest," Giles said as he hopped down from his horse. William helped Lily down, and she hissed as she reached the ground. Her hip felt like it was on fire.

"You *are* hurt," he whispered to her.

"I'll be okay," she put a hand on his chest, "I just need some rest." He didn't look like he believed her but let her walk away without a fight. She walked close to the creek and touched the water. Her affinity with the water god gave her the power to see that the water was pure, well, as pure as it was to get in the Shade anyway. It was safe to drink and wash from, at least. "The water's clear if anyone wishes to wash off. I think I will if no one objects." She was covered in dirt and debris from earlier and wanted to get as much of it off as possible.

"No objections here," Giles said, "it sounds like a good idea. We'll let you have some privacy Mother." They led the horses through some trees, and Lily found herself alone in the most evil place she'd ever been to. At the moment, there were no sounds other than the wind in the trees, so Lily disrobed and put her armor on the ground. She looked down and finally got a good look at her hip. There was a horrendous bruise blooming on it. But she didn't feel like anything was broken. More like she had gotten pinched between the horse and the ground. Keeping her underclothes on, she carefully walked over the smooth rocks and slipped into the water. The water was warm and felt good on her stiff muscles. It had been a while since she spent so much time on a horse, so she wasn't surprised her muscles were protesting. The water was a few inches deep, but she was able to lean back and dip her long hair into the water. It would have been nice if the threat of something bursting through the trees at any moment wasn't spoiling it. She heard footsteps and turned to see William walking over.

"Is it alright if I wash off with you?"

"Absolutely, there's plenty of room." She turned her back to him and heard him shed his armor and clothes. When he stepped into the water, she turned to him as he sat down.

"Let me see your hip." She wasn't used to people checking up on her and could hear how serious he was, so she acquiesced. She tilted onto her unhurt hip so the bruise was above the water. "Pippa's tit's Lily, that looks painful." Lily snickered at the curse. "I often wonder how the Goddess of Love feels about her holy breasts being talked of in such a way."

William chuckled. "I'm sure she finds it another way of revering her." He scooted closer and gently laid his fingers on it. The bruise was only a few hours old, but it was already a deep purple. The skin around it was a sickening green. "Lily, you have to heal yourself. You must be in agony." Honestly, the water was helping, but again, she didn't want to waste a spell while they were in the Shade.

She shook her head. "It looks worse than it is."

"I heard you hiss in pain," he shook his head and laid his entire hand over the bruise, "Blessed Otto, please heal your servant so she won't be in pain." Lily gasped as she felt the pain lessen a bit, and the bruise shrank a little.

She looked up at him. "You can heal?"

He looked up and met her eyes, his hand still on her hip. "A little, I learned how when I took the Seeker job. I figured it would be a good idea when I found those I was looking for. I didn't think they'd be in the best health."

She nodded. "That's smart." But he would not be deterred and stared into her eyes, she could see the pleading in them.

"Please, Lily, we won't die if you heal yourself." She looked back down at her hip, his hand still over the bruise. She slid her hand under his and cast a healing spell. The bruise was almost gone, and the pain was much more bearable. "Thank you." She nodded as he sat back and dunked his hair into the water like she had. She pulled her feet close and rubbed them under the water.

"So, Seeker William," he snickered and splashed some

water on his face, "do you have a sweetheart waiting for you after this?"

He shook his head and leaned back in the water. "No, no sweetheart."

Her eyes narrowed at him. "Really? I find that hard to believe."

William shrugged and washed some dirt from his arms. "Well, it's not like I'm actively looking. I always figured if it was meant to be, I'll know." He ran his wet hands through his hair. "Yesterday, you said we could ask you anything."

"I did." She wrung her hair out and started braiding it over her shoulder.

She noticed he looked cautious, even though he had permission. "You told Krag you didn't have children, is that true? You two were married for several years. I always assumed you had some."

She nervously licked her lips. She didn't often talk about that part of her life. "Yes, it's true. We were going to start trying when I turned thirty, but he got sick, and it happened so fast there was no time. I turned thirty last fall."

William shook his head in sympathy. "If any two people deserved children, it was you two."

Lily gave him a little nod. "Thank you." She glanced at him and felt her heart open to him in a way it had never opened before. "There was one child six years ago," William's eyebrows went up as he listened, "We were so excited, but soon after, I got sick. No one could help me, no one could cure me. It was something no one had seen before. And while I recovered... the child died inside me." The water spilled off William as he got to his knees and hugged her, his arms wrapping around her shoulders. She laid her head on his shoulder and wrapped her arms around him, "I think I'll always love that child, even though it barely existed," she whispered into his neck.

"Of course you love them. Mothers always love their children, no matter what."

She smiled against his wet skin. "I'm a mother?"

He sat back and held her face. "You *are* a mother, Lily, always, and I bet the soul of that little one is just waiting to come back to you."

She reached up and put her hands on his. "That is the sweetest thing I've ever heard."

"Well, you deserve to hear it, especially if you hadn't before." He sat back on his feet, his hands slid from her cheeks. She stared at him for a moment. It felt like she'd known him for years, more than just passing letters back and forth. Almost as if his soul was familiar.

"I feel all cooled off and less dirty. How about you?" She got to her feet, water dripping down her body, and she noticed William's eyes slowly moving up her body before he got to his feet. It had been a while since anyone paid her that kind of attention, and as she turned back to the shore, the corner of her lip tilted up in a smile.

As they stepped onto the shore, Lily cast a little spell that brought up a brisk wind and dried them both off.

William chuckled. "Handy." They dressed and made their way through the brush and found the others around a small fire.

"Have a nice dip?" Koizumi asked.

"For what it was, yes, the water is nice and warm." She began putting her chainmail back on while William buckled his leather armor back over his chest.

"Oh good." Leo stood and lifted his shirt over his head as he crashed through the brush.

Giles quickly got to his feet and went after him. "Leopold, would you be quiet!" He hissed as he crashed just as loudly through the bushes. Lily stifled her giggles and watched the other men get up and follow Giles and Leo, leaving her and William to guard the little fire. She didn't want her imagination going wild, so she decided to keep busy and warm some meat for everybody.

It didn't take long before she could hear them splashing around. "We weren't that loud, were we?" She smiled over at

William.

He chuckled. "No, we were perfectly silent. Not even the fish heard us." Lily laughed and turned the meat against the stones when she heard Giles calling out for her. They both sprang to their feet and rushed over to the little creek, where they saw Giles and Leo kneeling on the ground, looking at something.

"Lily!"

"I'm here, I'm here what?" She stopped next to him and saw they were looking at a leg. At least, she thought it was a leg. It seemed to have been rotting for some time, and she could smell the sweet smell of decay from where she was standing. It was also at least eight feet long which was something she'd never seen in person before.

Giles pointed at the disgusting thing. "Can you tell what this is?"

"Um… it looks like a leg."

"Can you tell what might have separated it from the owner?" Lily sighed and groaned internally, she would have to get closer, an extremely unpleasant prospect. Slowly, she kneeled and let her eyes study it. The leg was gray, and its knee was turned backwards like an insects. It was covered in deep cuts and if she had to guess, it was separated from its owner maybe two weeks ago. Leo handed her a nearby stick, and she began rolling it over when the young boy suddenly gasped and ran back into the water. Lily jumped at his sudden movements, thinking something was wrong. "What is it?" She looked around until she noticed Leo was kneeling in the water, staring at her, his hands below the surface.

Krag laughed and slapped him on the back. "I think the boy forgot he was naked!" She heard William snicker behind her. Truthfully, Lily hadn't noticed, but when she looked back at Giles, she saw he was naked as well.

"Leo there's no reason to be shy, I've seen just about every kind of body type there is," she turned back to the leg, "except for that." She used the stick and managed to turn the leg over. There was a huge chunk of missing meat just above the knee, and Lily held back a gag at the smell. "I'd say something big got it."

"Somethings in there." Krag walked noisily out of the water and reached into the big bite and grunted as he pulled whatever it was out.

Lily leaned a little closer and saw it was a tooth, a sharp, serrated tooth. "Blessed Otto, whatever got this thing was huge." She held out her hand, and Krag placed the tooth in her palm. It almost filled it.

"Blessed Otto," William whispered.

"Hope we don't run into whatever lost that," Giles said.

Krag laughed and strolled back into the water. "Oh, I don't know, might be kinda fun."

Lily dropped the tooth and wiped her hand on her robe. "Where did you find that?" she asked Giles.

"It washed downstream." He pointed in the direction it had come. It was the way they had to go.

"Of course it did." No one felt like relaxing after the leg was found, so the men quickly got dressed, and the group decided to hoof it to Artimus' keep instead of resting. Giles said he'd rather risk the old man's temper from waking him than be so exposed that night. They saddled up and followed the creek for another hour before Koizumi held up a hand.

"Does anyone hear that?" The horses stopped, and everyone strained to listen to what the young man had heard.

"I don't hear anything," Krag said. Lily's ear twitched and she turned just as a huge creature crashed through the trees. It looked to be a good fifteen feet tall with long arms that had two-foot-long claws at the end instead of hands. Its mouth was open, and she saw a tooth missing on the top, but it had so many she knew it wasn't hindered by it in any way.

"Run!" Giles spurred Malice through the woods, the other horses following quickly. William held Lily tight against him as Warden flew through the woods after Giles. She couldn't help but turn and watch the creature as it roared and followed them, running on its clawed knuckles. Krag's horse was the slowest and barely outrunning the monstrosity. The group burst through some trees, and Lily swallowed a scream as the horses suddenly stopped.

A tall, skeletal being wearing a tattered red robe was standing on a large rock about twenty feet away. It was surrounded by random undead creatures who were worshiping him. Dead humans, orcs, and goblins were on their knees, prostrating themselves before the skeleton. The evil that permeated the air threatened to overwhelm her, the power almost stole her breath, but she reached up and held her holy symbol and felt Otto's love flow over her.

"Blessed Otto, protect us." The giant creature that was chasing them smashed through the trees, and the undead looked up and finally saw they weren't alone.

The skeleton lifted a bony arm and pointed at Lily. "The Priestess first!" His voice was hoarse but rang loudly over the cracking sounds of the creature lifting a nearby tree out of the dirt. The smaller undead got to their feet and started running towards the group. Koizumi took a ready stance, and Krag unsheathed his weapon.

"My ax is calling for your heads!" He roared as half of the encroaching undead broke off and started heading towards the large creature. The other half was almost to Koizumi when Lily held her holy symbol high.

"Be gone, unclean beasts!" She yelled and felt Otto's power burst from her, and the nearest undead crumbled to dust.

"Koizumi run!" Giles yelled out and spurred Malice through the thicket and everyone followed. Lily turned and saw the rest of the undead leaping on the huge creature who was swinging the tree it had uprooted. When the forest's trees finally blocked the view of the horrible scene, she turned around and pressed close to William and thanked Otto that Giles didn't insist on fighting. The sounds of the weird battle rattled the forest as they ran through the dense trees. Loud roars, deep chirping, and wails of pain made her heart jump into her throat. Lily looked back once but didn't see anything chasing them.

"I think that creature running into us was a blessing in disguise," she yelled back to William.

He gave a quick glance over his shoulder and nodded. "I agree." *Please, Otto, quicken our pace,* she prayed silently. A few more minutes passed, and the battle sounds were long gone, but Krag yelled from the back.

"We got more company!" They all managed a quick turn and saw another horde of undead running after them. They were all wearing tattered tabards, and she could make out three horizontal stripes surrounded by circles, the livery of Mardensport. Something clicked in her head, and she remembered hearing about a missing squad from the large city about three years ago. Seems they've been found.

"There it is!" Giles yelled out, and Lily turned to see an incredibly, almost ridiculously tall, heavily gated tower in front of them. The horses came to a screeching halt, and both William and Lily hopped to the ground along with Krag. Leo jumped off his horse and stood protectively in front of Lily while Giles rattled the gates.

"Artimus! It's Giles Raventree let us in!" The gate rattled loudly but didn't open. "Artimus!" The undead stopped just at the edge of the clearing and surrounded the tower.

"Giles!" Lily yelled out. He turned and drew the sword from Malice's saddle and stood in front of the group.

"They're not moving." She heard Leo say.

"Nor will they, young man!" A voice sounded behind them, and they turned back towards the tower. An old man with long white hair was leaning out of one of the windows. "Giles, my boy, is that you?! It can't be. You were barely fifteen last I saw you. How are you!"

Giles sighed wearily and walked up to the locked gate. "Perhaps you could open the gate, and we could continue this reunion inside, old friend!"

"Oh yes, of course!" He waved his hand, and the gate creaked open. "Better hurry. That spell isn't made for so many!" The group hurried through, and the gate closed behind them as they ran to the steps of the tower. The undead finally overwhelmed whatever spell the old mage had created around his tower and smashed against the gate. But it was sturdy and didn't move, no matter how many piled against it. The front door opened, and the same man from the window started walking down the steps to the group. His white hair was long down his back, and he had a short, white, snowy beard.

"Giles, my boy, look at you!" He opened his arms and smiled, completely unfazed that his home was surrounded by undead whose numbers were growing by the minute.

"Artimus, thank you for letting us in." The old friends embraced, and Lily saw the old man studying them.

"Kind of old for traveling, aren't you?" he teased Giles.

He scoffed, "I wish. I came to ask a favor, Artimus."

"Well, why doesn't your boy there put your horses in the stable, and we'll talk about this favor over some dinner? How's that sound?"

"Sounds good, thank you." The old wizard turned and started back up the stairs. Lily felt Giles' hand on the small of her back. "Go on in. We'll join you in a moment." She nodded, and everyone but Giles and Leo followed the old man into the tower.

It was warm inside the tower, and it smelled of dust and herbs. Worn carpets and tapestries decorated the main reception room, and Lily assumed it had been many years since the old wizard had entertained guests. Who would willingly go to the Shade for a party?

"Please, let's all go by the fire. I'm sure you're all shaken, but I assure you, you're completely safe here," he said confidently, leading them into the next room. There was a long oak table in the middle of the room, it was covered with food, and there was a huge hearth with a friendly fire in it. Standing next to it was a light-haired half-elf man who looked up when they entered. He was wearing leather armor and Lily noticed a dagger at his side.

"Everything okay, Artimus?"

"It is now, young man," he turned to the group, raised his bushy eyebrows, then turned back to the half-elf. "I'd introduce you, but I'm afraid I don't know anybody's name."

The young half-elf smiled and walked over to the group. "That's okay, I'm Ivelios." He held out his hand towards Lily first, and she took it.

"Lily Marcel." She turned to the others, "This is Krag, Koizumi, and William Voltain." Ivelios shook hands with the others as a large gray wolf padded into the room over to the blonde man.

"He yours, I take it?" Krag asked. Ivelios scratched the wolf's ear, who proceeded to thump his hind leg quickly against the floor.

Lily smiled along with the half-elf. "Yeah, this is Bob." Lily's eyebrows lifted in confusion as the wolf's leg stopped thumping on the floor as he growled at Ivelios, who just laughed. "I'm kidding. He hates it when I do that. This is Yahul." The wolf turned to the group and stood regally next to his master.

"Now that's a much better name. May I pet him?" Lily had never touched a wolf before, but she figured this one was a lot tamer than the ones in the woods. Before the young man could answer, Yahul walked up and nuzzled her hand. His fur was soft, and he smelled like the wind.

She kneeled as he nuzzled her cheek, and she laughed. "He's amazing."

"Making friends, I see." They turned as Giles and Leo walked in.

"Trying anyway." She said as William bent down and used both hands to vigorously pet the wolf, who started growling happily, shaking his rump. "Giles, Leo, this is Ivelios and Yahul."

"Pleasure." He shook hands with the young man and then turned to the mage. "Artimus, I need your help."

"Help, eh? Why don't we sit, and you can tell me your predicament other than being chased through The Shade by every undead that resides here. Well done, by the way." Giles snickered as the wizard clapped his hands and cups appeared out of thin air along with bottles of wine. The drinks began pouring themselves and floating over to everyone, much to Lily and Leo's delight, whose smile could have lit the darkest cavern. Everyone sat around the fire, finding chairs or a bit of soft carpet, and Giles told his old friend what they were doing. After a couple of sips and a few bobs of his head, the old man clicked his tongue. "That is quite the job there, Giles."

"So, you'll help?"

He put his little glass down and shrugged. "I would like to help you, Giles, but I've already promised my time to Ivelios here." He motioned over to the half-elf next to Lily, who saw the lord's eyes wilt a little on the edges.

"I see."

"However," the old man raised a hand, "once I am done with that, I am glad to help. I'm sure Ivelios here wouldn't mind some extra help with what he's trying to accomplish, either. He may even be so inclined to join you when you leave."

"Yes, of course," Ivelios straightened up and looked at Giles, "I won't be needed here anymore so my life would need new meaning, and this is my kingdom as much as it is yours."

"Well, what exactly are you doing in The Shade young man?" Giles asked.

Ivelios cleared his throat and set his goblet down. "I first came to The Shade in hopes of cleansing it of the evil that had dug its roots deep into the land. Shortly after arriving, I realized this task was beyond me, but I still had to help. The faeries in my grove begged me to help them return to their plane of origin. But they needed the seed of life from The Shade and didn't know where it was. I've been searching for weeks and have come up with nothing."

"What is a 'seed of life'?" Lily asked.

Ivelios turned to her and clasped his hands together. "Every forest has a seed from which all life springs forth. The faeries need it to open the gateway to their world, which is in my grove. But without the seed, they are stuck here among all the evil, and their power is slowly waning. I must help them before this place kills them."

Lily looked over at Giles. "My Lord?" He sighed and rested his face in his hands. She could see the decision weighing heavily on his mind. Leave without the help he so desperately wanted and needed or help this young druid save a race of creatures known for their purity that could cost him what precious little time they had.

He looked over at the rest of the group. "What say you?"

Koizumi folded his hands in his lap. "I feel we should help the elf with his duty."

"Half-elf," Ivelios said, his eyes downcast. "Please don't lump me in with those inhuman abominations." Lily shouldn't have been shocked at his attitude towards elves. They were intensely xenophobic and kept to themselves in the forest. They rarely left their isolation, but when they did, things got violent.

"I apologize," Koizumi said, "I don't know much about the elves this far south."

The young man nodded. "It's all right. You don't really look like you're from around here."

Giles ignored the exchange and turned to Krag, who grunted a nod. "I'm always up for a fight, and the longer we stay here the more things I get to sink my ax into I'm bettin'. I'm willing to help."

Giles looked over at William. "What say you, Seeker?" William laid a hand on Lily's shoulder and she gave a little nod.

"We agree, it's a worthy cause, my Lord."

"All right then," Giles sat up straight, "Ivelios, we will help you with the understanding that when this is over, you help in our task."

The young man bowed his head. "You have my word.

Thank you so much for your help. I believe Artimus can locate the seed for us. After that, it shouldn't take long at all."

"Good." Giles sat back, making the old wooden chair creek. Lily could tell he still wasn't fully convinced that what they were doing was a good idea.

———

Now that the decision was made the group ate Artemis' food until they were bursting, except Giles. Occasionally, Lily would look over at him, picking and moving his food around the plate, barely taking a bite. She could almost feel how heavy his heart was just by looking at him. His eyes were down, and he only spoke when someone asked him something. When everything was eaten Artimus showed the group to some rooms and said he'd have the location of the seed in the morning. Giles thanked him and retired for the night while the others were still being shown their rooms.

"Mother, this is your room. I hope you find it satisfactory." Artimus pointed to the door across the hall from Giles' room.

"Thank you, master mage." She gave him a little bow and watched him show William to a room next to hers. He gave her a little nod and walked into his room. She held her hand over her doorknob, she wanted to go to bed, to lay down and sleep in safety. But she knew Giles was conflicted. Part of her job as a priestess was to bring comfort and clarity to the troubled minds of her charges, and Giles definitely fit that category. So, she quickly put aside her wants and walked across the hall. "My Lord, may I come in?" she asked as she knocked on the door.

"Please do." She heard from within and pushed open the door. Giles was sitting in an overstuffed chair, staring into the fire that blazed before him.

"I've come to lend you an ear. You seem troubled." She walked over to him.

His eyes moved from the fire to her. "That I am Mother."

She sat on an ottoman in front of him. "You must not feel that you're abandoning the first mission, Giles. If doing this can get us more help against whatever is holding the orc, it's a good thing. I'm sure whatever has Sobrei is something powerful and nasty, and I, for one, will be grateful for both Artimus and Ivelios."

He sighed heavily as his hand slowly moved to his lap. "I am grateful for their help as well. But I'm afraid my mind is more on how this current setback may impact my family. I left them in Raventree, and if this takes just a minute too long," his breath shuddered out, "I can barely think it, let alone say the words." Lily could sympathize with him, his family was in imminent danger, and all he wanted to do was finish this journey and make them safe again.

"I understand, Giles, I wish there was something I could do to ease your mind, but I'll say this. I'll make sure you make it back to your family. We will succeed and the world will not suffer that false emperor a minute longer after we get Sobrei. We all have families we want to be reunited with, but I know the happy memories that we have of them can sustain us and inspire us to do our best."

Giles gave a little chuckle. "I was just thinking about when my son was born. He was such a red squalling thing."

Lily smiled and reached out, laying her hand on his. "Just like that, the happy times can help ease our hearts."

He looked up at Lily, and she could tell he wanted to be careful with his words. "Do you still think of your husband?" Lily looked down and gave it some thought.

She licked her lips and met his eyes. "My grief is waning. Our happy memories give me joy again. I'm healing."

He patted her hand. "That's good. Losing one's spouse has to be one of the great tragedies of our lives."

"It truly is."

"I thank you for your council." He got to his feet and stretched his back. "I think I'm going to turn in. I suggest you do the same." Lily nodded and slowly moved to the door. "Goodnight, Lily."

"Goodnight." She walked out of Giles's room and saw William standing in the hallway, holding a tray with two mugs and she could smell chocolate in the air. "What's that?"

"Hot chocolate," he said with a smile.

Lily laughed and walked next to him. "Where did you get that?" She held up a hand, "I forgot we were in a mages tower, I'm sure you just asked for it, and it appeared."

William chuckled, "Pretty close, actually. Would you like a nightcap?" The hot chocolate smelled amazing, and even though she was tired, she admitted she wanted to spend some time with him.

"Sounds wonderful." She opened the door for him, and he walked over to the fire. There were no chairs, but there was a thick fur rug before the hearth, so he set the tray on the floor next to it and sat down.

"See, I knew you got a better room, my rug is threadbare, and the window is cracked." He sounded put out as he poured hot chocolate into some mugs.

Lily chuckled as she sat next to him. "I'm sorry, you can stay in here if you want. There's plenty of room." She motioned to the big king bed on the other side of the room.

"Naw, I'm just teasing," he handed her a mug, "but I appreciate the offer." She lifted the mug to her lips, but he put a hand over the top. "Not yet."

"Is it too hot?" He leaned back over to the tray then brought a spoon with whipped cream over.

"No, it's perfect, but this is what's really going to make it good." She lowered her mug and let him put a big dollop of cream in her mug. He let go of the spoon so she could stir it. "This is how my dad always had it." Lily smiled and stirred the cream into her hot chocolate, and took a sip. The chocolate was wonderful, but he was right. The cream added another creamy, rich layer of flavor to the drink, and she sighed.

"You could make a killing in Ardenry if you had a shop that sold this."

He laughed loudly, putting cream into his own mug. "Running a shop, that sounds like a nightmare." Truthfully, it did to her as well.

"Not the entrepreneurial type?"

He took a long drink. "Nope. I get why people like having their own shop, being their own boss, and all that. But you can be your own boss without that kind of responsibility."

"So, what do you want to be when you grow up?" she teased.

He looked over at her, his lovely blue eyes sparkling in the firelight. "Might be nice to be a Hunt Master for a Lord. Of course, I'd love to be a husband and one day a father. I think if I got those three things, I'd be the luckiest man in the world."

She nodded, taking another sip of her drink. "Those are noble aspirations."

He shrugged. "I don't know about noble, but they'd sure make me happy. What about you? Anything else you'd like to do?"

She finished her hot chocolate and put the mug on the floor behind her. "I'd like to pass the business on to someone else." His eyebrows went up at that. "I think I could do that now. I kept it up because it made me feel close to Henri, but lately, I keep hearing his voice in my head going, 'Go do what you love, my lovely, be happy in your own life.'" William gave her a little smile. "If I did that, I'd love to oversee a temple. But that's going to take a while as most want someone in charge that the people of the town know. So, first, I'd have to find a temple to take me in." She laid down on the rug, facing him, it was so soft, and the fire was keeping everything warm.

William put down his mug, and she could hear a little apprehension in his voice. "Would you...ever think about marrying again?"

She looked over at him, and as he turned to her, that wonderful, peaceful feeling flowed over her. It felt like happiness, and love, stability and devotion, all things she had been craving recently.

"I think...if I found the right person, it would be easy to marry again." While she knew that to be true, she was shocked that she was able to admit it out loud.

He nodded and laid on his back next to her. "That's a good way to look at it."

"I'm the kind of person to never say never, no matter the circumstances. Most balk at marrying clergy, though," she chuckled.

He turned on his side to face her, looking confused. "Why?"

She shrugged. "There are some people who think clergy put the gods above their loved ones. That they couldn't be counted on because of their staunch beliefs, just a bunch of reasons that don't really make sense." She noticed how his beautiful eyes burned into hers. She wasn't sure she'd ever seen dark blue eyes like his in her life. They reminded her of the sea before a storm, dark and churning from the flames of the fireplace.

"I'd think it'd be an honor to marry a priestess. That she felt I was special enough to be included in her life like that would be the ultimate sign of the devotion we would have for one another."

She felt her cheeks blush at that. "You just say whatever you mean, don't you?"

He chuckled, "Habit," he whispered. With the hot chocolate, soft rug, and warm fire, she felt her eyelids getting heavy. "Are you tired?"

"Getting there," her voice was quiet as she looked at him.

"Do you want me to go?" Her tired eyes roamed over him, his white tunic was askew, and he didn't have his boots on.

"No." She could barely keep her eyes open and laid her head on the soft fur. "Stay."

Her eyes closed, and she thought she felt something on her cheek. "As you wish, my priestess." She heard before she fell into a deep sleep.

CHAPTER 3
SEEDS, GOBLINS, AND MORE HELP

The next morning, Lily woke warm and rested, but it was clear she hadn't made it to the bed. She opened her eyes and saw she was still on the soft rug. She moved a little and felt a warm body against her back. Looking down, she saw William's arm around her waist. It was clear he was still asleep, breathing deep and even. Lily closed her eyes and savored the feeling of him so close. It had been so long since she fell asleep with someone's arm around her, with someone next to her. It was comforting. William was comforting, and she didn't want to move.

But as much as she wanted to lay there and bask, they had a job to do so she breathed in deep and turned to face him. The movement immediately woke him, and he opened his eyes but kept his arm around her.

"Morning." His voice was thick with sleep, and she brushed some of his long hair off his face.

"Morning. Hungry?"

He smiled, closing his eyes. "Mm, magical breakfast." Lily giggled and sat up. She fought not to blush as his arm slid off her side, his fingers almost lingering on her hip. She unbraided her hair and ran her fingers through it while William sat up and looked around.

"Boy, that hot chocolate really knocked us out."

Lily smiled. "I think it was an adrenaline dump after racing for our lives several times yesterday."

He nodded. "Or that, probably that." He got to his feet and held out his hands for her, which she took, and he pulled her to her feet. "How did you sleep?" He asked as they walked to the door.

"Better than I have in a while, you?"

"Same."

They were the first in the big hall, except the wolf, who was sleeping by the dying fire. She prayed to Otto, and the table disappeared under all the food and drink that appeared.

Yahul quickly lifted his head and sniffed the air, making both of them laugh. "I'm sure there's something good for you here, too," she said to him. He quickly got up and snuck a large ham slice from the table and ate it contentedly by the fire.

"A man of simple tastes, it seems." William piled a steak and eggs on his plate. Lily saw his eyes light up when he saw there was apple juice, and quickly poured himself a glass.

Artimus walked in next, and she heard his chuckle by the door. "I guess I've been outdone this morning." He waved his hand, and the dying fire once again came to life.

Lily smiled. "I figured your magic could be put to better use than feeding the strays you took in."

"You're not wrong there, young lady." He sat down and began spreading some jam on a piece of toast.

"Did you find the seed?" she asked as she poured him some juice.

He took a big bite as he nodded. "I did. It's not too far if I remember my way around. Mm, boysenberry!"

Lily relaxed and munched on a strawberry. "Good, I'd hate to have to walk much further around this awful place."

"Awful place?" He turned to her, his eyes were wide, and she had the feeling she had inadvertently insulted him. "This has been my home for almost twenty years!" William turned to her, his eyes wide as he tried to hold in a chuckle.

Lily cleared her throat to get rid of her own giggles. "I'm sorry, sir, it's just that, well, you don't have many neighbors for a reason, I'm thinking."

"Bah!" He waved his hand, and a piece of crust from his toast flew onto the floor. "A wizard needs privacy, can't get more private than The Shade, from people, at least." Lily had looked out a window when they walked down the stairs to the hall and saw they were still surrounded by the undead that had chased them the day before. It looked like a long day already. The rest of the inhabitants trickled in and ate Lily's breakfast heartily while Artimus explained where the seed was. "There's a hidden cave about half an hour east of here. The seed is in there. Now I know that particular area is crawling with goblins, so I'd prepare accordingly."

"After we get past all those undead," Leo mumbled into his milk.

"I wouldn't worry about that young man," Artimus said, "you have a rather powerful cleric with you. She ought to be able to get rid of them." Lily heard the mage talk about her as she stood behind William, tying his hair back with a thin leather strap as he continued to chat with Giles. His hair was thick between her fingers, and she was surprised at how much she liked playing with it.

"I will do my best." Lily knew it would take a great deal of power to get rid of all of them and wanted to save something for the cave. She wouldn't be any good to them if she spent all her magic before they even left the tower. She sat back down, and without a word, William began braiding her hair like she had the day before. His fingers were quick, and she tried her damndest not to close her eyes at the wonderful sensation. When he was done, she turned. "You know how to braid?"

"My mother insisted. She *said you never know you might have a gaggle of girls one day. You need to know how to do hair.*"

Lily laughed, "She sounds wise."

"Infinitely more so than me."

Giles smiled a little at the exchange and turned to Ivelios. "Do you know the cave?"

The half-elf nodded. "It shouldn't take long to get there," Ivelios laid his head in his hands, "I just can't believe I didn't think to look there." Lily could see he felt bad, so she reached out and laid a hand on his shoulder.

"I'm sure there are lots of places it could have been. Plus, if it's in a cave that's crawling with goblins, you're going to need help. So, it's a good thing you didn't go alone."

He sighed and nodded his head. "You're right, Mother. I'll make it right by getting the seed. I just need to focus on that."

"Good way to look at it," Giles said, "so I guess we need to get our things together then head out."

Ivelios stood. "Yes. I've been searching for too long. The quicker we can get out, the better." He started out of the room, Yahul following dutifully after.

Artimus sighed, "That boy's been beating himself up for a long time over this."

"His worries will be over soon, I hope," Giles got to his feet, "Let's start heading out." Everyone got to their feet and began filing out. Lily praying silently for a successful day.

———

The group walked down the stairs of the tower to the chorus of undead moaning at their arrival. "You want to clear a way for us, Mother?" Krag asked.

Lily held her holy symbol high and walked towards the fence. "Artimus, if you would open the gate, please?"

"Um, Lily," Leo stepped up next to her, "don't you think it would be safer with it closed?" She could understand his hesitation, but she needed to show them she wasn't afraid, and hiding behind a fence was like admitting fear.

"I *know* it would be safer, Leo." She glanced behind her at William, his sword drawn, and he gave her a wink. He knew what she was about to do. The gate started creaking open, and the undead began shambling inside. She could hear the men behind her unsheathing their weapons and hoped they wouldn't need them. "Foul beasts, I banish you in the name of Otto!" She yelled out, and her shell began to glow with holy power. The closest undead crumbled to dust, but others still flooded through the gate. "Otto, aid me in getting rid of these abominations!" Her shell grew brighter, but she could tell that these weren't normal undead. Being created in The Shade had made them more resistant to her holy power than usual. They would need direct divine intervention. Holding her shell high, she started running at the stubborn dead to the protests of her group.

"Lily, don't!" Giles yelled.

"Mother, what are you doing?!" Poor Leo sounded frantic.

"That's what I'm talking about!" She heard Krag yell and smiled a little as she reached the dead. Their bony hands closed around her robe, and she thrust her free hand on the closest one.

"I banish you from this world!" She yelled as her shell exploded with light and Otto's love. The undead roared, and she felt their hands fall away from her. When the light finally died, she saw she was alone just outside the gate. Krag's heavy footsteps stopped next to her, and she looked down just as he lowered his ax.

"Why'd you do that? I was looking forward to splittin' a few heads." She turned and saw everyone but Artimus and William running over. Leo looked so scared he was white, while Giles looked amazed but still a little worried.

"Why did you run away?" The young man asked breathlessly as they stopped in front of her.

"They needed a bit more, that's all."

"Are you okay? Did they hurt you?" She saw Leo's brown eyes roaming over her, trying to find some kind of wound.

"I'm fine, Leo, don't worry." She reached up and laid a hand on his shoulder. He was still trying to catch his breath but managed a little nod.

"You can't show fear when you banish the undead," William said, walking up, "She showed them how unafraid she is. And you can't do that from behind a gate or standing yards away."

"Exactly." She gave him a nod. "Now," she turned to everyone, "shall we?" Yahul happily trotted out of the gate towards what Lily assumed was the cave.

"This way." Ivelios walked out after his wolf, and the

others followed closely.

"Good luck!" Artemis called out before heading back into his tower. Lily didn't think he'd come on this particular venture but hoped he'd keep his word about joining when they were done.

Lily walked towards the back of the group, Leo and William diligently by her side. She could feel the drain that amount of power took on her. A nap sounded really good right now, and she hoped this wouldn't be a dangerous mission for her group.

Like Artimus said, it took about half an hour to reach the hidden entrance. After a quick spell from Ivelios, the vines and branches moved on their own to reveal the entrance that led into the earth.

"It's in there. I can feel it." The druid's voice was barely above a whisper as he made his way inside.

"Well let's not dawdle," Giles said and followed Ivelios inside.

"Otto, light my way." Lily's shell lit up with Otto's light, and she ducked her head as she entered the cave. Inside it was dark and smelled of wet earth, her shell the only source of light. "Which way?" she asked Ivelios. The half-elf's eyes were wide, and she could feel some kind of power surrounding him, and the smell of flowers replaced the smell of earth. "Ivelios?" He started walking down the passageway, his attention taken by something deep inside the cave.

They had been walking for five minutes when the sound of a sword swinging and a bow being loosed sounded just ahead.

Giles held up a fist, and everyone stopped and listened. "Someone's in here."

Krag stepped up next to his Lord. "Sounds too big for goblin weapons."

"Whoever they are, they better not have ill intent," she said. They could hear goblins chittering and yelling as they rounded one last corner. Lily gasped as her eyes focused on the activity in front of them. An orc and a young human woman were fighting a group of goblins. They both had big smiles on their faces as they cut down the little creatures.

"Help them out!" Giles yelled as he pulled out his sword and joined the fray. Krag laughed and ran after, quickly sinking his ax into one of the little jumping creatures.

"We don't need any help!" The young woman yelled out when she saw the newcomers. Lily watched her dance from goblin to goblin, her dark hair flying behind her. It looked almost effortless as the goblins died around her.

"Didn't think you did, but I've been itching to sink my ax into something all morning!" Krag yelled as another died by his hand. It was complete chaos as goblins jumped out of holes in the walls and tried to stab at the group. Leo moved in front of Lily, his sword drawn protectively, and William made sure nothing was coming up from behind. Giles stabbed the last of the goblins, and it made a pitiful squeal before it stopped moving. Everyone looked around and searched for more, but it was quiet.

"Is anyone hurt?" Lily called out. So far, everyone looked okay, but she knew the worst wounds could often be the hardest to find.

"No, we're fine," The woman said as she shook the green blood from her blade. She was wearing a black cloak and a worn leather brigantine. Lily didn't think she could be much older than Leo.

Giles turned to her and extended a hand. "Lord Giles Raventree."

She put her sword away and took his hand. "Sianora, you can call me Nora. This is Mal," she said, pointing to the orc at her back. Mal was huge, at least six and a half feet tall and muscular. It also looked like he had been shaving down the two tusks that protruded from his mouth.

He reached forward and shook hands with Giles. "Thanks for the help." Lily was too busy looking for Ivelios to be nervous of the large orc.

"Ivelios!" His shadow was flickering around the corner. *How did he get through the battle, and where was that light coming from,* she wondered and began pushing her way through the group. "Ivelios, wait!" Suddenly, a weight knocked Lily to the ground, and she yelled out as the tip of a dagger bit into her neck, right where her armor ended.

"Little shit!" She heard Nora curse as the sound of a sword sliced through the air a second before the weight was gone.

"Are you okay?" Giles helped her to her feet. She reached up and felt her neck. It was a superficial wound at best, more shocking than painful.

"I'm fine." She pointed up, "I'm fine. It wasn't a big blade, but keep your eyes up."

Everyone looked up and saw the holes. "Nasty little bugs." Krag growled and pushed past them. "Hey, elf, wait up!"

"Hurry," Lily pointed in the direction Ivelios went, "we need to catch up with him." Giles nodded and hurried after the young half-elf while Lily turned to the two new people. "You should stick with us."

The orc, Mal, nodded and put his bow away. "Took the words right out of my mouth," he said with a big grin. William pushed his way through the group up to Lily, his hand going straight to her neck.

"It's really a scratch," she said, but she knew William wouldn't let her get away with that.

He laid his hand on the little wound, and the pain was gone in an instant. "Now it's gone." He patted her shoulder.

"Thank you." They followed Giles, and Lily heard the young girl speak from the back of the group.

"So, what are you doing here?"

"We're helping Ivelios find the seed of life." Leo said, "What are *you* doing here?"

Nora flashed him a smile. "Just clearing out some rat holes." Lily thought she seemed rather excited about committing such violence. They turned one last corner and found themselves in a large cave with no way out except the way they came. In the middle of the cave was a small body of water about eight feet across, but the depth was hidden by unmoving, dark liquid. Ivelios walked straight toward the back of the little cave and fell to his knees as he dug into the wall. The others spread out and watched him dig, almost like something was controlling him.

"I hope it's in here," Leo whispered.

"This is it," Ivelios said quietly. He got to his feet and turned around, the smile on his face was pure joy as they saw he had a tiny white seed in his hand. "I found it. This is it!" The wolf licked his master's hand in his own little celebration, but it didn't last long. The hair on Yahul's back started prickling, and the wolf began growling at the water. "Yahul, what is it?" Ivelios slipped the seed into his pocket as the wolf began barking and running around the little pool.

Mal slowly drew his bow. "I think we need to go."

Giles nodded. "Yeah, we got what we came for." Ivelios quickly walked back across the room, and the group turned to leave.

"I hope there's no more go—" Leo yelped, and Lily watched as he fell to the ground and was quickly dragged by his ankle towards the pool of water by a huge tentacle.

"Leo!" Another tentacle slid out of the water and wrapped around his thigh. His scream made Lily's insides go cold.

"Mal!" Nora yelled out and started for the monster.

"I can't, I might hit the boy!" But as he said that another huge tentacle burst from the water and swiped at Nora, who ducked out of the way. "That'll do!" And he let loose, sinking an arrow into the thickest part of it. The tentacle quivered and quickly pulled back into the water but was replaced by several more. Giles dived forward, reaching out for Leo's searching hand, but missed by inches.

"No!" Krag threw his ax, but it landed just out of reach of the boy. Yahul leaped forward, his strong jaws clamping down on the nearest waving tentacle, ripping out a chunk before it sank back into the water. Lily ran and dived towards Leo, wrapping her arms around his torso before it disappeared under the water.

"I got you, I got you!" His arms braced against the edge of the pool, his hands slowly sinking into the mud. "William, help me!" Lily looked behind her and saw that the help she so desperately needed wasn't coming because the others were busy with goblins that had suddenly flooded the cave. Krag and Koizumi were knocking them back left and right, but when one flew away, two more replaced it. The large tentacle that was flailing in the air began swatting at the little creatures. When it missed its target, a goblin would hop on and start stabbing it with its dagger. It would have been a funny sight if they weren't in danger.

Suddenly, Lily heard a loud snap, and Leo screamed before he went lax in her arms. She began pulling and thanked Otto as he started coming out of the water. Leo wasn't very heavy, but he was wet, and it added at least twenty pounds to his lithe frame. Suddenly there was an orc arm reaching over her that grabbed the back of Leo's shirt. Lily squashed her fear of him. Helping Leo was more important.

"Pull!" He yelled, and with one last yank, they pulled Leo out of the water on top of her. "You got him?" Mal yelled.

"Yeah, help them!" She heard arrow after arrow leave the orc's bow as she dragged Leo back against the wall. "Leo, can you hear me?" She held his face in her hands, his eyes were closed, but he was breathing steadily, and his heart was strong.

Giles was suddenly next to her. "Is he okay?" The concern in his voice was overwhelming, and she quickly looked over the boy. He seemed fine except for his right leg, his femur was crushed, and his leg was bleeding profusely onto the ground.

Lily laid her hands on the horrible break and prayed. "Blessed Otto, please heal this boy of his horrible injury. He needs to be well to protect me on our journey. He is a sweet boy and doesn't deserve such pain." Otto's love and magic flowed through her, and when she felt it pour into Leo, she looked back up. His eyes were open, and he was staring at her.

Giles quickly leaned forward and held his face. "Leo, can you hear me? Are you all right?" His eyes moved from Lily over to Giles. He slowly nodded and licked his lips.

"Is it over?" His voice sounded tired and scratchy. Giles and Lily looked behind them and saw the ground was littered with dead goblins and the water was once again still.

"Yes, son, it's over," he said, turning back to Leo, "Lily, how's his leg?" She watched as her magic slowly put the bone and skin back together but knew it wasn't a hundred percent.

"He'll be able to walk on it," she glanced at Giles, "but it was too complex to heal fully so quickly." Her eyes searched and found Ivelios standing next to Mal, his bow still drawn. "You still got what you needed?"

He put his hand over his pocket. "I do."

"Good, I've had enough of this place." William was by their side in an instant, and together, they put their arms around Leo, and he stood up. He was a little wobbly at first but managed to take a few pain-free limps.

"I'll work it out," he said as he took a few stable steps.

"Yeah, you'll be fine, young man." William patted his back but stayed close as Leo insisted on moving under his own power.

Lily laid a hand on his shoulder. "Is there any pain?" Leo stopped a moment and gave it a thought before shaking his head. "Okay, then let's head out." Mal and Nora took point while Krag and Koizumi stayed in the rear. Lily and William stayed next to Leo, his father behind him. He could walk but Lily could see it pained him some.

They walked out of the cave, thankful there was nothing waiting for them. "Where is this grove of yours?" Giles asked.

"About five miles northeast of here, it shouldn't take long. I can meet you back at Artimus' tower." Without another word, he started into The Shade.

"Ivelios, wait, we can't let you go by yourself," Lily said.

She looked over at Giles, who sighed. "She's right, we'll go with you."

"If it pleases you," he said, without turning. The group started following the half-elf, Mal and Nora included.

"Don't mind, do you?" Nora asked, "Looks like our horses didn't make the wait." Lily didn't remember seeing any horses when they went in and felt sorry for the beasts.

"Doesn't look like it, does it? What say you, Giles?"

"The more the merrier," he said without turning. She had a feeling he wouldn't mind more help as long as nothing else stopped them from getting to Cyranar.

She held out her hand, "I'm Lily." Nora shook her hand, but when Mal reached out, Lily looked up and quickly took her hand back.

He looked startled for a moment, then smiled. "It's okay, I know I'm something to get used to."

She nodded, then looked back at Nora. "Why are you traveling with him?"

Nora laughed, "Mal's the best archer I've ever known, that's why."

Lily tried to keep the confusion off her face but felt she wasn't successful. "But—"

"He's an orc? Yeah, figured that out when I saw him naked that one time." Nora gave her a little wink and started after Giles. Lily knew she felt a little racist when it came to orcs, but she had never known a peaceful one. It was an unknown concept to her. Then again, she never knew a peaceful elf until her friend Ralan, so she knew they couldn't all be evil.

She slowly looked up and met Mal's eyes. "I'm sorry, it's just the only orcs I've ever known—"

"Were assholes?" Mal said as he followed his friend, "Yeah, most of us are, but after Sobrei was taken, I couldn't stand it at home anymore, so I left. I found Nora and haven't left her side." He said as he gave Nora's butt a healthy smack.

She quickly turned and elbowed him in the gut, but

it didn't seem to do much to him. "If you don't stop that, I'm gonna castrate you!" She said, but Lily heard the chuckle in the woman's threat.

"I'd like to see you try." Lily watched them interact and realized that her opinions of orcs had been highly twisted. Yes, most of them now worshiped their false emperor as a god, but humans worshiped Kore, the god of murder, and, to a lesser extent, the Shackled One as well. Who's to say that humans were any better.

She held out her hand. "It's nice to meet you."

"And you, Priestess," he said with a toothy grin as her hand disappeared in his handshake.

Sooner than anyone realized, they walked into a glade and were instantly calmed. Lily looked around and realized she had felt this kind of power before and recently.

"Here we are," Ivelios called out.

Lily stared at him, awe in her eyes. "It was you."

"What was me?" He kneeled and dug a little hole in the middle of the glade. Everyone watched as he carefully put the seed in it and covered it with dirt.

"I felt you running around The Shade yesterday. The one bright spot in all the darkness. I hoped that we would find you."

Ivelios smiled and got to his feet. "It seems I needed you more than you needed me. I'm glad we found each other." The group watched as little bits of light slowly began glowing and flying out of the trees around them.

"What is that?" Giles turned and watched them fly past him. Leo was leaning against a tree but when one of the lights popped out of it, he quickly moved next to the group.

"The faeries," the smile on Ivelios face was peaceful, "they're going home." Thousands of little lights surrounded them, and Lily swore she felt tiny wings flutter against her cheek. The little seed Ivelios planted began to grow exponentially, forming a large circle out of flowery branches. Slowly, the faeries started flying through one side but didn't come out the other.

Everyone could feel how happy and grateful the little sprites were to be going home. As the last one flew through, the light from the portal began to fill the grove.

"What's going on?" Giles went for his sword but didn't pull it free.

Ivelios shook his head. "Not sure." The light blinded them all, and Lily could feel magic pulling them in one direction.

"My Lord?" Leo called out, but it was so bright Lily couldn't see where anybody was. Suddenly, the light was gone, and the group was blinking furiously, trying to regain their composure. The woods around them were gone. In their place, they saw Artimus and their horses standing in front of them.

"Well, that was rude." The old man said as he crossed his arms over his chest.

Lily turned and saw The Shade was a few miles behind them. "What happened?"

Ivelios sighed, "It seems the faeries have transported us out of the Shade. I think they wanted us safe."

"Well, they could have asked first," Artimus complained. Lily and William chuckled at the old man. Malice walked over to Giles and nuzzled his cheek while the other horses began munching on the grass.

"Hey, boy," he said quietly.

"Can you tell which side of the Shade we're on?" Nora asked.

"Yes, the north side, west of the mountains." Ivelios pointed west, "Salthole is a week away." They looked to their right and saw the big mountain line in the distance.

"Convenient," Giles said, "Max told me he might have a contact in Salthole. We should check and see if they have any more information about Cyranar."

Mal put his bow up and nodded. "I agree we've—" he held up a hand, "Wait, did you say Cyranar?"

Giles nodded, "I did."

"Why in the nine hells would you go there?" Nora asked,

her eyes wide with amazement.

"This from a woman who voluntarily went into The Shade just to kill some goblins," Leo mumbled.

She walked over and held his chin so she could look him in the eyes. "The Shade and Cyranar are two vastly different things, boy. One is fun, the other is suicide." She let go, and Leo rubbed his chin as she walked over to Giles. "Why are you going? You don't look like treasure hunters."

Giles looked over at Lily, who nodded. "We're looking for Sobrei Re'vall. Our last reports have him being held captive in Cyranar."

Mal's jaw dropped as he stared at Giles. "You're serious, aren't you?" He quickly walked over and held out his hand. "I want to offer my help. Sobrei missing is the reason my home is gone to pot."

Giles shook his hand. "You're welcome to come along."

"Mal!" Nora walked over and tore her friend's hand out of Giles's, "What are you doing?" Leo limped over and held Nora's chin between his fingers like she had just done with him.

"It looks like he's lending his aid to a worthy cause." He let go and walked behind his Lord. Nora's eyes were glued to him as he moved. Lily thought she looked a bit taken aback that someone would stand up to her.

Finally, the young girl cleared her throat. "Well, where Mal goes, I go."

Giles nodded. "You both look like you can handle yourselves. We'll be glad to have your help."

Artimus sighed loudly. "Shall we go?" He waved his hands, and a carpet appeared on the ground. "I haven't been to Salthole in years. I wonder if that tavern by the dock still has that great apple drink." He sat down on the carpet, and Leo stifled a laugh.

Lily saw Koizumi look warily at Giles. "So, this man sitting on a carpet in the middle of nowhere is the reason we came here?" he asked quietly. Suddenly, the carpet hovered about four feet above the ground and started moving towards Salthole.

"Yep, it is," Giles said with a smile. "Leo, can you manage?" he asked as he got up on Malice. Luckily, the leg that was stiff easily swept over the horse, and he settled in.

"Seems so."

Nora helped herself up behind him and wrapped her arms around him. "Don't mind, do you?" Leo shook his head and gave his horse a little kick, and started after Artimus. William helped Lily up on his horse and then got on behind her as Giles sauntered over to them.

"That girl's trouble." Lily heard him mumble and gave a little chuckle.

"He's bound to run into a few in his life," she said, turning to him.

Malice diligently started after Leo's horse. "I know, I just hope she's not going to be a distraction." Lily looked over at Leo. He was staring straight ahead, not really paying much attention to the dark-haired girl behind him.

"I think he'll be fine," she said with a little smile.

CHAPTER 4
THE BATTLE OF SALTHOLE

As they traveled Lily thought about the last time she was in Salthole. It was almost eight years ago, and she wondered how the town had changed. It was a rough place when she was there, but she, Henri, Taren, and Dante had managed to bring a little bit of joy to the people. But eight years can change a place, and when they crossed the city's border, Lily's heart fell.

"Blessed Otto," she whispered. The city was crawling with Imperial orcs and Korites. The people seemed to go about their lives as normal, but to see such oppression was heart-wrenching.

"What the hell are Korites and orcs doing working together?" She heard William whisper harshly behind her.

"No idea, but I feel this place isn't as safe as we once thought." Everyone dismounted and began looking around.

"We were here just a few weeks ago," Nora said, "What the hell happened?"

Giles halted Malice until he was next to them. "They could be part of the legions that are camping between here and Raventree. Mother, do you think we might be able to stay at the Temple? I feel a regular Inn might be too dangerous." She could tell he already regretted his decision to bring them here.

Lily nodded and began leading the way. "I agree." The streets were dirtier than they were eight years ago. The smell of rotting food and too many bodies was constant, and the breeze from the ocean was almost nonexistent. Like it didn't want to come into the city. As they walked, Lily looked for some familiar faces but found none. After one last corner, they could see the gleaming white dome of Otto's temple in the distance. Artimus was still riding his little flying carpet when he suddenly zoomed off.

"Artimus!" Giles called after him, but he didn't stop. He flew up to an announcement board and pulled off a piece of paper before returning to the group.

"Seems you're a popular man, Giles." He handed him the paper, and Lily saw a drawing of Giles on it that said, *Lord Giles of Raventree, your presence is requested at the Dancing Bear Inn by Sergeant Derrick of the Ardenry Army.*

Giles folded the paper and put it in a pocket. "He's the prince's contact. Hopefully, he has some information for us."

Koizumi hurried next to Giles and leaned close to his ear. "There are Korites down the street staring at us."

Giles and Lily looked up and saw three red-clad figures staring at them. "So, there are. Let's just hope they don't start any trouble." Giles sounded a lot calmer than Lily felt and was glad he was the one in charge.

William put a hand on her shoulder, and she looked up at him. "We'll do what we need to do, then go, it'll be fine."

She sighed, "I hope you're right."

They walked down the alley, all eyes alert and thankfully found the Inn without any confrontation. Nora, Krag, and William decided to stay outside just in case while everyone else walked in.

"Lord Giles!" The voice was easily heard over the quiet din of the tavern. A man wearing Ardenry livery was sitting by the wall, waving them over. As Lily and Giles walked over, she noticed the prostitutes in the corner get up and start for the new men in the room. A redhead walked up to Mal, who shooed her away with a look.

"Damn orcs," she heard the woman mutter. One slid up to Koizumi. He gave her three gold pieces and bid her a good day. She smiled and walked away with the money she didn't have to work for. They sat across from Sergeant Derrick and shook hands.

"My Lord, I'm glad you made it here before heading to

Cyranar."

Giles leaned closer to the man with no tact. "If I were you, I'd keep my voice down," he said quietly.

The man looked around, "Ain't no one here gonna say nothing, just a bunch of whores," he said nonchalantly.

"Still, I'd advise you to be more careful." The bartender came over and set three mugs of ale down, and the man quickly started drinking. "So, what news?" Giles asked.

The man sighed and gave a hearty burp. "The prince has confirmed where in Cyranar Sobrei is being held."

Giles' eyes widened in shock. "Really? Leo!" The boy quickly walked over. Every time he limped Lily felt bad that she couldn't have helped him more. When they finally settled for the day, she'd have to work on it more. "Get me the map of Cyranar out of Malice's bag." He nodded and quickly did what his Lord asked of him.

"He can also confirm that the ones holding him are cultists of the Shackled One."

Giles breathed out and crossed his hands behind his head. "Almost nothing worse in this world than cultists."

Lily agreed as she nervously rubbed the cold, thick scar on her right hand. "Why did *they* want him?" she asked.

The man cleared his throat. "I don't know. Prince just wanted to know who and where."

Leo came back in and laid the map on the table. "Thank you, son." Giles unrolled it and held it down flat, "Okay, where is he?" The man took out a piece of paper and kept looking back and forth between the map and his paper.

"It looks like he'll be," he reached out and touched the middle of the city, "about here."

"Are you kidding?" Lily couldn't hold back.

The man shrugged. "Nice safe place if you ask me. Anyone coming after him would have to get through an entire city of Korites. Well, at least half a city. The other half is held by Efrits."

Giles almost choked on his beer at the man's words.

"Efrits?" The fire elementals weren't exactly known to be hospitable, and Lily hoped they could skirt around them.

"Yeah, seems them and the Korites are bidding for control of Cyranar at the moment. Kind of a tricky place to hide an orc prince, but what do I know," he said, shrugging. Lily sat back and held her holy symbol in her hands, *cultists and Efrits. What else could go wrong,* she wondered.

Giles quickly finished his beer. "I thank you for your time. We're going to stay in the Temple of Otto if you'd like to join us."

But Derrick just shook his head. "No thanks, got everything I need right here," he said with a smile, motioning over to one of the women.

"Well, I'm married so I'll just leave you to your business."

The man scoffed, "So am I, but she's not here, and I have needs."

Lily glared at him. "I feel sorry for your wife." She got to her feet and stomped outside, ignoring the man's jabs about stuck-up clergy.

Krag was sitting on a barrel, twirling his ax around by the handle, and looked up as Lily slammed the door shut.

"Something wrong, Mother?" She crossed her arms and looked up to the bit of sky where the temple's dome was visible.

"Some men are pigs," she hissed.

Krag laughed. "Don't tell me you're just now figuring that out."

"No. Just seeing it in front of me irks me."

Nora walked over, her hands on her hips. "Someone in there do something to you? I'd be glad to make him short an appendage or two."

Krag reached over and patted her shoulder. "My kind of girl."

Lily shook her head at him. "No Nora, nothing happened to me. But thank you."

"Good."

She looked around and didn't see the Seeker. "Where's

William?"

Nora motioned off to her right. "He's taking a wider watch." Lily nodded and leaned against the barrel Krag was sitting on.

"That boy's sweet on you," he whispered.

Lily looked over at him, and the dwarf was wiggling his eyebrows. "What?"

He chuckled. "You should have heard him that first night after he met you. Voltain fell hard."

"Krag, really." She turned away from him, desperately trying to keep her cheeks calm. The last thing she needed right now was getting teased by the dwarf. William walked around the corner, and the rest of the group started filing out of the Inn before she could fully process what he said.

"Shall we head to the temple?" Giles suggested.

"Yes, please. I feel the need to be surrounded by Otto." Lily put her hands in the arms of her robes and began leading the group back to the temple. She felt a hand on her shoulder, and without looking, she knew it was William.

"Are you all right? You seem annoyed."

She sighed and shook her head. "The guard we met with, he's an ass, but I need to forget about him. There are more important things to worry about." She looked up at him, "Did you see any Korites or orcs heading our way?"

William shook his head. "No, they seem to be avoiding the temple. Maybe that'll work in our favor later."

"Let's hope so." They saw no Korites as they walked the streets. For that, Lily was grateful. They made her almost as nervous as cultists.

———

The sun was a few hours from setting as she walked up the steps of the Temple, William next to her. Lily could feel Otto's love begin to radiate around her, and she relaxed. She smiled and looked back at her group and was shocked to see that William was the only one following her. Everyone else seemed to be waiting at the bottom of the stairs. "Well, come on, no one's going to bite you!" She teased and walked into the familiar temple with the sounds of her friends' footsteps behind her.

It looked the same, still clean and shiny. It even smelled the same, pine wax and seawater. There was an acolyte putting new candles in the holders who smiled as she walked in.

"Hello, Mother, what can I do for you?" he asked as he gave her a little bow.

Her group filed in behind her, and she smiled. "Good afternoon. Is Father Marco still here?"

The young boy's smile wilted a bit. "No, Mother, I'm afraid he died just last week."

"Oh, that's a shame he was an old friend. I'm sure he's at peace now."

"For sure, Mother. Is there anything else I can do?"

"Yes, I'm Mother Lily Marcel from Ardenry, and I was wondering if my group and I could find safe refuge here tonight."

The boy's eyes widened in excitement. "Lily? I wondered if that was you. I had hoped you would come back." He looked a little bit older than Leo, but she didn't know many youngsters so she couldn't place him.

"Do I know you, son?" She asked, trying not to seem rude, that she didn't remember him. He gave a little whistle, and a raggedy dog came in and nuzzled the boy's hand. "You gave me coin when I was starving about eight years ago." She gasped and took the acolyte's hand as the memory of that dirty little boy came back to her, and she laid her hand over her heart.

"Oh, Blessed Otto you're an acolyte now?"

"Yep, figured it was the least I could do. It's a lot more fulfilling than I thought it would be."

She quickly hugged him. "I can't tell you how happy it makes me to see you doing well."

He laughed and stepped back. "I'll let the Head Priest know you're here." He walked to the back of the dais and opened a door into the living chambers of the clerics while Lily turned to her friends.

"I knew him when he was just a little boy. He was half starved, sitting in front of a tavern with that old dog."

"Well, it looks like he's doing much better now," Koizumi said. The back door opened, and Lily watched a man with dark hair walk over and she wondered if he was the Head Priest. He seemed awful young for such a position.

"Mother Lily, it's wonderful to have you back. I'm Head Priest Rydell, I was but an acolyte myself the last time you were here, but I remember what you and your friends did for that family. Some still speak of it."

She took his hand and shook it, trying to keep her cheeks from blazing. "Thank you, Father. I have new friends this time and we're in need of safe harbor."

"Fear not, you all are welcome here. You can stay in my private quarters, I insist."

Giles stepped up and shook his hand. "Thank you, Father, it's most appreciated."

"Follow me. I'll show you to the room."

His room was on the third floor, it had a sitting area with a nice fireplace and behind the one other door was the bedroom. It was circular and spacious, with a big bed on the far wall.

Some acolytes had already brought some food and drink for them. "I hope you'll be comfortable here. At least it's inside." Lily walked over to the bed and sat down. She was about to take her boots off and rub her feet when a young boy ran into the room and looked around at the group. When he saw Lily, he ran over to her and handed her a piece of paper.

"Thank you," she said. She could feel a gold piece folded in the paper and opened it. It was a note from Koizumi. She had never read anything so lyrical before but managed to decipher that he and Mal were staying at an Inn across the street. She folded the note back up and handed the gold to the young boy, who smiled and quickly ran off.

"What was that?" Giles asked with a little chuckle.

"Oh, a beautiful note from Koizumi saying that he and Mal are staying across the street."

"I was wondering where they went," Nora said as she flopped down into one of the chairs.

"You should be comfortable here," Rydell said, "I'll leave you to rest now."

"Thank you so much for your hospitality, Father," Giles said, shaking his hand.

"Not a problem, you're most welcome. You have a traveling priestess of Otto in your company. A special one at that, and we thank you for keeping her safe." Rydell left the room, and Artemis crawled into the big bed opposite Lily and started reading.

"Leo, will you go see to the horses, please?" Giles asked, pulling his boots off.

"Yes, sir." He stood and hobbled towards the door.

"I'll go with you lad." William patted his back and opened the door.

"Leo, when you get back, I want to work on your leg some more, okay?" Lily called out. He gave her a quick nod and shut the door while Krag started in on the food.

"Good spread for a temple." Giles unrolled his bedroll on the floor and laid down, resting his head in his hands.

"Giles, would you like the bed?" Lily asked him.

"No, that's all right, ladies and old men get the bed."

She snickered and took a peek at Artemis, who didn't seem to hear him. "All right then." She swung her feet on the bed and laid back, closing her eyes in an attempt to relax. But something was nagging at her. She had a bad feeling, but honestly, at this point, it could have been anything. Would they be able to make it out of Salthole unaccosted, would they get to Cyranar in time, and would they have to fight the fiery Efrits that seemed to be vying for control of the fallen city?

So many things could go wrong. She took a deep breath and tried to shake the bad thoughts from her mind by thinking of the positives. They had more help than when they left Ardenry. They knew where Sobrei was, which cut down on their search a great deal. No one was mortally wounded, Leo's leg being the worst injury anyone had suffered so far. The morning she woke with William's arm around her was the best morning she'd had in a long time. Every moment with him was a bright spot in this quest, and she smiled.

"Shouldn't your squire be back by now?" Krag asked as he popped a few grapes in his mouth.

Giles got up and walked to the window. "He should, hope he didn't get lost." The sound of a wolf howling pierced the air, and they all looked at Ivelios. "Is that Yahul?" Lily opened her eyes and sat up in a flash and realized the wolf wasn't with them.

"Yes, something's wrong." Ivelios ran for the door, and everybody followed except Artemis.

"The stables are closer to the back of the temple. Follow me." Lily ran in front and led them down the stairs while acolytes and priests looked on in curiosity. They burst out the back door and saw the stables were just a few feet away.

"Leo!" Giles yelled out as he ran for Malice.

"William!" Lily yelled for the fighter, but all anyone could hear was Malice having a fit in its stall. They found him desperately trying to break the rope tying him down, but no Leo or William.

"Calm down, boy, calm down." Giles slid to a stop, his socks not providing much traction, and untied Malice, who quickly settled down. Yahul came running over and started biting at Ivelios' shirt and pulling him.

"Come on this way!" They started running out of the stable when everyone noticed the little dead thing on the ground.

"What the hell is that?" Krag walked up and poked it with his ax. It looked like some kind of rat, but rats didn't wear clothes, and no rat that size could possibly exist. It looked to be three feet tall, and the smell that permeated the air told Lily that it was infected with some kind of disease.

Nora knelt on the ground and pointed. "There's blood on its mouth, but it doesn't look like it came from whatever that thing is." Lily was inclined to agree with her. The mysterious creature looked like it had green blood leaking from a wound in its neck. The blood around its mouth was red, human.

"Leo!" Giles yelled and unsheathed his sword as he ran towards some nearby abandoned houses.

They quickly followed, and Lily heard swords clanging. "Leo, William!" They rounded a corner and finally found the young boy on the ground, another of those dead things on the ground next to him. William was standing over Leo, fighting off four of the twisted rat creatures as they stabbed at him with their own little swords. Lily could see Leo was holding his side, and his shirt was covered in bright red blood. Giles charged, and with the first slash of his sword, one of the creatures died.

"Leo, get back to Lily!" he ordered. Krag joined Giles with a loud laugh and was about to finally swing his ax when the one he targeted suddenly sprouted an arrow in its head and fell over dead.

"Damn it, that one was mine!"

Lily looked up and saw Mal and Koizumi running over. "There's another. I will catch him." The monk ran out of Lily's sight into one of the houses. Nora quickly joined Giles and William, flashing steel with the remaining creatures, and they quickly died. Lily ran over to Leo, who managed to get to his feet. But he refused to give up and tried to go into the house after Koizumi.

"Leo, stop, let me see." She grabbed his arm, and he stopped rather clumsily and would have fallen to the ground if William hadn't caught him.

"Those things, they came out of nowhere," he groaned.

"I've never seen such things. They're abominations." William gently laid Leo on the ground. As she kneeled next to them, she could see Leo's face was flushed, and his eyes looked feverish.

"Leo, did one of them bite you?" She slowly lifted his shirt, the blood made it stick to his skin, and it came away with a sickening squelch. She smelled the infection before she saw it and held back her shock. A four-inch round patch of skin on his stomach looked to be in ruins like one of those creatures had gnawed on him.

"Yeah, hurt like a bit— I mean, it really hurt."

She laid her hand over his wound and smiled softly. "I imagine it did hurt like a bitch Leo." He chuckled lazily and lay flat on the ground while she prayed. William and Nora stood next to them, their swords drawn, waiting for those things to come back.

———

Giles ran into the abandoned house and saw Koizumi in the doorway on the other side of the house.

"Where did it go?"

"Upstairs!" There was a crashing noise, and the monk turned and looked down the street. "He's there!" Whatever it was had smashed through an upstairs window and was still running.

"Pippa's bouncing tits, this thing is not normal!" Giles yelled as he ran through the abandoned house after Koizumi. The thing was covered in a black cloak and fast, but Koizumi was faster, and his hand wrapped around the flowing cloak. "Bring him down!" Giles yelled. He was almost to them when the thing twisted in the monk's hand and threw something in Koizumi's eyes. The monk yelled out in pain and shock, which gave the creature the opportunity it was looking for and started slipping away. "No, no, no," Giles said to himself. He thought the thing was going to get away until an arrow flew into the thing's back, taking it to the ground. He quickly turned and saw Mal was behind him, his bow still up. "Good shot!" He ran up to the figure and ripped the cloak off, but he was not prepared for what he saw and fought hard not to scream.

The person under the cloak was bone white, there was no hair on its body, and it looked emaciated and slimy. "What the hell?" He whispered and was about to kick it over onto its back when it suddenly burst into dust. Giles stumbled back a few steps and saw Mal ogling the dust pile. "Damn, Mal, what kind of arrows did you use?"

"The regular kind," he stuttered out in surprise, "I've never seen that happen before."

Koizumi walked over, still rubbing something out of his eyes. "Search the remains." Mal took out an arrow and started sifting through the ashes while Giles picked up the cloak.

"I've never seen a creature like that before. If I had to guess, I'd say it was some kind of undead." There was a little tinkling noise, and Mal lifted his arrow, and Giles saw a ring hanging on the end.

"He did leave something behind." He handed it to Giles, who took it off the arrow tip. There was a carving on the ring, but he didn't recognize it. "I don't know. Maybe Lily or Artemis will know what this means. Let's get back to them. I want to see how Leo's doing." He pocketed the ring and made their way back to where they last saw Lily.

———

The wound on Leo's stomach was almost closed and had stopped bleeding, but Lily could tell the young boy would need more than just healing to get rid of the disease that the creature had given him.

"Will he be okay?" Nora asked.

"He will be. Come on Leo, we need to get you back to the temple so we can make you well again. William, help me." He nodded, and the two of them got Leo to his feet. Whatever this disease was worked fast. He was already sweating, and it seemed to take a lot of effort just to pull himself to his feet.

"Thank you, Lily," his voice was quiet as he leaned against her for support.

"Leo!" Lily turned and saw Giles, Koizumi, and Mal running over to her.

"There you are. Where did you go?" Nora asked her friend.

"I was with Koizumi, and it's a good thing, too."

Giles stopped in front of Lily and pulled something out of his pocket. "Do you know what this symbol is?" He handed her the ring, and she passed Giles, his son who didn't put up much of an effort to stay on his feet. Lily wiped the ring clean and felt her blood go cold. Two hands bound with shackles were stamped rather hastily into the top of the chipped, pewter ring.

"Where did you find this?"

"I think from the one in charge of these little rat things. It looked like some kind of undead, but it was nothing I'd ever seen before. Do you know it?"

Lily nodded. "Yes, I do. It's the symbol for The Shackled One."

Everyone's eyes went wide. "Pardon me?" Giles asked. She heard William curse behind her as he sheathed his sword.

Nora started pacing and chewing on her lip. "I thought he was dead. Why does he have followers if he's dead?"

"He's not dead," Lily said, "he's not fully captive either. His presence will make a resurgence in our lifetime I have no doubt about that. But we can discuss that later. Right now, we need to get Leo back to the temple. He's been infected by those creatures, and he needs more than what I alone can give him."

"Okay, come on, Leopold, you don't have to go far." Giles started walking with him. The poor boy looked drunk as he slowly stumbled alongside his father.

"Pretty Lily can heal me," he mumbled, his eyes half closed.

Krag laughed. "I think he's going to be alright."

"He will be," Lily said as she wrapped the ring in a piece of cloth and put it in her pocket.

Giles carried Leo up to their room while Lily quickly rummaged through the Temple's herb room. Rydell walked in and started pulling the hardware she would need to make a poultice and a tea for the young boy.

"What exactly happened out there?" he asked, putting

glass vials in a big wooden box. She finished gathering her herbs and motioned for him to follow her.

"Seems The Shackled One has some new creatures he wanted to test out. Hopefully, they won't come back." As they climbed the stairs, she told him what happened and what seemed to be wrong with Leo.

"Sounds serious, but I know together we can get him up and around again," he said with a confident smile.

"I appreciate the help, Rydell. It's been a long day." They walked into the room and set their things down on the dresser. "If you can set up the equipment, I'll get the herbs ready," Lily said.

"Right." Rydell started putting the glass jars over the burners and filled them with water he called from Otto, while Lily quickly checked on Leo. Giles had put him in the bed, the poor boy was sweating profusely and mumbling nonsense.

Giles was sitting next to him, holding his hand. "He started up just after we laid him down."

She nodded and touched his forehead. He was burning up. "Leo, can you hear me?" He took a breath and locked eyes with her. "We're going make you better, okay, you just have to be brave for me, okay?"

He slowly nodded. "Brave for Lily," He mumbled and closed his eyes.

"Let him rest for now. It shouldn't be much longer." Giles nodded and turned back to Leo, fatherly concern all over his face.

She turned back to the beakers as the water started boiling. "Thank you so much, Rydell." And quickly grabbed the herbs she needed, squeezing them between her hands to release as much of the juice as possible before throwing them in the water.

"Here, add some white willow bark. If there's inflammation, it'll help bring it down."

"Thank you, Rydell." She took his suggestion and added just a little, "Giles, is Leo allergic to anything?"

"No, oh wait, uh cinnamon, he can't eat cinnamon."

"Good, I hadn't planned on using any." The leaves and roots mixed in the hot water and created a strong tea that smelled of mud and dandelions. Lily strained the liquid into a mug and handed the dregs to Rydell. "Father, if you could make a poultice for me, I'll get him to drink this."

"Yes, Mother," he said as she sat next to the afflicted boy.

"Leo?" His eyes fluttered open, "I need you to sit up and drink this all right? I can't promise it tastes good, but it'll help." Giles moved and helped prop Leo up so he could drink while Lily put the mug to his lips. "Drink Leo." He was a good patient, only sputtering a little while it went down.

"Tastes awful," he said as she put the mug down.

"I know, the best medicine often does. Go ahead and lay back down." She looked over at Rydell and caught a glimpse of Nora. She was pacing nervously at the foot of the bed.

"Nora?"

She stopped and looked up. "Huh? Do you need something? I can go get it."

Lily smiled for the girl's concern. "He'll be all right, Nora." She nodded and bit her lip, finally sitting down next to Ivelios, her hands wringing themselves in her lap.

"Here, Lily." Rydell handed her the wet, gray poultice, and she put it on the remains of his wound.

"This should help keep it from getting infected, well, more infected." She used some cotton wrapping to keep it secure on his body. It wouldn't do any good if it slid off. When she was satisfied with that, Lily pulled the covers down to his ankles.

"What are you doing?" he asked as he started fidgeting nervously. They had gotten him down to his underclothes before he got into bed, and she smiled up at him.

"I wanted to work on your leg some more, Leo, remember?"

He calmed down and stopped moving. "Oh, yeah you did say that, sorry I forgot."

"That's all right. You're allowed to forget when you're sick with something no one else has ever had." He gave her a brave smile and looked over at William, who was standing at the end of the bed.

"Did we get them?"

William smiled. "Yeah, we got 'em, you rest. You deserve it."

Giles hugged him, making sure not to touch the wet poultice. "We got 'em, Father," he mumbled, his eyes closing.

He chuckled. "I saw, you fought well." But Lily didn't think he heard his Lord Father as he fell asleep. Lily laid her hand on his thigh and could feel how tight the muscles were still. *Blessed Otto, I pray that you continue to heal Leo's leg. He is a young man and needs to be healthy to fight for his Lord.*

Lily prayed for an hour until she felt his leg was as good as it was going to get. When she opened her eyes, she saw Leo was still asleep, his mouth was slightly open, and he was snoring lightly. The sun was down now, and she saw that almost everyone around the room was asleep. Nora was in the chair, her neck at an odd angle as her head rested in her hand. Ivelios seemed to be meditating rather than sleeping, but his wolf was fast asleep next to him, kicking the air in his dreams. Giles was asleep, still holding Leo's hand. The devotion he had for his adopted son made Lily smile. William was sitting on the floor against the bed next to her, his head back on the mattress.

Krag was the only one not in the room. She suspected he was somewhere around the kitchen since all the food in the room was gone. Lily started feeling the excitement from the day catch up to her as her eyelids grew heavy. She used a lot of her power, and she could feel her body screaming at her for rest. So, she didn't fight as she sat next to William, laid her head on his shoulder, and quickly found sleep.

———

Lily felt something touch her cheek, and she woke. When she opened her eyes, she saw William looking down at her, his eyes soft.

"Why didn't you crawl into bed?" he asked quietly.

She wasn't sure what to say, if she could admit it aloud. "I..."

"Evening, Mother," Giles's voice broke the gaze they held with each other. She saw the Lord, Nora, and Ivelios were eating, "They brought us some more food," Giles said. She wasn't sure how long she slept, but she felt much better and quickly got to her feet.

She bent down and put a hand on Willam's cheek. "Go get something to eat." He nodded and pulled himself up, and joined the others while she checked on Leo. He was still asleep. His fever was down from what it was but not completely gone. "He's doing much better." She reported and slipped off the bed. Her stomach rumbled at the smell of the meats and cheeses on the platter.

"He is," Giles said, "I can't thank you enough, Mother. He seems to be a little accident-prone lately."

Lily waved him off. "We all have our moments, I'm sure. What time is it?"

"Almost midnight, I believe. They came in about an hour ago with the food." Her stomach rumbled, and she picked up a piece of meat.

"That was good of them." She had barely taken a bite out of a piece of her turkey when an acolyte ran in breathless. He looked rather upset.

"Um, Priest Rydell wanted me to tell you that it seems a legion of Korites are heading straight for the temple." Lily almost choked on her food, and she felt William's hand on her back.

Giles swore and started putting his armor on. "We'll help any way we can." The acolyte nodded and left the room. "Leo's in no shape to fight he'll have to stay here," Giles said, glancing at his son.

"I can stay with him," Nora said, "unless you'd rather I come down with you, either way," she quickly added. Giles looked over at the young half-elf, who was putting on his own leather armor.

"Ivelios, do you think Yahul can watch over him?"

The wolf sat up and gave a bark. "He'll watch over him with his life, my Lord."

"Good," he turned back to Nora, "we may need your blade." She nodded and gathered her things without protest. "Where the hell is Krag, and could someone wake Artemis?" Giles started giving orders and people hopped to. Ivelios walked over and nudged the old man, who woke with a start. "There are Korites coming. We need you," the young man said.

"Bah, damn Korites always interrupting my naps." He slammed his book shut and climbed out of bed. "Can't a man get any sleep around here?" He walked angrily out the door, even though he had probably gotten more sleep than any of them.

Giles threw a big piece of meat over to the wolf, who deftly caught it in the air. "Keep Leo safe, and there's more where that came from." Yahul barked and jumped up on the bed, and laid a paw on Leo's arm. "Good boy, okay, let's go see what's going on."

As the five of them ran down the stairs, Lily prayed. "Otto, we are about to defend your house from a dangerous foe, please be with us this night, make our swords sharp and swift, make our arrows true and our spells powerful." She could feel that Otto blessed them, but she wondered if it would be enough.

They reached the first floor and saw all the priests and paladins gathered around the door. Nora was pacing nervously behind them. "Mal's still out there."

Lily could hear the concern in her voice. "I'm sure he'll be fine, Nora. It may even be a good thing he's across the street. That bow of his is rather deadly he can snipe from the tavern." The young woman huffed and started swinging her sword in the air around her without a word. Lily was worried about the others as well but there was nothing she could do now. She walked up behind Giles, who was standing next to Rydell at the open doors of the Temple.

"Forgive my lack of battle vernacular, but exactly how

many is a legion anyway?" she asked.

"Anywhere from five to six thousand men," Giles said.

Lily felt her heart sink at the realization. "There are six thousand men coming here. What are we going to do?" The thought almost paralyzed her. Six thousand men against barely a hundred, mostly priests. The odds weren't good.

"We're going to choke off their charge." Giles pointed down the road with his sword. "We'll keep the doors open and surround it with our fighters. The healers will be behind us," he turned, eyes on Lily, "keeping us alive."

"How do we know they're coming here?" William asked, "maybe they just want to attack Salthole?"

"Not that I wish Salthole be burned to ruins," Rydell said, "but a scout reported their men talking about hitting Otto's temple and leaving the town alone. This attack is especially for us."

"Wonderful," she groaned, and her ears picked up a rumbling noise in the air. "What is that?" William walked up and put a hand on her shoulder.

Giles sheathed his sword and took a deep breath. "The sound of six thousand men coming for us." She and Willam turned and looked out into the street and watched as it slowly filled with marching men wearing Kore's red livery.

William's arm slid around her waist, and she did the same to him. "Otto, be with us," she whispered and felt his lips on her forehead.

"He will be Lily. We're in His house," he said the words against her temple.

She looked up and put a hand on his cheek. "Blessed Otto, protect him from injuries that would be catastrophic. Let him be strong during battle." She felt the spell sink into his chest, and she felt a little better that he had a little extra protection.

He hugged her. "Thank you, my priestess." He stepped back and unsheathed his sword. "Stay safe." She watched him walk over to Giles and talk strategy. Her heart was pounding.

She had never been in a battle before and hoped she had rested enough that she would be able to keep up with the injuries she would need to heal.

Ivelios came running from the back of the temple. "We only have to look after this one door, I've taken care of the back they won't get through ten inches of stone."

"Good thinking," Giles gave him a nod, "now prepare yourself. We've got a long night ahead of us. Mother, stay back if you can."

"Yes, my Lord."

Giles looked up to the second-story balcony. "Artemis, just keep throwing spells at them for as long as you can!"

The old wizard peered out the window. He had a perfect view of the army. "Will do, young man!" The noise stopped, and Lily glimpsed the army in the street. There were several figures in red robes standing in front of the regular rank and file.

"Shut the doors for now," Giles said. The paladins started shutting the doors when Lily saw the robed figures start moving their hands.

"Look out!" But she was too late, and everyone within ten feet of the door was thrown back by the blast of three huge fireballs. The noise was deafening as the doors splintered and people screamed in pain and shock. Lily landed hard on her back and heard Nora scream somewhere behind her. When she finally came to her senses, she sat up and saw Rydell a few feet to her left. He was burned and shaking. "Rydell!" She crawled over to him. The skin on his hands was black, and his chest was bleeding. "Hold on, you're going to be okay." She laid her hands on him, and he groaned. "Blessed Otto, this protector of your house is badly injured. Please give me the power to heal him so he may keep defending his people." Otto's love flowed quickly from her hands, and she watched the burns start to heal. She looked up and saw William helping Nora back up to her feet. He looked unhurt, and she thanked Otto for that little miracle.

"They're coming!" She heard Giles yell and looked behind

her. The doorway was filled with paladins, preparing for the charge. When the Korites finally made their way up the stairs, the noise was deafening, metal on metal as sword and shield met, but she could see Otto's paladins clearly had the advantage. The choking method seemed to work as the first wave of enemies died quickly with little damage to the paladins.

Rydell coughed and sat up. "Thank you, Mother, I need to get to my people." She helped him up, and he raised his hands in the air. "Blessed Otto, help me protect your temple!" he cried out. Lily could feel magic in the air and watched as lightning struck the first third of the army waiting to charge the temple. They fell to the ground and didn't move, "Maybe that'll help a little." He said and moved behind his men.

———

Koizumi was looking out the window and noticed the town seemed rather empty. Since they arrived in Salthole, the guards were an ever-present force on the streets, now, there was no one.

"Mal, something is not right."

The Orc put his bow over his shoulder and walked next to Koizumi. "What's wrong?"

"Look at the street."

Mal opened the window and poked his head out. "It looks rather peaceful. You're right. That is odd." He said with a smile and was about to pull back in when his eye caught something in the distance. "What's that?" The monk got to his feet and crawled onto the window ledge. There was a large group of people making their way down the street. They didn't bother anything as they walked, and the longer he looked, the more of them there seemed to be.

"Whoever they are, there are a lot of them." His eyes caught movement and saw a single guard quickly make his way into a house across the way. "Perhaps he knows." Koizumi quickly climbed down the building while Mal watched, amazed.

"I'll just meet you over there," Mal mumbled and quickly

ducked back into the room.

The large group of people hadn't quite come into view at the end of the street, but Koizumi didn't lower his guard as he ran across the street and flattened against the building he saw the guard run into. Mal made his way over, his bow still slung over his shoulder.

"Perhaps we should take an alternative way inside." The monk suggested.

"My thoughts exactly." They snuck around to the back of the building and pried open a window.

Both listened for a moment and heard fighting inside. "It seems they are in need of assistance." The monk said and quickly hoisted himself inside.

"Get the door. I won't fit!" Mal whispered after him. The back door clicked, and he ran up the stairs, an arrow ready in his bow. It was dark in the house, but it wasn't hard to find the guard. They could hear him yelling in the front of the house. As they made their way through the hall, they could see several dead guards, some had their throats slit, and to Koizumi, it meant they weren't expecting it. The others had deep wounds in their chests. They all had met violent ends. They heard a man give a death cry, and they ran to the front of the house as the guard Koizumi saw earlier pulled his sword from one of the Korites that had been occupying Salthole.

He quickly turned and flashed his sword at them but stopped. "You're not Korites." He said. He had a big bruise on his face, and his leg was bleeding, but otherwise he was fine.

"No, we are not, but we noticed something was wrong and wanted to help."

The man nodded and wiped his sword clean. "There are more of us upstairs. The Korite Captain is holding my men hostage. They heard the Korites talking about a legion coming, and they plan on marching on the temple."

"An entire Legion!" Mal almost dropped his bow, "That's what we saw? It's a bit overkill, isn't it?"

"They're Korites. Everything is overkill with them." The guard took a calming breath and held out his hand. "I'm Corporal Whitmore, you can call me James."

"Koizumi, this is Mal."

He nodded. "I don't know how many are alive upstairs, but I've got to try and save them."

"Lead the way," Mal said, and they followed James up the stairs.

The floor creaked under his footsteps, and Mal saw shadows moving around them. When they got to the second-floor landing, they saw a door at the end of the hall was open, letting the moonlight spill into the rest of the house.

"Donovan!" James yelled out and headed towards the open door. It was halfway open, but he made the effort and kicked the door wide anyway. The three of them walked in and saw a man standing in the corner. The skulls on his shoulders told them he was indeed a high-ranking Korite. He was smiling as he pressed a dagger to the throat of one of the town guards who was tied up on the floor.

"Ah, James, so nice you could join us." He quickly slit the man's throat and wiped the dagger on his pants as the poor man fell to the ground.

"No!" James rushed forward, but Mal held him back.

"Wait, it could be a trap," he said in his ear.

"You will die, Donovan, I promise you that!" James yelled, pointing his sword at the man.

The man just laughed. "You think death scares me? My god will bring me back so that I may continue to serve him, WE DON'T FEAR DEATH!" he screamed, and the windows exploded. Mal and James covered their heads as shards of glass scraped and bit at them. Koizumi flipped to the back of the room and saw shadows on the floor coming from around Donovan.

"There are three more next to him!" he yelled out and rushed the first one. Mal fired an arrow and it sunk into nothingness, but he heard a groan just as a man appeared.

Donovan unsheathed his great sword and charged James. "Kore will love having you in his service, James!" He swung, but the guard was able to avoid the worst of it as it barely grazed his shoulder.

"He'll never have me!" Their swords clashed back and forth while Koizumi and Mal took care of the invisible foes. One by one, they groaned and appeared on the floor, bleeding and bruised.

"Untie the guards, Koizumi." Mal took out his short sword and quickly dispatched the unconscious Korites while the monk deftly undid the knots on the men's bonds. The sounds of swords clashing filled the air, and when all the guards were untied, they picked up what weapons they could find and joined James.

"You're outnumbered Donovan, give up!" James' sword made a wide arc up and caught the Korite in the chin, and he stumbled back into one of the now-freed guards, a waiting knife in his hand. He twisted it, and a slight crack sounded in the room.

"Or just die. I really don't care, you piece of shit." The man growled and let Donovan slump to the floor while the others made a pin cushion out of him.

James leaned against his sword, the tip stuck into the wood floor. "Are you all okay?" He asked the guards.

The men wiped their brows and nodded. "We're fine, Corporal, just a little shook up."

"Understandable, but now we're really in it. The legion is marching on the temple as we speak."

"Should we try and evacuate?"

Koizumi moved next to James. "I don't think that will do much good, besides do you really think the priests would abandon their temple?"

The men looked between them and shook their heads. "No, they wouldn't." Suddenly, the little bits of glass on the floor started tinkling lightly against the wood.

"What is that?" one of the men asked.

James walked over to the broken window. "Bright Alar

help us," he gasped. Everyone moved to the window and saw the street was filled with Korites, as far as the eye could see. "We do what we can. That's all anyone can ask of us," James said.

"My thoughts exactly," Koizumi said and snaked his way out of the broken window onto the roof of the building. He had seen a lot of armies in his day, and he could tell that the bulk of the enemy was just rank and file troops, nothing special about them. They would be lucky if their weapons were of decent quality. Koizumi watched as three Korites who made the army deadly started their way towards the temple. They were wearing red robes, and Koizumi smiled. He knew just what to do with them.

Mal climbed up onto the roof through the access panel and sighed. "I don't have enough arrows for all of them."

"Do what you can," James looked up at the Orc, "We can ask no more of you." An explosion shook the Temple and they both saw the doors were blown open and bits of fiery wood littered the ground.

"Have fun down there, Monk," Mal called out.

"Oh, I will." He watched as the lithe man quickly climbed down the building and ran over to the three spell casters.

"Crazy monk." He drew his bow and covered Koizumi as best he could.

———

Koizumi was smiling as he ran up behind the nearest spell caster. "Hello!" he called out and swept his legs under the man's feet, tripping him. The caster fell hard to the ground, and the monk was already on the next one. This one saw it coming, and Koizumi barely dodged out of the way of another fireball that erupted from the man's hand. "Almost!" he yelled tauntingly and took that caster to his feet just as easily as the first.

He looked up at the last one, who was shaking with anger, "Kore will make good use of you," Koizumi didn't let him finish before he took him down, too. "Let him try it!" he laughed and moved back to the first one, who was back up on his knees. "I don't think so!"

Mal watched as Koizumi moved from spell caster to spell caster, taking them down before they could get up. He laughed as the monk easily did this repeatedly, barely hitting them, but it was enough that they couldn't cast anymore against the ones inside the temple. His eyes took in the rest of the field when he realized his friend didn't need any help, especially after James and the other guards started running interference for him.

"I hope he knows what he's doing," he said to himself. Mal glanced over at the temple steps and gave a little impressed whistle. There were so many bodies, they were already piling up on the steps, and he felt lucky to be up high. He drew back his bow, but before he could fire an arrow, a searing pain stopped him. He reached back and pulled a dagger from his side and saw a man dressed all in black standing behind him. Mal reached out and, with his big hands, gripped the man's head before he could duck away. "Big mistake." Mal shoved him backwards and threw the dagger off the roof. "Let's see how you do when they know you're there." He slashed down as quickly as he could, but the assailant jumped back and brought out another dagger. "That little thing's not going to do anything." Mal tried to intimidate the man, or who he assumed was a man, they were completely covered, and he couldn't tell anything about his opponent.

The assassin rushed forward, and their dagger went slicing up at him, and he moved to block, but the man feinted, and he noticed too late as the dagger bit into his other side. He roared, anger feeding his aggression, and slammed his arm into the back of the person as they tried sliding around him. "You little shit!" He wrapped his big arm around their neck and lifted them off their feet. "Try shuffling around now!" He squeezed his arm together while the helpless assassin flailed around, trying to break grapple, but Mal was so much stronger, and he didn't let go until the man stopped moving.

Mal made a sudden jerked and heard a crack. "No one stabs me," he said as he threw the body like a rag doll off the roof. Mal made sure his insides weren't leaking out, and when he was satisfied, he wouldn't die. He looked back up at Koizumi. "Shit," he mumbled as he realized the monk was being engulfed by lightning from one of the casters. He quickly drew his bow and fired an arrow. It hit the caster in the chest, and the spell instantly ended, but not to Mal's surprise. Koizumi kept moving around the remaining casters. "He's got guts. I'll give him that," he mumbled.

He heard a scrabbling noise and saw a hand come over the side of the building. He walked over and poised an arrow at the person but quickly held back when he saw it was Ivelios. "What are you doing here?" He reached down and helped the young man up to the roof.

"I wanted to see how you two were doing." Ivelios looked down at the monk, "Looks like you're doing okay."

"We're both a little beat up, anything you can do?" He showed the half-elf his wounds, and he quickly laid his hands on them.

"I got a little, nothing like a real healer, but you won't bleed to death."

Mal could see the blood flow stem and sighed. "Thanks. How about Koizumi?"

Ivelios made his way over to the edge of the roof. "I can't heal him from here, but I may be able to help." He put his hands together and started chanting in a language Mal didn't know. When he looked back at the Monk, he saw that one of the spell casters was occupied by vines growing up out of the ground. They quickly wrapped around him and brought him hard to the ground, unable to move.

"I think that'll do." Mal turned and began firing arrows at the high-ranking Korites. They were easy to spot sitting on their horses away from the battle. Korites were dangerous in numbers, but when they had no leadership, they easily fell apart. It took three whole arrows and only one General left standing before they noticed where Mal was.

He watched as the man dressed in bone armor sent some men over to the building, but Mal wasn't really concerned. None of them were going to climb the building. They would have to come up the way he did, and he knew he could easily dispatch them.

He stepped back from the edge and laughed as he picked up his sword. "Let them come!" he roared.

"Mal, wait, something's happening." Ivelios sounded worried.

"What he's sending more? Let him."

"No, Mal, look." He walked next to Ivelios and saw the men the General had sent were running back to him.

"What are they doing?"

His eyes followed the street, and his face fell. "Gods," he whispered. "Get back to the temple, Ivelios. Let them know we've got company."

"What is it? I can't see it yet."

"Orcs."

———

Wave after wave of Korites tried to breach the line of Otto's paladins, but they were pushed back by the faithful fighters. Lily was surprised when no other spells were cast by the Korites, but she wouldn't complain. Those spellcasters could have wiped them all out with just a few more spells. She took her place behind Giles and saw no end to the enemy. She dodged swords that aimed between the paladins, one hit her side, but her armor kept the worst of it at bay.

"Blessed Otto, your warriors need stamina to keep defending your home." She prayed and felt the blessing, thanking her God for another spell she wasn't sure she had the energy for. There were so many dead bodies on the stairs the Korites were climbing over their fallen comrades just to get to them. "How long has this been going on?" she cried out.

"Several hours, Mother," one of the paladins called out, "Goes fast, doesn't it?" She had never been a part of such a big battle before and never imagined it could be like this. The last Korite at the front died, and no one else charged.

"Okay, bar the doors the best you can!" Rydell cried out and cast a spell on the pile of dead bodies so they couldn't be raised to fight against them. The paladins worked quickly, throwing the heavy wooden pews and the larger parts of the broken door against the large opening. Giles walked back to Lily who was kneeling on the ground, healing an arrow wound one of the acolytes sustained. "Where's Ivelios?" he asked breathlessly.

She looked up and realized it had been a while since she'd seen him, "I don't know, maybe he's checking on Yahul?"

Nora jogged over. She looked tired but didn't have a scratch on her. "I saw him climb out the window a few hours ago."

Lily's eyes widened. "What?"

"He said he wanted to find Mal and Koizumi."

Giles sighed and put his hands on his hips. "Well, he's a big boy he can take care of himself." William sheathed his sword and helped Lily to her feet. He looked worn but unhurt. "You look how I feel." He chuckled and sighed. "Are you hurt?"

He shook his head. "No, I'm unhurt, you?" One hand slid behind her neck, and she closed her eyes as he kneaded her muscles. It was exactly what she needed after hours of healing.

"I'm fine." She laid a hand on his chest and prayed to Otto for him to be refreshed and he sighed as he laid his forehead on hers. "How long is this battle going to last?" She didn't really expect an answer but couldn't help but ask.

"Hopefully, not much longer. They're just throwing themselves at us at his point. They're desperate." She opened her eyes and met his lovely blue eyes. "But we're doing better than I think they expected."

"Are we?" She could smell sweat, blood, and sword oil, the smells of battle, things she had never smelled together before.

He gave her a little smile and, again, kissed her forehead. "Oh yeah." She wondered why he was giving her those kisses, but she was grateful for them. She swore whenever he did that, the peaceful feeling he radiated swept over her, and she wanted to keep feeling it.

Rydell came over and helped the acolyte to his feet. "Choking the door worked, but we can only take so much. We're all exhausted, and we can't take another wave like that."

Giles sighed wearily, "I agree, but there's not much else we can do." There were chunks of the door still missing, and they could see other Korites dragging away the bodies peacefully. Apparently, they needed a rest, too.

"How long before they start again?" Lily asked.

Rydell shook his head. "I don't know, fifteen minutes, half an hour. Not long either way." "There are only about five more bodies left, Father!" One of the paladins yelled out.

Rydell sighed. "Blessed Otto, help us." He turned back to the door and took a sword from one of the men who was too injured to fight. "For Otto and Salthole!" he yelled and thrust his sword into the air.

"Otto!" Everyone yelled and got ready for another wave of Korites.

"My Lord!" Lily gasped at the familiar voice and turned back towards the windows as Ivelios climbed back in.

"Ivelios, where did you go?" she yelled out as he ran over to them.

"I wanted to see what else was going on. I found Mal and Koizumi they're all right, but I don't think the monk's going to last much longer."

"That's true of us all, unfortunately," she said.

Giles quickly ran back to them. "Ivelios, what news?"

Lily watched as the young man seemed almost scared to say what he knew. "My Lord, it seems there are about a thousand Imperial orcs marching towards us."

Lily's heart sank, and she felt tears in her eyes. "No." She covered her mouth as Giles vigorously rubbed his face. William pulled Lily close, one hand on her back, the other on the back of her head. She could hear his heart pounding frantically under his armor and knew hers was doing the same.

"Then this is where we make our last stand. Ivelios, could you make sure Leo gets out of here?"

"If it comes to that, I promise." He walked over to the door and drew his bow.

Giles laid his hand on William's shoulder. "I want you to get Lily and Leo out of here."

"Yes, my Lord."

Rydell ran over. He looked rather shocked. "I don't think you're going to have to worry about that." Everyone ran back to the door and saw the Korites had turned their backs on the temple.

"What are they doing?" Lily asked.

"Perhaps they fear the orcs at their backs more than us?" Giles suggested.

"Either way, we can use the time to better reinforce the door. Come on!" William yelled out and everyone grabbed what they could and braced it against the door and heard the sounds of battle outside.

"Did they really cut through the rest of the Korites already?" One of the paladins asked.

Rydell stood on a cabinet and looked out the window. "They did, I can see their banner, but I don't recognize it, Giles?"

He quickly ran over and climbed next to Rydell. "Um, well, I know it, but I don't believe it," he said incredulously.

"What is it?" Lily called out.

"It's The Burned Hand." He turned to her, "I thought they were all dead. It was said they were all killed about four years ago."

"What's the Burned Hand?" Ivelios asked.

One of the paladins walked up beside them. "I've heard of them. They were fiercely loyal to the last Orc Emperor, the one who died about five years ago. I heard they were dead, too."

"They're not undead orcs, are they?" Nora asked, an

uneasy grimace on her face. "I don't think I could take on that many undead."

"No," Giles looked back out the window, "they look alive. They're making handy work of those Korites, too." Lily climbed up on another cabinet and watched. The orcs were well-trained, and their weapons were a great deal more impressive than the Korites. It only took them half an hour to cut through the army. It was incredibly impressive.

When the ground was covered with human bodies, the orcs began cleaning up the street, putting the Korites in piles and burning them. They made no move towards the temple, and Rydell moved towards the door.

"Do we open it?"

Giles stared at the door for a moment, holding his chin in his hand. "They've made no aggressive move towards the temple or Salthole. We thought they were gone, and yet here they are, essentially helping us." He looked at Lily, "What do you think, Mother?" She agreed with everything he said. They hadn't made any violent moves except against the Korites.

She nodded. "Open it." She walked next to Giles as the paladins quickly un-barricaded the door.

"I can't believe we're doing this." She heard Giles mumble.

"We're going to Cyranar to re-capture a lost orc prince and you can't believe this part?" She looked at him, one eyebrow raised, and he smiled a tired smile. The door creaked open but quickly fell apart with a crash, leaving the temple completely exposed. Giles, Lily, and Rydell walked to the top of the steps and watched as the orcs stopped what they were doing to watch them. An older orc with a big scar across his blind left eye walked through the crowd and stopped at the foot of the stairs.

"My name is Father Rydell. I am the head priest here."

"Father, I am General Horg, leader of the Burned Hand. I hope you don't mind we took care of your little rodent problem."

Rydell smiled. "Not at all, but you can understand my hesitation about the help?"

Horg nodded. "Indeed, I can. We are what's left of the Burned Hand, the last legion loyal to the rightful Emperor, Sobrei Re'vall. We've been searching the world for him since he disappeared, but so far, all that has come from our search is bloodied feet and disappointment. When we heard a legion of Korites was heading for Salthole, we thought we'd find an honorable death in trying to rid the world of those filthy maggots, but it seems we have things yet to do in this world."

Giles walked slowly down the stairs, his hand extended in friendship. "I am Lord Giles of Raventree. I believe we can be of service to each other." Lily watched them shake hands when her eyes spied Koizumi and Mal walking up to the temple. Both looked rather beat up, and she ran down the steps.

"Are you two okay?" Her hands immediately went to the bruises on the monk's body, but he gently pushed her hands off.

"I am fine, Lily, but Mal is gravely injured."

Mal's head whipped over to him. "What? Am not you loopy monk!" Lily managed a smile while she quickly gave them both a once over and determined neither was dying of their wounds.

"Mal, I think Nora is worried about you. You should go see her."

He shook his head and slung his bow over his shoulder. "Bah, she wasn't worried about me," he mumbled as he walked up the stairs, but she could hear how relieved he was that his friend was still alive. Lily watched Giles invite the orc General into the temple as his warriors continued to clean up the Korites. She walked among the butchered bodies and thought about the scene. It was hard to feel sorry for the Korites, but she felt ashamed that she was glad they were dead. *Otto, such violence,* she thought.

Her eyes caught movement towards one of the buildings, and she ran over. A hand was slowly lifting into the air, and she saw it belonged to a man dressed in the guard attire of Salthole. He was down on the ground and looked near death. "You'll be okay now," she said as she kneeled and took his hand. He was breathing erratically, and blood poured from a wound in his neck. "Blessed Otto," Lily barely started her prayer for the man when an arm came from nowhere and stabbed the guard in the chest. He gurgled, and Lily felt his soul leave his body. "No!" She screamed and looked up. A Korite had crawled over to them. The smile on his face was manic and bloody. "How could you!" Hate seethed through her. She thought they were safe, but the illusion was shattered.

The Korite started laughing. "Kore will reward me in death," he gurgled. Lily's hand wrapped around the knife that was still in the guard's chest and pulled. His body shuddered from the movement, and she felt a tear roll down her cheek.

"Then let me help you meet him." She thrust the knife as hard as she could into the Korites neck. His warm blood flowed quickly over her hand. He didn't make any noise as his body shook around the knife. Lily pushed it in further and sliced through his skin, completely opening him up. His life's blood flowed freely from his body as he fell forward on the ground and didn't move again.

"Lily!" Running footsteps stopped behind her, and she dropped the knife, but the evidence was all over her. The man's blood was still warm on her skin, but she could feel it quickly cooling.

Hands touched her shoulders. She gasped and turned to see Giles. "No, don't touch me!" She cringed away, but he held her still.

"Lily, are you okay? What happened?" He kneeled next to her and started wiping her cheeks. They were so wet, she didn't realize she had been crying.

"I killed him," she whispered. Her hands were shaking, and she felt her tears now, "I hated him, and I killed him, Giles." Her voice shaking as much as her hands, she wanted his blood gone but didn't know what to do.

Giles lifted her head. "It's okay, Lily, he deserved it."

"Did he? Who am I to take a life from this world?" Giles pulled a rag from his pocket and started wiping the blood from her hands. "I killed a man, Giles."

"I've killed a lot of men, Lily. It's okay, really." Her hands were dry but still stained as Giles helped her to her feet. "Come inside now, Leo needs to be checked on." She nodded numbly and let him lead her back into the temple.

When Rydell saw her, he gasped and ran over. "Lily, are you all right?" He reached up and touched her shoulder, but she was still staring at her red hands.

"I need to check on Leo." Her voice was breaking as she walked away from the priest towards the stairs.

"Lily?"

"I need to check on Leo." And started up the stairs without another word.

William walked over to Giles. "Did Lily have blood all over her hands?"

He nodded. "Seems there was still one Korite alive, I'm not sure what happened exactly, but she killed him." He looked up at the fighter, concern in his eyes. "I don't think she's killed before."

"What?" He glanced up the stairs, then back to Giles, "But what she said in Ardenry, it sounded like she understood what it was like to take a life."

"It did. Maybe it was just from being around others who took life."

"Damn." He took a step towards the stairs but felt Giles's hand on his shoulder.

"She's checking on Leo. She'll be fine."

Giles could tell the young man didn't believe him. "I'll check on her later then." Giles gave his back a pat and moved back to Rydell, hoping William would heed his words.

———

It was hard to move. The guilt of what she had done was crushing her. She pushed open the bedroom door and saw Yahul was still on the bed next to Leo who was sleeping peacefully.

Lily slowly walked over and sat next to him. *He's so innocent,* she thought and didn't hold back as she cried into her hands. *Otto, forgive me. I'm so sorry,* she thought as her cries filled the air.

"I'll never take another life with a blade as long as I live, I swear." She had never felt so ashamed and guilty in her entire life. "I'm sorry, Otto, forgive me." Yahul crawled over Leo and started nuzzling Lily. He pushed her arm away from her face and started licking her cheeks. "Oh, what are you doing?" she asked him wearily.

"Mother?" She looked over and saw Leo was awake and looked healthy.

She quickly cleared her throat and wiped her cheeks. "Leo, how do you feel?" she asked, trying to keep her voice steady.

He sat up and didn't hesitate in wrapping his arms around her. "What's wrong?"

She hugged him tight and fought hard to regain her composure. "Nothing, Leo, it's just been a really long night." She felt his hands rub her back, and her thoughts drifted to William. If only she could feel his arms around her. She knew it would make everything better.

"Where is everyone?" he asked and sat back. She gently pushed him back and gave him a once over, there was no poison in his system, and he was healthy again.

"Downstairs." She told him what had transpired while he slept, and he jumped out of bed and started putting his clothes on.

"Everyone's okay?" he asked quickly.

"Yes."

He stopped and looked at her. "What's wrong, Mother?"

"Nothing you need to concern yourself with, Leo. I bet Giles would like to see you, why don't you finish getting dressed and come downstairs."

She stood and started for the door when he caught her

arm. "Please tell me what's wrong."

"Nothing, Leo!" She didn't mean to snap at him and instantly felt bad, but she didn't want to put her burdens on him. She took a deep breath, "Nothing, I'm fine." And she hurried from the room.

CHAPTER 5
TIME HEALS

Lily sat in one of the darkened confession booths in the temple. She was exhausted but didn't want to sleep. She knew nightmares were waiting for her. Otto's house was now filled with injured humans and orcs. She probably should have been helping bandage up what she could, but all she could think about was the feel of the Korite's blood as it flowed over her hands, the look in his eyes as he died, shocked, scared, and somewhat triumphant. She didn't think she could concentrate enough to help anyone now.

"Leo!" She looked up through the little slits in the door and saw Giles run over and hug his son. "You look much better. How do you feel?" He held Leo's face and looked him over while the young boy just looked around the room. He didn't bother hiding the shock on his face.

"Better, what exactly did I miss?"

"Battle, but everything's okay now. We have some more unexpected allies as well." Lily watched as the young man seemed unconcerned about the orcs walking around.

"My Lord, what happened to Mother Lily?"

"What do you mean?"

"Something's wrong. Her hands were bloody, and she... was short with me when I asked what was wrong."

Giles nodded his head and led Leo over to one of the empty pews. "We all had a long night, son. We thought it was over and started to relax when I heard Lily scream. I ran over and saw she had killed a Korite. I was rather proud of her, but I don't think she took it that way." Lily felt her lower lip tremble as she listened to Giles talk about what she had done. She was so ashamed she didn't know how she could face anyone.

"But she killed a bad guy. She should be glad," Leo said.

"Son, I don't think she'd ever killed before."

Leo's eyes looked confused. "But what she told me that night, surely—"

"If you saw her reaction, you'd know. We're just going to have to give her some time to deal with it. I think she took it rather badly."

Leo started biting on his thumbnail. "You don't think she'd leave, do you?" The thought never occurred to her that she could leave. But she didn't want to. They needed her.

"No, son, I think she just needs to deal with what she did. No one blames her. That man killed a guard in front of her. Truthfully, the man deserved worse."

"Where is she?"

Giles shook his head. "I don't know, hopefully getting some rest. I feel about ready to pass out myself."

"She's not in the room. She left before I came down." Giles sat back, and Lily watched Nora walk over to them.

The relief in the girls' eyes was obvious to Lily. "Leo? How are you?"

He got to his feet and straightened his shirt. "I feel much better. You look good for having been in a battle all night." Lily didn't think Nora took a single hit during the night, which was a miracle, but the girl hardly stood still as she fought and wasn't too surprised.

"Just tired, I'm glad to see you up." She gave his hand a little squeeze and walked over to Mal who was talking with one of the Burned Hand Orcs. Lily could see the young woman seemed to care about Leo, but how much was unclear. Nora was good at keeping to herself and Lily knew if she wanted Leo, the subtle route might not work. Lily jumped as the little wooden window of the confession booth slid open. William was sitting in the booth next to her. His eyes were tired and full of worry.

"Found you."

She nodded. "Found me."

"Are you feeling any better?"

She shrugged and looked down at her hands, covered in dried blood. "I might feel better if I got some rest. But I know the moment I close my eyes, all I will see will be that Korite, taunting me with what I've done." That was the last thing she wanted to see.

"Happens to me, too, after I've killed someone." She realized that she was most likely responsible for him having to kill when there were no other options while rescuing those taken. "Do you want to talk about it?"

She swallowed hard. She didn't but knew it would help eventually. "I've never killed before. I've injured, sure, incapacitated, knocked unconscious but never killed."

"We were wondering about that." He slipped out of his side of the booth and joined her, sliding next to her. The booth was really only made for one person, so they were a little squished together. But she wasn't going to complain. "Rest will help. Right now, your mind and body are running on fumes and can't process anything correctly."

"I don't think I've ever been so exhausted in my life, and that's saying something."

He chuckled. "Same." He rubbed his eyes, "Otto will forgive you, I know you know that, but you also need to forgive yourself. Take your own words to heart. What you said to Leo in Ardenry was the truth, so go easy on yourself."

She nodded. "I'll try." He gave her a little smile, and she wanted to do nothing else in this world than sleep with his arms around her. "Shall we go rest?" He nodded and slid out of the booth, and she followed. Giles looked up and smiled at her as she shut the door behind her.

"There you are. We were worried about you."

"I'm fine, I just didn't want to sleep."

Giles got up and laid his hands on her shoulders. "I suggest that's exactly what you do. We're going to need your help later."

She nodded and didn't fight him. "I'll try."

She started for the stairs, pulling William with her, when Giles called out to her. "Lily, what you did wasn't a bad thing. People die in battle, which means someone must kill them. He was a Korite, a nasty piece of work, and I, for one, am glad the world is rid of him."

"He *was* a Korite, Giles," She slowly turned to him, keeping William's hand in hers, "but he was someone's son. He may have been someone's husband and father, and I took him away from them." Her voice wavered as she spoke. Not even holding William's hand could keep her from feeling like she was about to fall apart.

Giles quickly walked over and hugged her tightly. "Those are things you can't think about, Lily. It'll drive you mad, and we still need you. Remember what you said to Leo in Ardenry. Don't take it to a bad place."

She hugged him tightly. "I'll try."

"Take it from someone who's taken a lot of lives," he stepped back and held her face, "Focus on what could have been lost if those people hadn't died. That's how I get through it."

She nodded. "Thank you, Giles."

The trip up the stairs took longer than she thought it would. When she opened the door, she saw Artimus was snoring on the left side of the bed and Ivelios and Yahul were sleeping on his bedroll under the window. Lily took her robe off and slowly slid to the middle of the bed under the covers. William slid in behind her and pulled her against him. He was so warm she let an appreciative sigh escape her lips. The pillows were so soft, and William was with her, so she didn't bother fighting the sleep that quickly pulled her under.

———

Giles was exhausted, but knowing Leo was healthy again helped immensely. He rubbed his face and willed himself to stay awake as he spoke with Horg about their mission. The old orc sat still as he tried to process what Giles had just told him.

"So, you're looking for Sobrei as well?"

"We are. We know where he is, but we've been a bit sidetracked. Last night being a good example of that."

The orc's good eye widened as he leaned on the table. "Where is he? We've looked everywhere."

"Cyranar."

Horg sat back and shook his head. "No wonder we never found him. We didn't think anyone would be crazy enough to take him there."

Giles sighed. "Crazy doesn't begin to describe the situation. Cultists from Dal En Val have him, and Korites are vying for control over Cyranar against Efrits who have also taken up residence in the old city."

Horg groaned. "God, I hate Efrits." He whispered and wiped his face, "Well, it seems that you will need an army just to get to him. We can accompany you and keep you safe."

Giles licked his lips and sat up. "Actually, I was thinking you could make your way to Raventree."

The orc sat up in surprise. "Raventree? Why would we go there?"

"When we left Ardenry, we learned several legions of orcs loyal to the false emperor camping between Raventree and Salthole. I'm afraid they could march on my city if the mood strikes them. If you marched to Raventree it would ensure the city would remain safe. And could be a safe place to bring Sobrei." There was no way he was going to tell the General of the Burned Hand that they had planned to capture Sobrei themselves. He hoped if he made it seem like they were just trying to free an orc who was falsely imprisoned, it might endear them to Ardenry and Raventree.

Horg held his chin and thought for a moment. "Fewer would have a better chance of going unnoticed in the crumbling city. And getting to bash some heads of the orcs who refuse to acknowledge their true leader sounds fun. I see the wisdom in your plan, Giles. I shall discuss it with my men and get back to you." He got up and held out his hand, "Thank you for speaking with me. I know it must be rather uncomfortable."

Giles shook his hand, making sure to give it a nice, good grip. "Not uncomfortable, Horg. It's always good to make new friends, even in unexpected places." He gave Giles an orcish grin and walked from the room. Sighing, he sat back down and laid his head in his hand. It would be a lot easier for them to move around Cyranar without a thousand Orcs trailing behind them, no matter how safe they could make them.

If cultists saw that many orcs marching on the city, they might move Sobrei, and they would have to start all over. He prayed to whatever god would listen that the Burned Hand would march to Raventree and help his people. *Gods, I miss you, Siddah*, he thought before his eyes closed and sleep found him right there at the old wooden table.

———

When Lily woke, it was late afternoon. Her head was laying on William's chest. He was still asleep. She didn't blame him, he fought a long time and needed rest. She took a deep breath and felt much better. Her head was much clearer, and while she still felt sad, she understood that in a battle like that, it would have been a miracle if she hadn't killed anyone. She looked back up at William as he breathed in and opened his eyes. "Morning, er, whatever time it is."

He snickered, and that arm around gave her a squeeze. "Sleep well?" His eyes were sleep-laden as he looked down at her, and she quickly realized she didn't want to move.

"I did, I feel better. How about you? Sleep alright?"

He took a breath, his eyes burning into hers. "Better than I have in a long time." She smiled. His peaceful nature around her made her not want to get out of bed for a long time.

The door opened, and Nora walked in. "Hey, you're finally up. The town brought a bunch of food for the temple. We're all eating downstairs if you want to join us." She walked over to her pack and pulled something out of it.

"We'll be down in a minute," Lily said as she finally sat up, her side cold now that it wasn't pressing against William.

"No rush." Nora gave Lily a wink and walked out of the room, closing the door behind her. Lily snickered and shook her head while William laughed. She reached up to run her fingers through her hair, and she saw how red they were.

"Gods, I forgot."

"Here, let me help." He took her hands, and they got out of bed. There was a bowl of fresh water next to the side table, and he put her hands in it. He rubbed his fingers over her stained skin, and eventually, the water ran red, and her skin was clean. "How's that?" He dried her hands with a nearby cloth. She smiled down at her hands, grateful the blood was gone, but also because of how gentle he was as he washed her skin. She could feel the strength his hands held, but they felt like a healer's hands, comforting.

"Thank you."

She looked up, and he had a little smile on his face. "No problem."

They quickly got dressed and made their way down to the main temple. Halfway down the stairs, they could smell the food.

"Mm, I'm hungrier than I realized," he said.

Lily felt her stomach grumble as he opened the door. "Same." Before them, the temple was filled with tables, and the paladins, priests, and orcs filled the seats. The sounds of talking and silverware scraping on plates filled the air. Lily could smell meat and bread in the air. It was good to know that there were still good people in Salthole and that they cared about the temple.

"Lily!" She turned at Leo's voice and saw him waving at her from down the table, "Come sit. I'm sure you're hungry," he called out.

William put a hand on her back. "Every man for themselves." He gave her a wink and found a seat between two of the Burned Hand orcs. They gave his back a hearty pat as he sat down, and they shoved a mug of ale to him. Smiling, she made her way to the little space between Leo and Mal and sat down. She couldn't help but chuckle when she saw Leo's plate hidden under a pile of potatoes and meat.

"Got your appetite back, I see?"

"Doubly, it seems," he said and shoved a big spoonful of potatoes in his mouth.

"How are you, Mother?" Mal asked.

Slowly, she turned while he started putting food on her plate. "Better, I think, thank you. How are you?"

"Oh, I'm fine, glad we all made it out alive. I know you tried to help James. He was a good man."

James, she thought, *who was James?* "I tried to help a lot of people. I'm afraid I don't remember a James."

"He was the guard the Korite killed when you were trying to help him. I know he would have appreciated your intervention."

"Hmm, well, I wish I could have done more for him." She ate whatever Mal put on her plate for half an hour, several hunks of meat, a large spoonful of fried potatoes, and three rolls before Giles came up behind her and put his hands on her shoulders.

"Nice to see you up," he whispered in her ear before he stood straight, "If everyone would follow me back to the room, we all need to talk and re-group." Everyone stood and followed Giles. Rydell's room seemed a bit crowded now that everyone was there. Lily stood by the window. The smell of the ocean blowing in comforted her. William stood next to her, leaning on the windowsill. Leo, Nora, and Artimus sat on the bed while everyone else found a place to stand, not on someone's toes.

"Salthole is safe for now," Giles said. "I'm proud of all of you for contributing any way you did. I am confident that with all your help, we will retrieve the prince and succeed in our mission. Now, speaking of the mission, we have gotten a bit off track but now we'll be able to continue towards Cyranar."

He started pacing between the bed and the door. "Some of you know that Max was able to figure out where in the city he was being held." He turned to Leo, who jumped up from the bed and unfolded the map of the old city on the table. "It is in the middle of the city," Giles laid a finger where the Sergeant indicated, "and there will be Korites and Efrits between us and him. Hopefully, we can circumvent most of them. I'd hate to see what would happen if we ran into the others."

Lily walked over and studied the map with Artemis and Mal. The middle of the city looked to be a good twenty miles from the surrounding edge. "When will we leave?" she asked.

"We need to replenish our supplies and rest from the battle. As good as we may feel, it takes a few days to really heal from a fight like that. The Burned Hand will be marching to Raventree. They'll make a wide berth around the Dal En Val legion, so if they decide to start trouble, Raventree won't be completely helpless. We, however, will head towards Ral Hava and go through the mountain to get around all that."

"How do we know they won't just slaughter us all when this prince is free?" Nora asked, "They've been looking for him for years I'd think they'd be desperate to get him back."

Giles nodded. "I understand your concern Nora, but nothing would really change for them once we freed him. The false emperor is still sitting on the throne and is surrounded by his entire army. They would need a lot more than what they currently have to take back Dal En' Val. They'll need a place to rest and recoup as well, and we need them to help keep Raventree safe."

William cleared his throat. "Do they know what Max asked of us? That we're supposed to keep him detained? I'd think if they saw us doing the same as his kidnappers, they'd get pissy."

Giles sighed and shook his head. "No, they don't know that, and no one is to tell them either. I'll deal with it later. One problem at a time now."

Artemis laughed. "Giles, my boy, you are really taking to this Lordship well, I must say."

"I don't have much choice, do I?" he said with a smile.

"Rest up. In two days, we leave for Cyranar and face things we've only seen in our nightmares." He rolled up the map and walked from the room. Koizumi, Krag, and William followed after he gave her arm a little squeeze while the others just sat around the room and processed what they just learned. Lily's nightmares could be horrifying, so she tried not to take Giles' words to heart.

Nora crossed her legs and cleared her throat. "How are you, Leo?" she asked. Lily could hear the concern in the young girl's voice and hid a small smile.

"Oh, I'm fine. Lily works miracles," he said as he pulled his sword from its sheath and sat down in one of the chairs, and started sharpening it, not paying Nora much mind.

She stood and walked over to him. "I really thought you were going to die."

"Nah." Lily could hear him hiding the fear in his voice, "I doubt any of us will die as long as Lily's around."

She gave a little chuckle as she sat on the bed. "Thank you for the vote of confidence, young man." Nora sighed and sat in the chair next to Leo, and started picking at the hole forming at the bottom of her shirt.

"So, where are you from, Mother? How did *Giles of Raventree* get you mixed up in this?" she asked, mimicking the lord's lazy drawl as she said his name. Lily chuckled and looked over at her. Nora's long dark hair was in a messy bun at the nape of her neck, and she looked tired. There were bags under her brown eyes making her appear older than her twenty years.

"Fairwinds originally."

Nora smiled. "I've never been, but I've heard it's nice."

Lily nodded and sat back on the bed. "It is. It's profitable and safe. You can smell the ocean no matter where you are. When I was a child, I spent almost every day at the beach with my father and—" she paused for just a moment, "and my sister. We would make necklaces from the seashells we gathered, and then we would pile them on my father until all you could see was the top of his head," she said with a smile, remembering that carefree day. It had been a long time since she had thought of it. "I haven't been back for a few years. My husband and I lived in Ardenry, but we'd go visit my father every so often."

She noticed Nora's eyes go wide. "You're married?" Lily forgot they picked her and Mal up like stray cats in a cave and didn't know much about them. She was most likely thinking about when she found her in bed with William a few hours ago. Not the best look for a married priestess she would admit, but she wasn't married.

"Widowed, these past two years."

Nora's shocked eyes quickly turned to sorry. "Oh, I'm sorry, I didn't know."

Lily shook her head. "It's all right, I'm healing."

Ivelios snorted. "That's obvious." Nora looked at him, confused. He leaned down and whispered in her ear, and she covered her mouth as she laughed and nodded in agreement.

"What?" Lily looked between them.

"You and the Seeker," the half-elf patted his leg, and Yahul quickly joined his master as he walked towards the door, "you're inseparable." He walked out of the room as Lily hoped her cheeks weren't red.

"So, you said you went home to visit your father. What about your mother?" Nora asked. She turned back to Nora who had her feet pulled up in the chair, her arms around her legs.

"She died when we were born."

Nora's face dropped. "Oh, mine too."

Mal also got to his feet and moved towards the door. "Well, I'm going to go pump some gold into the local economy by purchasing a great deal of ale to fill my belly, Nora?"

"In a minute, you go on." He gave her a little wink and walked out after Ivelios.

Lily turned to Artemis, who was once again reading one of his books. "Have you ever encountered an Efrit, Artemis?"

He nodded and slowly put his book down. "I have, tricky creatures made of fire but incredibly intelligent. It does not surprise me that they are trying to take over Cyranar. It's said there are lots of treasures from the old ages still buried beneath the city. Treasures like that are inclined to attract powerful beings."

"What kind of treasure?" Leo asked.

"Oh, nothing we could really use, I'm sure. They probably want them for sentimental reasons or some such drivel. Now, please let me get back to my book," he said like a grumpy old man and hid behind his book.

Nora rolled her eyes and got to her feet. "Come on, Leo, let's go drink ourselves silly."

He snickered and put his sword away. "I don't know about silly, but I'll have something," he said as he followed her out of the room. Lily glanced over at Artemis and deemed him not good company at the moment and decided to go to the beach and watch the sun go down.

"I'll see you later, mage," she said and left the room.

———

The docks were full of boats, so Lily decided to walk down to the rocky shores of Salthole. The tide was coming in, but there was still a good twenty feet between her and the ocean. For the first time since they reached the port town, she could truly smell the salty air that reminded her of Otto and home. The worn rocks were slimy with algae, but she knew how to walk on them without falling and got as close to the water line as she dared. Water gently lapped against the rocks, and Lily closed her eyes.

"Blessed Otto, I pray you'll be with us as we travel to Cyranar. I know it's a cursed place where not even the gods like to go, but we need peace, and if freeing Sobrei Re'vall is the path to that peace, then we will walk that path willingly. Please give me the strength to keep my group safe from the evil that roams free in that blighted city. Keep us safe so that we may see our loved ones again."

"Lily?" She opened her eyes and turned to Giles who was standing on the nearest dock looking down at her. "You're getting wet." He pointed at the water, and she looked down. The tide had come in up to her ankles.

"Oh, I didn't realize." Lifting her robes, she quickly made her way back up the beach and onto the dock next to her friend. "I was just praying. I guess I lost track of time."

He smiled and looked out at sea as the sun finally disappeared over the horizon. "That's all right. I just didn't want you to get swept out to sea."

She chuckled, "I won't, I promise."

Giles cleared his throat. "Now that we're no longer under siege, I wonder if you can tell me more about that ring we found on that creature?"

"Oh. I almost forgot." She pulled the folded handkerchief out of her pocket and held it in the palm of her hand.

"What did you mean he would make a resurgence? Do you know something?" Giles reached into the folded cloth and pulled out the ring.

Lily nodded and put the handkerchief back in her pocket. "A few months before Henri and I settled in Ardenry, we visited the Citadel. While we were there, it was discovered that the Cup of Kurr had been stolen and replaced with a replica." The cup acted like a lock of sorts on the magical prison that held The Shackled One. It was guarded just as fiercely as the prison, but somehow, someone managed to take it. "Neither the paladins nor the dragons had realized it was gone and had no idea how long ago it was taken." The Citadel was created especially to guard the old god, and everyone there took their job seriously. Sometimes too seriously, but she understood the importance of it. The Shackled One had been imprisoned by the other gods so long ago, no one knew their true name anymore. But that didn't stop the worst of the worst from still worshipping them. Anyone caught doing so was immediately put to death. That was one law that every god agreed upon.

Giles groaned and wiped his face. "Gods, that is bad. Mighty fortuitous that you happened to be there. I wonder if Max is aware of this."

She shook her head. "I don't know. Maybe that's why he was so insistent that we get Sobrei. One less front to worry about?" She turned to him and crossed her arms. "But there's a feeling in the pit of my stomach like he's gaining power exponentially."

"Scary thought." They stood on the dock, watching the stars slowly pop into the dark sky. It was a rare peace, Lily thought. Giles pulled his arm back and threw the ring into the ocean as far as he could. *Good riddance,* she thought as he turned back to her, a little more subdued.

"Anyway," Giles turned back to her, "I just want you to know how grateful I am. I've wanted to thank you for saving Leo but that battle kind of took a great deal of all our time."

"It did, and it's my pleasure, Giles. Leo's a good boy. I hated seeing him so sick."

Giles sighed and looked up at the stars. "I can honestly say I feared the worst," he looked back down at her, "but now I know as long as you're with us, Otto is with us. He truly favors you."

"Thank you, Giles," she said with a little nod.

He started walking back towards the city. "I believe the rest of our group is at the tavern across from the temple, what do you say we join them and enjoy each other's company while we can? I have a feeling a certain Seeker is itching to dance with you," he teased, with a little smile on his face.

She walked next to him and took the arm he offered to her. "You people are relentless," she chuckled.

He laughed and patted her arm. "I'm not the one who keeps waking up in his arms." Lily chuckled, shaking her head. "He's been enamored of you from the moment he saw you that night at the castle. Don't tell me you don't see it."

She nodded. "I do." It was the truth, and she wondered if anyone saw how she felt about him. "He's wonderful, he really is."

"But?" She looked over at him, a 'really?' look on her face. Giles laughed, "My wife isn't here, and I miss her whispering campaigns of those around us, indulge me."

Lily laughed and patted his arm. "Yes, my Lord. There's no 'but', not really. I am not married. I am healing to the point where my heart yearns for things I once had that William has been giving me. I suppose I am a little...shy. It has been a long time since I've been with someone and I want to make sure I want that person, and I'm not just using them because I miss my husband. Does that make sense?"

His eyes met hers. "It does. That's incredibly wise of you."

They found the others save for Artemis in The Wailing Whelp. People were buying them drinks and Mal was standing by the bar telling a story about how he and Nora escaped a band of Korites, and everyone was listening intently.

Giles and Lily sat down next to Leo and William. He gave her a smile and raised his arm for an ale, passing his untouched drink to her.

"I see Mal enjoys a crowd," Giles said.

Nora shook her head. "He wants to be well known and thinks telling stories at every tavern we visit will do it. Honestly, I wish he'd stop, I hate the attention."

"Well, maybe you should go to a different tavern," Lily suggested, "you know, where there's dancing and music instead of storytelling."

Nora smiled. It looked like the idea had never occurred to her. "You know that doesn't sound half bad." She quickly finished her mug and turned to Leo, "How about it, Leo? Want to find some music?"

He looked excited for all of a second before he relaxed. "I would, but I'm bound to serve my Lord if he needs anything."

Giles chuckled, "Leo, I can fend for myself tonight. Go have fun."

Lily saw Nora give Giles a little smile as she got to her feet. "Oh okay, um," he looked over at Nora, "I guess I'm all yours, I mean um."

Nora laughed. "I know what you mean, come on."

Lily and Giles held back laughs until they were both out of

earshot. "Does Leo not have many girls back home?"

"There's a few, but I think he's so focused on his duties he tries not to let them distract him."

"Perhaps Nora's good for him after all."

Giles took a few good gulps of the ale Leo left behind. "Perhaps."

———

The sun had been down for a few hours, and everyone was occupying themselves with different activities. Mal was still telling stories about his adventures to whoever would listen, mostly young women. Giles and Krag were talking strategy by the fire. She and William had found a table in the corner and had been talking for hours about everything.

"So, I have a silly question." Lily chuckled at him and rested her head in her hand, waiting for what she was sure wasn't a silly question, "Why do you smile at your ale?"

Lily burst out laughing, her head going back. "Oh, gods, do I still do that?"

He laughed and nodded. "You do."

She settled down and wiped a tear away. "Ale makes me think of my friend, Taren. I didn't drink it before I met him. I remember the barmaid set it down in front of me, and I sniffed it. He teased me for it, saying you drink it, you don't smell it. But I had never had one I wanted to smell it." William chuckled. "So, ale makes me think of him."

"He's your friend who died from a cultist attack?" Lily nodded. "You never thought to bring him back?"

She cleared her throat. "At the time, I was unprepared for such a spell. A year after he died, I did try and raise him," he noticed how far away her eyes looked. He reached out and put a hand over hers, "He didn't come back." He could tell that still bothered her.

"I take it the spell was performed adequately."

She nodded. "It was, but I never heard a reply. Usually, when you raise someone, you ask if they want to come back, and you hear their yes or no, but with Taren, there was nothing."

"Huh," William rubbed his chin, "why wouldn't it work?"

"No idea. There are only two reasons a spell of mine wouldn't bring someone back, they don't want to come back, or they're not dead."

He lifted his chin at that. "You don't think he's alive, do you?"

"No, there's no way he'd be alive and not make himself known. He was like a brother to me. Not for a moment do I believe he would stay away."

William nodded. "I agree, I guess it's just one of life's great mysteries."

She shrugged. "I suppose so." He reached out for her hand, and she let him hold it. That peaceful feeling flowed over her once again. "Okay, I have to ask, what is that peaceful aura you have? I feel it almost every time I touch you."

He looked shocked at her words, but his thumb ran gently on her hand. "I have an aura? This from someone with the most peaceful spirit of anyone I've ever met?"

She smiled and laid her free hand over his. "Yeah, you do. I noticed it when you walked into the dining room at the castle. I could feel your peaceful presence from across the room. I honestly wondered if you were a priest as well."

He chuckled. "No priest, just me. I wish I could tell you what it is, but no one ever told me that before." He looked at their hands, entwined on the table. "Can I ask—" he stopped, and she could see the hesitation in his eyes.

She slid a hand from his and laid it on his cheek. "You can ask me anything." He reached up and put his hand over hers, pressing her hand to him. He closed his eyes and turned, his lips kissed the palm of her hand on the thick, white scar that ran diagonally across it. While she couldn't feel the kiss because of the scar, her racing heart more than made up for it.

His other hand wrapped around that wrist by his head. "I feel I should apologize for my behavior," he whispered and finally looked up and met her eyes, "I have no business, putting my arms around you, kissing you. But from the moment I saw you…I will stop if you ask it of me. I will stop if you aren't ready." She could feel the truth in his words. He would do whatever she wanted, stay or go. It was up to her.

"William," She whispered his name, and he kissed her palm again and a flash of her whispering his name in the dark made her stomach tighten.

"I'm willing to wait for you, no matter how long it takes," he says against her palm.

She smiled. "You still haven't asked your question."

He looked up, their entwined hands against his lips. "Could your heart ever see me?"

"Does your heart see me?" she countered.

He smiled, "I've never known a more wonderful woman in my life. Your brains and beauty and faith call to me. I want to kiss you from sunup to sundown. I want to roll around in bed, naked, ignoring the world with you." She laughed and held his hands tighter. "So yes, my heart sees you and only you." She swallowed and decided to once again give her heart what it desired, despite it barely being over a week of knowing him as William and not just someone in a letter.

"My heart sees you too." An unexpected wave of grief washed over her for just a moment, a stray tear betraying the moment. "Otto, help me, I see you."

He reached over and brushed the tear away. "Are you afraid?"

"A little." He moved his chair to the corner next to her, and she laid a hand on his knee.

"Me too." The way he looked at her stopped her breath. His eyes were full of love and understanding, something she wasn't sure she'd ever find again. His handsome face gave her all his attention, and she wrapped her hands around the back of his neck and pulled him to her lips. His lips were soft on hers, and she felt his arms pick her up and put her in his lap, his arms once again wrapping around her waist. He kissed her deeply, her bottom lip between his, and she opened for him, their tongues swept together like they'd been kissing their entire lives. His arms tightened around her as she held him against her. Kissing him made her feel like a hole in her soul was filled, that she'd know only love for the rest of her life. That this peaceful man, this Seeker, had been made her for.

————

Giles got up to get another mug of ale when he noticed Lily and William in the corner, kissing like their lives depended on it. He smiled and said a silent prayer to whoever listened that they would both make it through this dangerous time.

————

Nora and Leo had been dancing for hours. They found a nearby tavern with a group playing music and had hardly sat down since they walked in. Nora couldn't remember having more fun. Leo was a good dancer, never stepping on her toes or accidentally twirling her into someone else. She assumed that was from growing up the son of a Lord. Even if he was adopted, it was clear Giles loved him like his own and gave him everything the son of a Lord would have growing up, including dancing lessons. The musicians started playing a slow song, and to her surprise, Leo took her hand and put her other one around him. The last few slow songs were when he suggested they take a break, but apparently, he didn't want a break this time, and she fought not to blush.

"How old were you when you left home?" he asked her. They talked while they traveled on his horse, so they knew a little about each other. The first thing they learned was they were both orphans.

She took a deep breath and glanced at her hand in his. "I was eight."

"Eight?" She could hear the shock in his voice. "What happened?"

"Hmm, well, my mother died when I was born, and when

I was seven, my Da was killed. I tried sticking around, but it was hard. I had no family, and my friend's parents didn't want to help. They had their own kids to take care of, so I packed what little I had and left."

"Gods, Nora, how did you survive?"

She chuckled. "It wasn't easy, but a few months after I left, I found a Suya camp, and they were more than glad to let me tag along." Nora smiled as she thought about her Suya family, always willing to let her stay in whatever tent she wanted, showing her how to cook, hunt, dance, and fight. Suya were nomadic, moving their colorful camps every few weeks. Nora liked it when they moved somewhere new, but she longed for a home that she didn't have to pack up.

He smiled at that. "I've never met a Suya, always wanted to."

"They're wonderful. That's where I learned to fight like I do. Well, let me rephrase that. I learned to dance from them. I put the blade in my own hand."

He smiled down at her, and she felt the butterflies in her stomach go wild. "I've never seen anyone fight like you do. I'll admit sometimes it's hard not to stare as you whirl around with your sword."

"Oh?" She teased, and he laughed. She felt the hand at her back pull her closer.

"The way you move is ethereal, Nora. Hasn't anyone ever told you that?" His lips were so close, that she wondered if she'd dare close those last few inches.

"No one." She gasped as he spun her around and pressed her against him again.

"Well, you are." She watched his eyes move back up to her eyes. Was he staring at her lips? "You're the most interesting woman I've ever met."

"Interesting?" Her eyes narrowed at him. "Just interesting?"

He laughed. "I'm afraid I don't have the words to describe

you the way you deserve, so interesting will have to do for now."

She rolled her eyes. "Fine, interesting it is," she teased.

"What about me? How would you describe me?" She met his eyes, so many words flew through her mind, but she wasn't sure she could say them without making a fool of herself. But if he found her ethereal, what harm would it do if she told the truth.

"Marvelous."

He smiled. "I'll take it."

CHAPTER 6
SHOCK OF UNKNOWN ENEMIES

The next few days flew by for the group. Giles encouraged Leo to spend more time with Nora before they headed out, and Lily could see how happy it made the young girl. They spent a great deal of time walking around the town and talking. Lily hoped that one of them would make a move, but so far, they were just friendly. But she swore she caught Leo staring at the dark-haired girl more and more. She and William relished the peace of the days. He splurged and got a room at a nearby inn just so they could have some privacy from the groups near constant teasing. She knew it'd stop eventually but was glad for the privacy. They mostly talked, their arms around each other in bed, getting to know each other. He said he loved to cook and couldn't wait to make her, her favorite dinner, cottage pie.

She told him the story of how she met Henri. He seemed enthralled the entire time. It was a rather exciting story. He said he loved hearing how their business endeavor began, and she loved that he didn't mind hearing about Henri. He said he hoped she'd talk about him whenever she wanted. After all, if she loved him, he must have been a great man.

The morning they left Salthole, everyone was gathered in the stables of the temple, putting their things back on their horses.

Lily walked over to Malice, her hands behind her back. "Hello, gorgeous boy." Normally, he'd snort and stamp his annoyance, but instead, he rubbed his snout against the side of her head.

Lily laughed and patted him. "I think he's getting used to others."

"Perhaps he realized that a little more grace in his life isn't a bad thing." Giles hauled himself up and turned to the group. Artemis was still riding that ridiculous carpet. Leo and Nora were both riding his horse while Koizumi and Ivelios chose to run alongside. Krag still had his mountain of a horse and seemed rather fond of his mount. Lily stayed with William on his horse, sitting in front of him. As his arm went around her waist, she laid a hand over his and leaned back into him. She felt him kiss the back of her head and smiled.

"We have to go through Ral Hava to get to Cyranar," Giles said, "We shouldn't encounter any problems with the dwarves, but be on guard anyway." He turned Malice towards their destination, and they rode out of Salthole. Lily prayed they would get to Ral Hava without any trouble.

———

It took another week to get to the mountain pass that would lead them to the dwarven city. From there, they would take the road through the mountain to Cyranar. It was warm traveling in the cavern, the rocks radiated the sun's warmth, and soon everyone was sweating.

"Gods it feels like summer in here," Nora complained as she tried to stretch the collar of her shirt out to catch some breeze.

"Be glad it doesn't feel like winter," Lily called back, "You and Leo would have to huddle together on that horse just to stay alive," she said with a smile only Giles could see.

"What? I just meant, well—"

The girl started sputtering, and Mal laughed. "She's teasing you, Nora."

"Oh." Lily saw her tanned cheeks turn a light shake of pink as she turned away from the group. She had a feeling Nora didn't get teased a great deal. Krag rode his huge horse up to Giles, the noise it made bounced off the cavern walls and made it a little hard to hear.

"I think I'll ride ahead and make sure they don't mistake us for people with bad intentions."

Giles nodded. "Go ahead, we'll catch up." With that, the

big horse took off down the narrow cavern.

"How long do you think it will take to reach Ral Hava?" Lily asked.

"I'm not sure. I've never come this way before, but it should be before the day is out," Giles called back. Lily had never been to the big dwarf city. She was looking forward to it. Her father used to tell her stories of the engineering feats they used to create the underground city. There were giant stone and metal golems that quickly made tunnels big enough that armies could march through. He talked about the intricate carvings that decorated the buildings according to a family's standing. The richer the family, the more complicated the design, usually telling the family's history.

It took almost all day to catch up to Krag, who was sitting around a fire with a few dwarven sentries when they found him.

"Ah, here they are," the bulky dwarf got to his feet, "This is my group I was telling you about." Everyone dismounted and walked their horses over to the fire but were quickly taken off guard as the other dwarves slowly started drawing their weapons.

"Krag, what exactly did you tell them?" Giles asked as William stood protectively in front of Lily.

Krag turned and saw the three sentries had their axes ready to strike. "Hey, what are you doing? We don't mean you any harm!" he yelled, waving his arms frantically in the air.

"We believe you, Krag," the dwarf in front said, "but that bitch right there is going to answer for her crimes." Everyone turned and saw they were pointing at Lily.

Her eyes widened, and she pointed to herself. "Me? What did I do? I've never been here before!" They started moving forward while everyone else put themselves between Lily and the guards. "Look, we lost a lot of good men because of her and those abominations she was with, so we're going to take her in!" one of them yelled.

"Sirs, please believe me when I say I have no idea what

you're talking about, but I'm sorry for your loss." She couldn't believe this was happening. Lily was so confused her mind was spinning.

"You may have changed your hair, but we won't let you get away this time!"

"Hair?" She and William looked at each other, confusion on both their faces, "I've never changed," she stopped when she realized what must have happened. "Sirs, could you describe the others that were with the woman who looks like me?"

"What good will that do?" She heard Ivelios whisper behind her.

"I think I know who they're talking about," she murmured.

"Three Korites," the dwarf in front said, "one of them rode a horse that flew on fire, a giant and a man who only wore pants who seemed to have an affinity with acid. The only thing I see missing—"

"Are undead?" She finished.

Giles turned with a confused look on his face. "Lily, what's going on?"

"Yeah," one of the guards said, "you must have gotten rid of them when you joined these poor people."

"Lily, how did you know there were undead?" Giles asked. She slowly walked through her friends. William stayed behind her as she stopped in front of the guards.

"Sirs, I'm afraid you had the unfortunate pleasure of meeting my sister. I don't know what she was doing with those people, but I assure you I am not her." She held up her holy symbol and prayed, "Blessed Otto, I ask that you gift me with water to cool my friends." Suddenly, a bucket full of water from nowhere dumped onto Krag's head.

"What the bloody hell!" he sputtered.

She heard chuckling behind her and looked at the guards. "Surely you can see I am not her. May we please pass?"

The guards looked between each other, and finally, one of them nodded. "All right, but you'll still find your way blocked and not by us."

"What do you mean?" Giles asked.

"Krag said you're heading towards Cyranar, but our tunnel's blocked at the moment. Just follow us, we'll introduce you to the General. You'll have to leave your horses at the stables in the front, though. They won't like it under the mountain." They put up their axes and started for the city.

"This one will be fine, I assure you," Giles said as he patted Malice's neck.

"Suit yourself," one of the dwarves said, shaking his head.

When they got out of earshot, Giles turned to Krag. "Did they mention anything about their tunnels being blocked?" Giles asked.

He shook his head, spraying the rocks with water droplets. "No, wish they had."

Everyone filed in behind the guards and followed them into the city of Ral Hava. It was just as expansive as Lily's father said it was, and she marveled at how the houses and stores were built directly from the surrounding stone. It was dark inside, but the numerous torches and lit sconces gave them just enough light to see. She wondered if the air would be stale under the mountain, but it smelled of moist earth and, to her surprise, food.

"It's wondrous," she said to no one.

"We'll see how wondrous it is if we can get through," Nora mumbled.

As the group followed the guards, William took Lily's hand. "So, your sister looks like you?" he asked quietly.

She took a breath and nodded. "Twin," she held up her hand to show him the scar he had kissed so many times. "She did this to me."

"Gods, I wondered what happened."

She lifted his hand to her lips and gave it a kiss. "It's a long story. I'll tell you sometime, but there's a reason I haven't seen her in ten years." He squeezed her hand, and they continued down into the mountain.

The guards led them about three miles into the mountain, and when they took one last right, they saw a ramp leading to a large stone door barred with a large metal bar. It was surrounded by elite dwarven guards. They were all wearing heavy plate mail, and their weapons looked sharp and reliable.

Ivelios walked up next to her. "I wonder what's on the other side." Lily looked over at the druid and noticed the hair on Yahul's back was on end and hoped the wolf wouldn't cause a scene.

"Is he all right? He seems kind of bothered."

"I think he can smell what's on the other side. Whatever it is, it's bad." They walked up, and the guard introduced them to the General in charge of guarding the tunnel.

"General Thorton, this is Lord Giles and his people. They want to use the tunnel to get to Cyranar." The General was tall, just over four feet, and the ax he wielded was so shiny Lily could tell it was magical.

"They do, eh? I take it you told them the tunnel is impassable at the moment?"

Giles walked up and offered his hand. "He said they were blocked but didn't say by what."

Thorton shook his hand, "Blocked," he scoffed, "in more ways than one. About nine ways." Suddenly, the large stone door shuddered, and Yahul barked angrily at it. Ivelios quickly quieted him while they stared at the door.

"Nine?" Lily asked.

"Those things came through the other entrance. We can only assume all our guards are dead by now. We don't know why they're in there or why they're trying to come through Ral Hava. They had to have known it wouldn't work." he looked up at Giles, "If you want through, you're going to have to deal with what's on the other side of the doors."

Giles turned back to the group, "Looks like we've got another hurdle. Does anyone want to take the long way around the mountain?"

Everyone looked at each other. Nora turned and nodded at Mal. "We're hunters, Giles," she said and turned back to him, "and it sounds like big prey back there. We're in."

"I go with you, my Lord," Leo said.

Ivelios got to his feet. "Whatever is behind that door is an abomination against nature, I can tell. I made a vow to destroy such beasts. We're with you."

Artemis zoomed up on his carpet. "Son, you say you're too old for this sort of thing, yet here you are helping dwarves with something they should take care of themselves."

Giles chuckled. "Probably, but if we can do some good, we're going to do it, and I'm sure we couldn't do this without you."

He hmphed. "I know you couldn't," and flew up to the door.

"Awfully confident, isn't he?" Lily said quietly to Giles.

"I think you get that way when you're older than dirt," Giles teased.

"I heard that!" he yelled back, and Giles laughed. Surprisingly, the sound calmed Lily. *If Giles is laughing, then there's hope,* she thought.

She held up her hands. "Blessed Otto, protect us as we face an unknown foe so that we may continue our mission and restore peace to our lands." Otto's blessing filled all their hearts with bravery and confidence.

"I've never felt such a thing." Nora was staring at her hands like she'd never seen them before, "I feel like I can do anything."

"With Otto's blessing, even the most impossible task is within your reach," Lily said. She watched Leo stand next to Nora and whisper something to her before joining Giles. She swore the girl was trying to hide a smile.

"Well said, Sweets," William whispered and gave her a kiss. He had been calling her that lately. She absolutely loved it.

The dwarves moved to the big metal bar that held the door

shut. "We'll help the best we can. I think with all of us, we have a chance," General Thornton said, "Open the doors!" The front line consisted of a few Dwarven guards, Giles on Malice and Krag. Lily made sure to stay towards the back and Leo stood guard in front of her, William at her side as the doors cracked open. Wind blew in from the tunnel, and Lily quickly realized it was going to be pitch black in there. She reached into her money pouch and grabbed a handful of pennies.

"Otto, give us light!" She pulled out a handful of glowing coins and threw them into the tunnel. The little lights flew over the group's heads and landed a good thirty feet into the tunnel, some kept rolling, and they finally saw what had been trying to break through.

In the front were four large bugbears. Their beady little eyes glowed with the coins' light. They roared and charged the group, raising their giant, bloody flails as they ran. Lily looked around for the other enemies and spied three hill giants stumbling forward. It looked like they were wielding tree trunks, and they started swinging before any of them were even close enough to feel the wind from the top branch.

Odd words filled the air, and Lily's eyes were drawn to the back of the group. A large blue giant dressed in white fur was chanting, his arms raised above his head. A nalux ran around the shaman, clicking and slashing its sharp, spider-like legs at anything its way. She could tell the shaman was casting a spell, but the words were cut off as her group clashed with the bugbears. Krag yelled as he sank his ax into the knee of one of them. It roared loudly and swung its weapon wildly but missed everything except the ground, and everyone was sprayed with bits of rock.

Ivelios stood next to Lily, and she watched as vines sprouted from the mountain and wrapped around one of the hill giants. Luckily, it seemed to confuse the creature as it just sat down and started calmly untangling itself. That's when Yahul struck, clamping his powerful jaws around the giant's neck.

Blood squirted violently from the creature, and with a powerful shake of the wolf's head, a loud crack filled the air, and the giant went down. The giant in front yelled in some deep, guttural language, and Nora started screaming. The whirling fighter was still spinning, but her sword wasn't cutting anything. It looked like she was trying to get away from something.

"Nora, I'm coming!" Lily ducked from a flail and slid on the ground and managed to catch Nora as she fell to the ground.

She was screaming and scratching at her skin, "Get them off, get them off!" Lily saw large red welts appear on her face and arms and gasped when she saw what did it. There were black centipedes crawling all over Nora, biting and stinging. It was no wonder she couldn't fight.

"Blessed Otto, I need water to wash away these vile bugs!" Water crashed down on Nora, washing away the critters, but she lay still in Lily's lap, whimpering with every quick breath she took. Lily laid her hands over the blistering bites. "Otto, give me the power to heal this girl of her wounds. She's poisoned and needs to be well to fight." Otto's love flowed from her hands and infused Nora with health and vitality while nullifying the poison.

She took a deep breath and opened her eyes. "Priestess?"

"You're going to be alright." Lily gave her one more once over as Leo ran over.

"Is everything okay?" He reached out and cupped Nora's cheek. Lily could see his eyes searching for wounds.

"I'm fine, I'm fine." She let him help her up, and she quickly ran next to Krag, and together, they took out the last bugbear. Lily looked around to assess her friends. William was handily taking care of the giant with the flail, dodging the deadly-looking weapon and slashing at its legs while dwarves hacked into it with their axes. Ivelios was healing Mal, and Artemius was throwing lighting at the Shaman in the back.

She turned and found Giles and the nalux engaged, and so far, Giles seemed to be winning. His sharp lance had impaled the giant spider-looking monster between its shells, and one of its pincers was trying to pull it free while the others were gnashing at Giles. He blocked with his sword and ducked just as the creature spit a white, sticky-looking substance at him. It screeched angrily and started running away, filling the cave with loud clicks. Now that Giles found himself without an opponent, he charged the Shaman, who didn't stop casting when he saw he was about to be engaged.

"Lily!" Mal's frightened voice drew her attention, and she saw two of the remaining hill giants bearing down on him. He had dropped his bow and was wielding his sword, but he already looked a little beat up. His right leg was bleeding profusely, and his left elbow seemed to be broken. It seemed Ivelios had to help Yahul, and the orc was left to fend for himself.

Lily quickly raised her hands. "Otto, help me shape stone!" She prayed and watched as one of the giants was quickly engulfed in a dome of stone that had been pulled from beneath its feet. It wouldn't hold it long, but it was better than nothing. Koizumi appeared out of thin air and kicked the free giant in the head so hard she thought she heard something break, and apparently, it had. The giant immediately stopped and fell to the ground, its spine sticking out at odd angles.

If the monk was lucky, he could do that again. "Koizumi, go help Giles!" Lily yelled as the others converged on the monster as it broke free of the stone dome. But the giant didn't stand a chance as William, Nora, and Krag all brought their weapons down at the same time and split the creature's head with a deafening crunch. Nora quickly gave Mal a potion, and Lily saw his arm heal.

Lily turned and watched as the Shaman hit Giles in the chest with his large staff. The Lord flew backwards off Malice and hit the wall hard. Her feet were running to him before he slid to the ground, her hand already clasping her seashell. The shaman yelled something in giant and was knocked to the ground as Malice reared up and kicked him with his powerful hooves. Koizumi appeared behind him, and with a mighty kick, another loud snap filled the air and the giant fell without another word.

Lily quickly landed next to Giles and thanked Otto that his eyes were open, but she could see he was struggling for air. His breastplate was in ruins, the metal had a deep crack, and she could tell the sharp edges had broken his chest bone. Her fingers tried to quickly undo the straps of his armor, but they were soaked in blood and kept slipping through her fingers.

"Otto, please help me," she prayed. When the buckles were finally undone, she heaved the ruined armor aside. His shirt was torn, and she could see there were indeed deep wounds in his chest. His breastbone was broken and blood poured out in time with his heartbeat.

"Close your eyes," she whispered and covered his eyes with her left hand as her right reached up and held her holy symbol. "Blessed Otto, please give me the power to fully heal this brave man so he may keep the world bright with his presence."

"My Lord!" Leo yelled and ran for his adopted father, fearing the worst. He slid on the ground across from Lily and took his father's free hand. "My Lord, you'll be fine," he whispered and listened to Lily pray. "Please, Father, please don't give in." Tears filled his eyes, and he willed them not to fall. He had to be strong, so he closed his eyes. *Please,* he thought, *please don't leave us, Papa, please.* He looked up at Lily and saw her holy symbol glowing. It had never glowed while she was healing, and he wondered if it was because her power was growing or his father was that severely injured.

He looked back at his father. His shirt was covered in blood and was torn, but as he slowly sat up, it was clear that he was fine, no longer bleeding, and he could see no wounds.

"Father!" Leo forgot all formality as he flung himself forward and hugged his Lord, who gratefully hugged him back.

"I'm all right, Leo," he patted his back, "I'm all right, son."

Lily reached out and pulled his shirt up. "Are you all right? Are you in pain?" She ran her fingers over his skin and was thankful it was no longer a ruined mess.

"I'm fine." He stopped her hands and held them, "Thank you."

"Of course." She patted his hands and looked around. The fighting was done, and a troop of dwarves were making their way through the tunnel. "Where are they going?" William helped Lily to her feet and laid a hand on her cheek.

"All right?"

She nodded. "You?" He nodded and kissed her cheek.

"They're checking the route before us," Mal said, "They want to see if any other dwarves made it out alive."

"I pray they did."

An hour later, Giles had another breastplate, courtesy of the dwarves, and everyone else was healed enough to keep going and headed into the mountain. They could see where the troop of dwarves had walked through, making sure the road was clear by moving debris and bodies. They could also see the wrath the creatures had wrought on the dwarves that lived on this route. Every home that they passed was empty, and blood ran in the streets. They stopped when the dwarves said it was late and settled next to a fountain in the middle of one of the small, deserted towns.

"I'm so sorry for your losses," Giles said as Leo started a fire for them.

"Thank you, sir. We'll rebuild, repopulate, life goes on," one of the dwarven guards said. "The houses still have running water if you want to wash off. Bugbear stink can linger." Lily was grateful for the tip and watched as several members of their group found nearby houses to take advantage of a bath. Lily motioned to William and walked into one of the houses. There were still a few pieces of furniture, one of which was a huge comfortable-looking couch. She spread out her bedroll on it. Her mind still racing from the fight that happened a few hours ago. She knew a nightmare was waiting for her. Then realized she had thought that before, that her dreams would be haunted by all manner of horrid things, but they weren't. Not since she met William.

He walked in and smiled. "Comfy."

"I thought so." He spread out his roll next to hers on the big couch.

"I'm going to wash off." He gave her cheek a kiss and took his shirt off. The corner of Lily's mouth tilted at the sight of his muscular chest.

"Me next." He winked and disappeared into another room. Lily walked from the house and sat by the dry fountain. She cast a little spell, and clear water began flowing through it again. The sound of burbling water filled the air.

"Mother?" Lily looked over as Mal made his way over.

"What can I do for you, Mal?"

"I wanted to thank you for taking care of Nora back there. She'd never do it herself," he said affectionately.

"That's all right, no thanks are necessary. It's my job."

He gave a little chuckle and put his large hands on his hips. "That girl runs into trouble more than I can keep her from."

She smiled, it was clear he cared about Nora like she was family. "Young people are often like that. They think they can take on the world by themselves."

"I won't argue with you there, Mother."

"How long have you two traveled together?"

He took a mighty sniff as he gave it a thought. "About three years now. Found her in Buckland. She had just left her Suya camp and was looking for some people to travel with her. I volunteered first, and since Suya don't have the same prejudices against orcs, she was happy to let me tag along. But it kept others from joining us. So, it's just been the two of us."

"Nora is Suya?" Lily had never met anyone from a Suya camp, but she had heard they were known for their dancing and storytelling. It made sense if she was. The way she moved when she fought, it was almost like a deadly dance.

But Mal shook his head. "No, she just stayed with them after her Da died." He stepped close and leaned down, his voice lowered, but she had no trouble hearing him, "What do you know of Leo? My eyes are not so blind that I don't see that my friend seems to be fond of him." Lily sneaked a glance behind her. Nora was sitting next to Leo, talking about something. He was nodding his head at the appropriate times, but she wondered if Leo was really listening to the girl.

"I see the same as you, Mal, Leo is a good boy. He'll be a great man I have no doubt. I'm not sure he sees her in the same light. But then again—"

"He's male and therefore a bit blind?"

Lily chuckled and turned back to Mal. "I think Nora's going to need a more direct approach when revealing her feelings for Leo." The boys' laughter filled the air, and Lily wondered if Leo could love a wild cat like Nora.

"Maybe I'll give her a little push. Thank you for your time, Mother."

"You're most welcome." She turned back to the fountain as the tall orc made his way back to the fire. Lily sighed, and rubbed her temples as thoughts of her sister came to her mind. She figured it had something to do with what the dwarves said about her, but normally, she was good at keeping memories of Lavinia away. She thought about their fifth birthday. Their papa made them each a little cake, which they still shared with each other. A neighbor came by and gave them each a bow for their hair, Lily's had a little seashell in the middle, and Lavinia's had a shiny purple bead, it was one of their happier birthdays.

When they turned fourteen, they snuck out of their room early and found their father crying by the fire. Their birthday was also the anniversary of their mother's death and the only black spot on the day. They quickly ran over and hugged their father, who tried covering his tears, but he couldn't fool them, and they cried for their mother along with him. *Why am I remembering these now?* She thought to herself. Suddenly there was a pain in her soul deep down. It stole her breath, and as quickly as she felt the pain, it was gone, like a violent, shocking rip. Something was taken from her. She couldn't stop herself from gasping a bit from the shock.

"Lavinia." Her hand went to her chest as she sat on the lip of the fountain.

"Lily, are you okay?" Someone asked, but all she could think about was that feeling. She was alone in the world, there was a hole that wasn't there before, and she knew what it meant. Lavinia was dead.

"Lily, what's wrong?" A hand touched her cheek, and it woke her from her internal mourning, and she saw Giles in front of her. "Are you okay?"

The feeling slowly ebbed away, but the heartache stayed. "I, uh, I'm okay. Sorry, I didn't mean to worry anybody."

"It's all right. We thought you might be praying, so we left you alone, but then it sounded like you were crying."

She reached up and felt her cheeks were indeed wet. "Seems I was."

"What's wrong?" He reached up and wiped the tears from her cheek.

Lily sniffed and rubbed her chest over her aching heart. "I think… I think my sister is dead."

His eyes went wide. "Oh, I'm sorry. What makes you think that?"

She shook her head. "Just a feeling. She's my twin, I've felt things from her before, but now there's nothing. Like a hole in my soul, like something's missing." His face looked sympathetic as he tucked some hair behind her ear and rubbed his thumb against her golden hair.

"This is the same sister I take, who attacked the dwarves with undead and Korites?"

She slowly sighed and looked down at her feet. "Yes. She follows…followed The Shackled One."

Giles shook his head. "I can't imagine what got in her head to be that way, but I'm sorry."

"Thank you." Lily looked up, but she couldn't lock eyes with Giles. They were full of pity. "Part of me wonders if someone will bring her back."

"Do you want her to come back?" Lily had never thought about that. Her sister was evil, a worshiper of the most evil god the world had ever seen, and had almost killed her. But she was still her sister.

"Yes," she whispered, almost afraid someone would hear.

He gave her a little smile. "I kind of figured you'd say that. But it doesn't surprise me. You've got a good heart. I think the world would be a better place if more people were like you."

Lily gave a little chuckle. "Thank you." She couldn't stifle a yawn and felt Giles' hand on her neck, his fingers rubbing gently.

"You should probably lie down. I still don't think you're a hundred percent from healing my sorry butt."

She nodded. "Okay, good night then, Lord Sorry Butt." He chuckled as she walked back into the home where her bedroll was.

As she walked in, William walked out from the bathing room, his hair damp and his clothes clinging to him.

"Bath is free," he said with a smile.

She sighed and shed her robe. "I don't think I've ever needed a soak more than I do now." She walked past him to the bath, but he stopped her with a hand on her stomach.

"Sweets, what's wrong?" She closed her eyes, concentrating on the feeling of his hand on her. He stepped close and laid his forehead on the side of her head, his thumb making little circles on her stomach.

"Let me wash, then I'll tell you. I need some time."

He nodded. "If you're sure, but I'm here."

She turned to him. "I know." She kissed him, a little brush of lips that she treasured, and he dropped his arm and let her pass. The room was still warm from William's bath, but she saw he had refilled the stone bin for her, and the clear water was steaming. She slipped out of her armor and clothes and stepped into the water. The heat felt amazing on her tired body, and she laid back, getting as much of her body under the water as she could. As she let the water hold her, she could still feel that empty spot in her heart where Lavinia lived.

It was a different kind of hurt than losing her husband or Taren. It was sharper, deeper and she felt tears roll down her cheeks. It had been so long since she'd seen her, but she had forgiven her years ago. She had wanted to see Lavinia but wasn't sure how to go about it. She didn't know if Lavinia would even want to see her. Her shoulders began to shake as she thought about the good times with her sister, how they'd stay up talking, how they'd make a cake for their Papa on his birthday. And that they could never agree on the flavor so one layer was always chocolate, and one was always vanilla.

A sob escaped her lips as she thought about sleeping under the stars in summer, always re-naming the constellations different things. Elephant was always one of Lavinia's favorites. She laid her head in her hands and sobbed. Her twin, so alike yet so different, was gone, and her heart broke. She felt arms around her but didn't care who it was and threw her arms around them and sobbed into their neck.

Their hand ran over her hair, trying to comfort her. "I got you, Sweets." Of course it was William. Who else would it be? "I got you." She held him as tight as she could, sobbing over the loss of her sister.

When she calmed down, she wiped her face with her hand and sat back. "My sister is dead," she whispered.

"Oh, Lily." He hugged her again, "I'm so sorry."

"It felt like a piece of my soul being ripped out of me. I can still feel it." She tapped her chest.

"I can't imagine feeling something like that." He kissed her temple and moved behind her. "Just relax." He picked up a ladle next to the stone bath and dipped it in the water. "Lean back." She sniffed and pulled her knees under her chin, and did as he asked. He poured the water over her hair until it was soaked. He grabbed the hair cleaner and poured some in the palm of his hand. She felt him rub his fingers against her scalp, soon covered in bubbles. She sat in the water, letting him wash her hair as silent tears slid down her cheeks. He rinsed her hair until all the bubbles were gone, then grabbed the soap and washed her. She watched with raw eyes as he rubbed the soap along her arms, her legs, and her stomach. He didn't hesitate as he ran the soap over her breasts and then up and down her back. He rinsed her off, then got a big towel from a rack across the room. "Let's rest," he said quietly as he held the towel out for her. She stepped out, and he wrapped it around her.

As tired as she was before her bath, she felt like all her energy had been consumed by her grief, and she could barely walk to their bedrolls. He set her down on the couch and pulled out a comfy shirt from her pack. "Let's get this on you, then we'll lay down." She nodded and took the shirt. The towel slipped down her torso, and she put the shirt over her head. William took the towel and rubbed her hair until it was just damp. He opened their bedrolls and helped her down. Lily immediately settled into his arms and closed her eyes. "Sleep, my love," he whispered but she didn't hear him because she was already fast asleep.

——————

Nora was on duty with a few of the dwarves. She didn't mind night watch, especially since she wasn't alone. It gave her a chance to let her mind wander a bit. Her eyes landed on Leo, sleeping a few feet away. She was never one for happy endings or romance, but ever since he grabbed her chin and stood up to her outside of The Shade it flipped her world upside down. Most men were intimidated by her. She knew she didn't make it easy on them, but the way she grew up, you had to stand up for yourself or be flattened. The Suya women taught her how to be strong, and she might have taken it a bit too far. She had gotten used to the idea that she would go through life spending only a little time with a partner before they would get sick of her and move on. But with Leo, it was different.

He was a few years younger, but he didn't really look like it. He was tall and muscular. He could have passed for twenty if he wanted to, but she knew he never would. Leo was kind and truthful, he never presented airs, and she wondered why. Most men she knew fluffed themselves up to be more than they were, but not Leo. He was kind and funny, loyal down to his bones and his face. *God's his face,* she thought, he was so handsome she thought her knees might give out. She loved riding on the back of his horse with her arms wrapped around his waist. She hoped they would get out of this mountain soon so she could do it again.

Nora wasn't used to feeling like this, and she started wondering if she was in love, but she couldn't ask Mal. He'd just tease her. Leo gasped, and his eyes opened in a panic, looking around for something.

"Are you all right?" she whispered.

He turned to her and sighed heavily. "Had a nightmare." He sat up and rubbed his face, and picked up his waterskin.

Nora shook her head. "Hate nightmares. I used to have them a lot as a child, just after my Da died." She sat down next to him. "He was murdered by some defectors from Ardenry. I found his body the next morning." He was under his blanket. There was blood everywhere, so she knew. Without looking, she knew.

"That must have been awful for you," he said, taking a drink of water.

She shrugged. "Could have been worse, I suppose." She looked over at Leo, "How'd your Da die?" He talked endlessly while they traveled, so she knew a little about his past, but not as much as she wanted, and hoped he'd open up a bit.

"Oh, um, it was a hunting accident. His horse got spooked and fell on top of him, crushed his chest. Lord Giles said he didn't suffer much. I suppose I should be thankful for that." Nora didn't understand why a person would be grateful when a family member died, no matter how quick or peaceful it was.

"I'm sorry."

"S'okay, it was a long time ago. I'm grateful my Lord took me in. I didn't have any other family. My life could have turned out different if he didn't."

"I'm glad he did, too. That way, we got to meet."

He gave her a tired smile. "I'm glad we met too. I think I'm going to try and get back to sleep."

"Okay." He lay down and she waited for him to close his eyes, but instead, he reached out and took her hand. His skin was calloused, and she swore she could feel his hand shaking a bit as he squeezed hers.

"If it looks like I'm having another nightmare, would you wake me?" he asked, without looking at her. She laid down facing him, her right hand holding his and she reached up and laid her other hand on his cheek. His eyes met hers, and despite how tired he looked, she could see how much he didn't want to tempt another nightmare. His kind brown eyes, which shone with happiness and joy most of the time, were scared.

"I'll keep the nightmares away," she whispered.

"Promise?" he asked just as quietly. She leaned forward and gently kissed him, her lips covering his bottom lip.

"I promise," she said against his lips.

"Thanks, Nora." He pulled her close, and she watched his eyes finally close.

"You're welcome, Leo." Her own life might have turned out differently if she had a Lord to take her in like he did, but she didn't begrudge him. While her life was hard, it made her into the woman she was today, and right now, she loved her life.

A week later, they finally emerged from beneath the mountain into a grassy field. The dwarves said their goodbyes and mentioned there was a village about ten miles to the west where the group might get some horses if they wished.

When the dwarves disappeared back into the mountain, Giles turned to the group. "I think we will stop in that village. We need to be well rested when we get to Cyranar, and sleeping in some beds will help us get over the last few rocky days." He put a hand on Lily's cheek when he said that. Everyone knew that she was mourning her sister. She was grateful for the support, but she was determined not to let it distract her. There will be a time to properly mourn after this was done.

William was amazing. She told him everything the morning after her breakdown. He didn't run when he learned about Lavinia and what she had done. He kept his arms around her and listened as she poured her heart out to the first person in almost a decade about her sister. She told him when they were done with this, she wanted to go home to Fairwinds and let her father know. Hopefully, she'd be able to put up a little memorial for them to visit. He kissed her forehead and said he'd happily go with her.

Malice was the only horse they had now, much to Krag's dismay, so Giles let him rest and didn't ride him. Everyone spread out and walked. Koizumi ran ahead to scout, just in case. The day was sunny, and the grass was lush and green. Lily could see wildflowers in the distance and took a deep breath. *Thank you for this lovely day, Otto* she prayed and tilted her face towards the sun. She wasn't claustrophobic but it felt good finally being on the surface. When she opened her eyes, she saw Nora and Leo walking rather close together and smiled. Artemis was flying by his lonesome as usual, and Krag and Ivelios were talking as they walked. Yahul seemed to be having the most fun as he repeatedly ran and dived into the ankle-high grass and rolled around on his back. He must have hated being underground.

Lily gave William's arm a little squeeze. "I'm going to catch up with Giles for a moment."

"Okay, Sweets." He gave her cheek a kiss, and she quickened her pace and caught up with Giles.

"It's nice being out of the mountain, isn't it?"

"Immensely," he said with a grateful sigh. "I know Malice would behave, but I could tell he was uncomfortable," he said, petting the horse's neck. "So, how are you?"

She took a deep breath. "I'm sad, but better. Anxious to get this over with."

"Same. I swear I'm missing Siddah and my boy more every day." She could see the worry in his eyes and wanted to help him get his mind off that worry.

"How did you meet her?"

A smile instantly spread on his face. "I was twenty-three, and my father brought me to Ardenry to meet with the King and Max. Max and I had known each other already so I was looking forward to the trip. I don't have any siblings, and Max filled that hole rather well. When we got there, I could see he was already scheming. The smile on his face was like a sneaky cat." They laughed, and Lily put her arm through his when he offered it. "We went to this tavern on the other side of Ardenry, kept our hoods up and all that so no one would recognize him. We got drinks, and Max nudged me with his elbow, 'There is a bard singing tonight. You will love her'."

"A singer, huh?" The smile on Giles's face was peaceful, and she hoped it would lift his spirits talking about her.

"She came out in a pretty red dress, and I swore she didn't need to sing a word. My heart was already flying out of my chest. She was so beautiful. Her long dark hair was braided behind her head, and her lovely brown eyes were so kind. But when she started singing, I thought I had died and gone to the gods. Her voice was bright and lovely. I made Max wait until her set was over because I was not leaving that tavern without meeting her. Which, of course, was his plan all along."

Lily giggled, "Sounds like love at first sight."

"It really was," he sighed, smiling at the memory. "You and William seem to be getting along."

She snickered. "Yes, we are. This would be the second time I've found a companion while traveling. Well…maybe third." She waved her hand nonchalantly.

He patted her arm. "I'm glad you return his affections. I got to know him a bit before we left Ardenry. He's a good man."

"He is. He's taken care of me in a way I wouldn't expect someone who has only known me for what, three, four weeks, too? I can't remember when we left. These days are blending together." They laughed. Traveling did that to the days, you focused on what you were doing at the moment, and the days and weeks would blend seamlessly into each other. "I feel so loved and cherished. Most importantly, I feel excited to love again and excited that it's him." She smiled as she spoke about him and couldn't wait for all this to be over so they could really get to know each other.

"You sound very much in love."

Her heart leapt at the realization. "I am."

Giles sighed heavily. She thought he looked ashamed for some reason. "My wife didn't want me to go on this mission."

Ah, poor man, she thought. "I imagine she knew it would be dangerous. I don't blame her."

Giles shook his head, "I fought with her the day I left. I said I was keeping Raventree safe for my family and my people. She said we should just abandon the city and go to Ardenry, where it would be safe."

Lily clicked her tongue in sympathy. "I'm sure she was just acting out of panic. Most don't think things through when they're in a scary situation."

He nodded, "I've come to the same conclusion. But at the time, I was so angry with her, thinking I could just leave my homeland, my people. Like they didn't mean anything. I was so mad at her, I told her maybe she should go to Ardenry and not come back. Then I left. I didn't even tell her I loved her." Lily could see how bad he felt for saying such things to his wife. Especially since they were getting closer to Cyranar, he must have been afraid he wouldn't make it back. "When Max said two legions of orcs were camping close to Raventree, I felt as if the gods were punishing me for saying such things to her. I started to believe I'd never see her again."

"Oh," she gave his arm a little squeeze, "of course you'll see her again. All couples fight, but when you see her again, it will all be forgotten. She loves you, and when she's in your arms again, you'll see just how much."

He gave her a little smile and kissed her hand. "Thank you, Lily."

"You're welcome, Giles."

———————

Nora smiled to herself when Leo started walking next to her. "So glad to be out of that mountain," he said, stretching like a happy cat.

"Me too. One can only take so much nothingness to look at and stone to smell."

Leo chuckled, "It does smell a lot better out here."

"So, when we're done with this absolutely insane, impossible mission, what are you going to do?" She looked over at him, gods he was handsome. His eyes were brown, and she never really thought brown eyes were pretty until now.

He shrugged. "I imagine I'll complete my training with my Lord, and then..."

He paused, and Nora could tell he was hesitating. "What?"

Leo shook his head, a shy smile on his lips. "Naw, it's silly."

She reached out and laid a hand on his arm. "I'm sure it's not."

He looked at her from the corner of his eyes. "Hmm, promise you won't laugh?"

She chuckled, "I promise." She watched the decision cross his face, from shyness to being excited.

"I want to go to the Citadel and be a Dragon Rider." He turned and watched her, waiting for the laugh, but she smiled.

"That sounds amazing. Is that something you can do?"

He shrugged and she could see how relieved he looked that she didn't tease him. "I don't know, I sure hope so. That's why I'm hoping if I go when I'm a Knight, they'll listen to me and not go, 'We don't let nobody orphans ride dragons.'"

Nora chuckled, "No, they wouldn't say that." She sighed, "I bet they have the best weapons there."

Leo smiled down at her. "Well, you could go with me if you wanted." Her heart jumped into her throat. She wanted nothing more than to stay by his side, no matter where he went.

"Really?" She didn't bother hiding her smile.

"Yeah, I mean, you'd have to wait in Raventree for a bit, or, not, I suppose you could write and tell me,"

Nora laughed as he stammered. "No, I'd like to stay in Raventree. It sounds nice."

He stared at her for a moment. "Really?"

She nodded. "Really." She swore she saw his cheeks turn pink.

"Good, that'll make it easy."

Nora stared ahead, a big smile on her face, and took his hand. "Yes, it will." She waited for him to let go, but he didn't.

Lily finished her conversation with Giles and waited for William as he walked up to her. As she watched him, she couldn't help but feel at peace. This handsome, sweet, noble man loved her. She knew it in her heart. She knew she wanted to feel loved again, and she wanted to feel it with him. He reached out as he stepped next to her and took her hand.

"Have a nice chat?" He kissed her head, and they began walking.

"Yes, it was enlightening." They walked for a bit, just holding hands, before she looked up at him. "William?"

He looked down. "Yes?" She met his eyes, glittering in the sunlight, with nothing but love in them as he gazed down at her. A smile slowly spread on her face. No fear about what they were about to do, no fear about going to the cursed city and facing Efrits or Korites. None of it mattered anymore as she stared into his eyes. As the words sat in her mouth, she had no fear about the future.

"I came on this trek to make the world a better place. That was the only thing I hoped for, but now there's so much more I want." He smiled and ran his knuckles along her cheek. "I was not prepared for the way you make me feel."

He leaned down and gently kissed her cheek. "And how do I make you feel?" He whispered in her ear in a way no one had in years and felt her stomach tighten. She looked up into his eyes, his lips so close it wouldn't take much to feel them on hers.

"Loved. Cherished. I feel as if your love has marked my soul. That you will give me everything in life I've dreamed of."

"I will give you everything, my heart, my soul. Whatever you ask of me is yours."

The words fled her mouth, knowing a new chapter of her life was beginning. "I love you."William quickly pressed his lips on hers as his arms tightened around her."You love me." It wasn't a question, it was a statement, and she nodded. "You love me," he lifted her up, spinning around in the wildflowers around them. "The most wonderful, beautiful, faithful woman in the world loves me," he said into her neck. "And I love her, with every beat of my heart and every fiber of my being." She laughed and kissed his cheek. "And I will love her the rest of my life and beyond." He set her down and held her face. "From the first moment I saw you, I loved you. I didn't understand it at first, but I know why now."

Tears were sparkling in her eyes. "Why?" She whispered, her hands covering his.

"You're my soulmate, Lily. We were made for each other." Her tears became too heavy to hold in, and they rolled down her cheeks. "We were so close, yet so far all these years, but those years led us to each other now." His own tears tumbled down his face, and she kissed them away, one by one. "I love you, my priestess." He wrapped his arms around her, and she pressed him as close to her as she could.

"I love you, William." As the words fled her lips, there was a completeness she felt, something she had never felt before, and she knew he was right.

They easily made it to the town the dwarfs told them

about. It was small, but thankfully, they found plenty of rooms at one of the taverns. William and Lily walked into their room, fully expecting to be squeezing into a twin, but were pleasantly surprised to find a queen-sized bed.

"Oh, happy day." William teased and put his pack on the floor. Lily pulled her robe off and hung it behind the door. She turned, and her chain mail gleamed from the sun streaming in through the window. William smiled and walked over to her. "You look like an angel." He stood in front of her and unbuckled the buckles at her sides. He lifted the chain shirt over her head and laid it on the back of the chair. She watched his fingers go to the belt that held up the chain over her legs. He unbuckled it and pulled the leather out of the rings. He snuck a kiss against her stomach before he bent down so she could step out of it. He laid the leg armor over the chain shirt and Lily stood in front of him in her underclothes and did the same to his leather armor.

She unbuckled the three straps on his left side, one at a time, and after each one was undone, she tilted her head up and kissed his neck. One, two, three. She moved over to the buckles on his right side and did the same thing. Kiss, kiss, kiss, and helped him shrug out of the leather. She took his left arm and turned it over so she could unbuckle his bracers, one, two, three. She lifted his hand to her lips and kissed his palm, then put the bracer on the bed. She did the same to the one on his right arm. She turned it over, one, two...she looked up and smiled as she kissed the palm of his hand, three.

"We should wash." William nodded as Lily summoned water for the wash bin in the room. Thankfully, there was already soap in the room, and the bin was big enough for two. Lily pulled his shirt over his head, dropping it to the floor as she leaned in and kissed his chest. With a sigh, he buried a hand in her hair as her lips moved from one side to the other. Slowly, her hand trailed down his chest, down his stomach, and unlaced his leather pants. They fell to the floor, and she noticed his tan skin held little scars in random places, no doubt from his work as a Seeker. Her fingers gently touched them. One on his stomach was raised like it was still healing. There was a small one between his ribs that she was grateful wasn't deeper.

He picked up her hand and gave it a kiss. "Shall we?" He stepped out of his pants, and her eyes roamed over him as he got into the water. She admired his body as he lowered himself down. His muscular arms that she knew would hold her tight. His legs, the corner of her mouth tilted in a sly smile as she thought how those powerful thighs could hold her up against the wall. His sapphire eyes burned into hers, and her stomach tightened with desire, something she had felt in years. She stood by the bin and started to take the fabric over her breasts off, but he turned to give her privacy. "William," he looked over his shoulder at her, "you don't have to turn around." He had already seen everything. Besides, she loved him. She wanted him to see her. His eyes went wide for a moment before they filled with hunger as he turned to her. A hunger she hadn't seen on a man's face in years. A hunger she wanted to satisfy. In one movement, she pulled the fabric around her breasts over her head and let it fall to the floor. She hooked her thumbs in her underclothes and pushed them down until they fell freely to the floor. William's hands clenched in the water and she watched him lick his lower lip as his eyes took in every inch of her body.

"I was wrong." His voice was low, and an unexpected throb between her legs made her gasp. "You aren't an angel. You're a Goddess."

She smiled and stepped into the bin and sank into the water. "Sweet talker." He laughed, and she picked up the soap. "Turn." He obeyed, his eyes lingering on her a moment. She kissed his back, then ran the soap over the same spot. He chuckled as she kissed his neck while she ran the soap over his lower back. William reached over his head and laid his hand on her head as she moved to the other side of his neck, kissing and gently sucking his skin. An appreciative noise rumbled out of him as she made little circles with the soap along his side and stomach.

"What are you doing?" He teased as his hand rubbed the back of her neck.

"Nothing." She nipped his ear, and he laughed as her hand went lower. "You need a bath, is all." She moved the soap to his thigh when his hand landed on hers, taking the soap. He turned towards her, and she was taken aback. She had never seen such heat in a man's eyes before. He held one of her legs and slowly rubbed the soap on her calf, then up to her knee, then her thigh.

"Hmm, I suppose I do." His voice was low, and she spread her legs, letting him run the soap on the inside of her thigh. The pressure felt amazing on her tired muscles, and she let him hear how good it felt as she moaned and leaned back against the edge of the tub. Her nipples hardened as they came above the water, the chilly air teasing her. "Gods," he breathed out and rubbed the soap on the inside of her other thigh. Lily looked at him, ran her foot along his leg, and smiled at him.

"What?" She teased as he ran the soap up her torso, but he didn't go any higher than her stomach

He chuckled as he dropped the soap and leaned down to her exposed breasts. "Whoops." She laughed as he ran the tip of his tongue on her nipple. She gasped at the sensation as he kissed and gently bit that sensitive, hard skin. "Gods, Lily." He kissed her neck, his teeth gently bit at that thundering pulse. She laid her hand on his chest and could feel his own heart beating fast. Slowly, she ran her hand down his body and grasped the hardness between his legs. He moaned and stayed still as she rubbed her palm against him. "Gods, can we do this?" he asked.

She chuckled, "Of course we can." He wrapped his arms around her waist and sat back, bringing her onto his lap, straddling him. "We love each other."

He smiled, breathing hard, "I've never felt this way about anyone." She kissed him deeply, coaxing his tongue into her mouth, and felt his hand go between them. "Can I touch you?" His hand kneaded at the inside of her thigh, slowly moving closer to her middle.

"William Voltain, if you don't touch me right this minute —" she didn't get to finish as he slid a finger inside her. The sensation stole her voice and breath. "Gods, it's been so long." He rubbed on that spot inside her, each stroke more mind-blowing than the last, and she couldn't stop the movement of her hips, her body demanding more. It felt as if something inside her was ignited, something she forgot existed. She leaned back and felt him slip another finger inside her. Her moan echoed in the room, but she didn't care. They were together, and they were going to enjoy every moment of being alone.

"I will worship you the rest of my life," his voice was low and husky as his fingers slowly pumped into her. He pulled her closer with his other hand as her sensitive nipple disappeared in his mouth. Lily cried out, the pressure between her legs growing. "I will worship every bit of you, your love, your body, your soul," he kissed the space between her breasts, "You are the most beautiful woman I have ever known, inside and out." She kissed him furiously as his thumb found her clit, and her head flew back, unable to hold back. "I have never loved anyone as I love you, my beautiful priestess and I want to make you feel this way the rest of your life." His fingers went deep, and she felt the tips of his fingers rub on a spot that hadn't been touched in years and the pressure between her legs was almost too much.

"Gods, yes, William, yes." She looked down as he took one of her nipples in his mouth again. She held him against her as he rolled his tongue around that hard, sensitive flesh. Tingles spread down her body, and she felt a release was close. "Please, William, please, I need you." His fingers pressed on that spot, and the release was so sudden she bucked against him. It had been so long that she didn't know if she wanted to laugh or cry as the intense waves of pleasure throbbed inside her. She cried out, pressing him against her, and she felt his other arm doing the same to her.

"Oh gods," she whispered and felt a tear fall down her cheek. She looked down at him, and he kissed away the tear.

"I love you." He smiled. "I want you the rest of my days." She angled her hips and inch by inch, lowered herself onto him until he was deep inside her. His head flew back, and his eyes closed at the sensation. She sighed at how he filled her, complete and perfect. Slowly, she moved, her hips making him hit that spot inside her once again. "I want everything about you," she gasped as his hand slid over her breast, his thumb running over that hard, sensitive flesh, "everything only you can give me." He took her nipple in his mouth and sucked until she cried out again. She could feel his teeth gently scraping against her skin. It had been so long since she had just let go, just given herself what she wanted. She moaned and buried a hand in his hair, "Oh gods, I love that, yes."

Her hips moved faster, and he moaned. "Fuck Lily, you're exquisite." She laughed and deepened her movements, and it was his turn to make a noise that echoed around the room. His hand moved between them, and she cried out as he ran his finger around her clit. "Later, I'm going to do this with my tongue." He practically growled it next to her ear, and she captured his lips with hers as the mere promise of him kissing her there made her stomach tight.

"Oh, gods, promise?"

He chuckled, "Promise."

She wrapped her arms around him when she felt another release building inside her. "I'm close," she whispered, and he moaned into her neck.

"Gods, me too." She felt his teeth gently bite her neck, and she pulled him closer.

"William," she bit her lower lip as she laid her forehead on his. "Do you want to finish in me?" His hands gripped her ass and held her in place."Fuck yes, I want to feel you pulsing around me." One more thrust of her hips and the pleasure broke inside her, and she cried out louder than the last time as wave after wave of euphoria filled her. William echoed her a second later, his arms holding her against his chest. He moaned every time her body pulsed deeply around his. When her body was finally done, she looked down at him. His eyes were closed, and his face was a mask of pleasure. When he finally opened his eyes, he sighed and kissed her deeply. "That was fucking amazing."

She laughed, "It was." She laid her head in the crook of his neck, "I think we need to dry off," she sat back and held his face in her hands, "and try that in the bed."

He chuckled as a cheeky smile spread on his face. "I believe I have promised you something."

Hours later, they were laying in bed, satisfied for a second time. She was laying against him, his arm around her. Her eyes and fingers taking in the little scars he had.

"You must have seen a lot of action." Her fingers touched the scars on his chest and stomach. They didn't seem big enough to be life-threatening, but he must have bled a lot.

"It was for a good cause," he kissed her head, "another reason I learned to heal. I was tired of paying for potions." She chuckled and saw an unusual scar on his hip. It was bone white and shaped like a crescent moon.

"How did you get that?" She touched it, and a little tingle of magic ran through her. That was no scar.

"It's a birthmark," his fingers touched hers as she ran her finger over it, "my father had one too. He said it meant we were favored by the Gods."

"Interesting." She had never heard of anyone being marked by the Gods before, but as she touched it, she could feel a familiar holy power. It was faint but unmistakable. "Do you feel favored?"

She looked up, and he met her eyes. "I do."

———

That night, they joined their friends downstairs in the tavern. Mal was once again spinning tales while everyone else gathered at a big table with their ales. William's arm laid across her shoulders while under the table, she laid a leg over his and hardly a minute passed between the kisses they'd give each other.

She couldn't remember the last time she felt like this, if ever. While she loved Henri and he loved her, there was something different with William, almost like the gods approved.

Thankfully the teasing had stopped, and everyone acted like they had been like this the entire time. Lily laid her head against him and looked around. Leo and Nora were dancing, they moved well together and were all smiles. Giles and Krag were sitting at the bar, no doubt talking more strategy. She saw Koizumi doing balancing tricks in the corner, people were clapping while some tried to copy him, to no avail. There was no sign of the old wizard, but he usually stayed in his room to read anyway.

Lily spied Ivelios, sitting by the fire with a mug of ale that he wasn't drinking. He was just staring at the burning logs while Yahul had his head on his master's thigh.

She laid a hand on William's arm, and he leaned down. "I'm going to speak with Ivelios for a moment." He nodded and kissed her head before she stood and walked over to him. "May I join you?"

His eyes moved from the burning logs up to hers. "Of course."

She pulled up a chair and gave Yahul's neck a scratch. "Having a good night?"

"I suppose it could be worse."

Lily nodded. "True. You look almost sentimental, if I may say so."

He leaned forward and put his elbows on his knees. "Being in a tavern always makes me think of my childhood. Probably why I avoid most of them." He looked up at her with a snicker.

"Bad memories?"

He shrugged. "I don't know about bad. Sad maybe. My mother was a server, so I spent a great deal of time in the corners listening to travelers and handing out ales when I could. Those times weren't bad."

"Where are you from?"

He finally took a drink of his ale. "Blackridge."

She smiled. "I've been there a few times. First time I got punched in the face was in Blackridge." Her smile was proud as she thought back to that day.

Ivelios looked at her with wide eyes before he started laughing. "What could *you* possibly do to get punched in the face?"

"Oh, it's a long story, but the short version is I told a father whose daughter ran off with an elf that I married them, and she was going to have a child," she said with a wave of her hand as she sat back in her chair. He stared at her like she was an idiot. She didn't blame him. Most looked at her like that when she told them about the first wedding ceremony she ever performed.

"You…married a human and an elf? Was that wise?"

She smiled and nodded. "Ralan is different from most elves. He wanted peace, and for that, they shunned him, so he lived in the forest a day outside of Blackridge. He is a good man, and he loves his wife and children so much. I know most elves aren't willing to set aside their differences, but he is. If you'd like, I could introduce you one day. Just say the word." He sat still for a moment. She knew most half-elves hated their elven parents, whoever it was, since most abandoned them. But she felt if one half-elf could see that not all elves were heartless monsters, then maybe she had done some good.

"Maybe. I'll think about it." It wasn't a no.

"Do that. So, when did you feel the call of the forest?" She wanted to get him onto another topic, she came over to ease his mind, not create more strife.

He sighed and leaned back in his chair. "I must have been twelve. I know my mom didn't understand, but I couldn't stand it in the city. I felt choked and stunted, even though Blackridge isn't all that big. It was too much. So, I spent a lot of my time on the very edge of the forest. Scared her to death, I know," he said with a little smile. "She died when I was fourteen. A fight broke out in the tavern, and someone stabbed her when she tried to break it up. After that, I dedicated my life to the wilds."

"I'm sorry." She squeezed his arm, and he gave it a pat. "Did you ever know your father?" Lily knew it could be a raw subject to half-elves, but she didn't think Ivelios would take offense.

"No. Don't even know his name. I could care less, really. He didn't love my mother or me, so why should I waste time thinking about him." He didn't sound particularly bitter, just tired. "You think they'd care about our world to put our differences aside and help against the orcs, but they seem content ignoring us in the forest, letting the world burn around them."

Lily shrugged. "Perhaps the right ambassador can convince them."

"He'd have to be insane," he said, staring into his mug.

"Who said the lot of us aren't insane for what we're doing."

He sighed loudly and chuckled. "I'll drink to that." He held up his mug, and they cheered their insane endeavor.

"I'll leave you alone." She started to get up when he laid a hand on her arm.

"Thank you, I needed that."

She gave him a hug. "We all do sometimes." She took a step back and Yahul gave a whimper. "What, you want a hug too?" His tail thumped loudly on the wooden floor. Laughing, she bent down and hugged the wolf. "There you go." He growled happily, shaking his rump.

With one last smile, she walked back to the table and sat down next to William. "All good?"

"Yep. Just making sure our druid is all right."

———

The music stopped, and everyone clapped for the musicians. Nora fanned her face with her hand. "It's so hot in here."

"I blame the dancing." Leo wiped his brow with his sleeve, "Want to take a walk and cool off?" She grabbed his hand without a word and dragged him outside as he laughed. A cool breeze instantly hit them, and they both sighed. "Maybe we should dance outside," he teased.

"Taverns need windows downstairs, not just in their rooms."

"Agreed." They started walking down the dirt road towards the bridge that went over a wide river. Nora didn't remember the name of this town, it was so small it was more of a hamlet anyway. Anyone who wasn't at home was in the tavern, so the streets were quiet. The occasional dog going from one place to the other was the only thing they really saw or heard.

"So, when did you meet Mal?"

"Three years ago, in Buckland. I wanted a bigger group, but no one wanted to travel with an orc, so it was just us. Or they thought I was annoying. Either way, it was just us."

Leo scoffed, "Some people are assholes."

She nodded. "True, and they're not worth my time." They walked onto the curved bridge and stood in the middle. The cool breeze from the river felt amazing, and Nora leaned her back against the railing, tilting her head back to get more breeze. The sound of the bubbling river made her smile. "Reminds me of a song."

"What does?" She felt him scoot closer to her. She turned towards him and motioned to the water.

"The river." She flipped over, putting her arms on the railing, and her dark hair fell over her shoulder. "One of the Suya elders would always sing a song when we camped near a big river."

He was quiet for a moment. "Would you sing it?"

Her eyes narrowed at his request. "Sing?"

"Yeah, I'd like to hear it." He reached out and moved her thick curtain of hair over her shoulder. "I bet you have a lovely voice." He wasn't wrong. She just didn't have a lot of chances to sing.

"Hmm, all right." She took a breath and thought about the words for a moment.

"Down by the river, where the willows weep, murmuring secrets, old, wise, and deep."

She watched him smile as she sang, her stomach flipped with nerves.

"Oh, river of wonder, river of light, carry our burdens into the night."

She noticed he was leaning closer to her, and she did the same.

"Whispering waters, eternal and true, binding us all, in a mystical hue, river of life, in your loving embrace, whispering waters, lead us to grace."

He was so close she could feel his breath on her skin. "I knew you could sing."

"Yes, you're so smart."

He chuckled, "Can I ask you a question?" She nodded. "Why did you kiss me that night in the mountain?" His voice was low, and she fought not to kiss him instead of answering his question.

"I wanted to comfort you." She noticed his eyes move from her eyes to her lips and back. "Should I not have?"

His hand cupped her cheek. "Your kiss comforted me more than anything ever has." She smiled and turned her face into the palm of his hand, and she sighed as his thumb gently ran over her lips. "Has anyone ever told you how beautiful you are?" Her breath caught in her throat as she turned back to him, his thumb making little circles on her cheek.

"No." She kissed his thumb, and his other arm wrapped around her and pulled her close.

The corner of his mouth tilted into a wicked smile. "Shame." She chuckled and moved in to kiss him when a big, slobbery, warm tongue popped up between them. They both leaned back in shock as Yahul growled happily and started spinning in circles.

"Yahul!" Nora saw Ivelios walking over the bridge towards the nearby woods, a huge smile on his face. "You." She pointed at him as Leo groaned and wiped his mouth.

He laughed loudly, his hands up. "I told him nothing." He walked past, and the wolf joined him as they walked over the bridge.

Leo laughed and hugged her. "Never been kissed by a wolf before."

She sighed and wrapped her arms around him. "Could have done without that experience."

"Shall we head back?"

She leaned back, her arms still around him. "Sure." She watched as he moved closer to her lips.

"I don't know about you," She didn't let him finish before she pressed her lips on his and held him tight against her. His hands pressed against her back, and she felt his tongue run lightly along her lips. It was so easy to part her lips and let him in, his tongue swept in, and she met it with hers. Her hand went to the back of his neck, and she held him in place as she sucked and licked. She felt his hand move down and cup her backside as things low in her body started to tingle. She gave him an appreciative little moan before his hands moved up to her back, and he took his tongue back, simply pressing his lips on hers. When he finally parted, he sighed. "What was I saying?" Nora burst out laughing and pulled him back towards the tavern, her arm around him.

"No idea."

CHAPTER 7
THE DEAD CITY

After a few good days of rest, they all got horses and headed for Cyranar. They were a week away from the evil city, and with every mile they traveled, Lily could feel that evil getting closer. No matter how hard she'd grip William's hand, nothing could calm her. Ivelios and Yahul seemed unnerved as well, and that didn't surprise her. The young man and his familiar were deeply tied to the land. What happened to Cyranar left it decimated, cursed, and devoid of life, so she wasn't surprised the druid felt uneasy.

That first night they camped away from the town, Leo walked up to her as she was gathering some wood for a fire.

"Um, Mother, may I ask you something?" She stood straight and started walking back to the camp, a bundle of sticks in her arms.

"Of course, what's on your mind?" She dropped the sticks into the pit, and Ivelios cast a little spell, and a healthy fire roared in front of them.

"I know I'm supposed to protect you," she smiled and walked over to her pack, Leo following, "and I take that job seriously,"

"But?"

He licked his lips and cleared his throat. "But...I was wondering if you would be okay with me sleeping by Nora instead?"

Lily smiled as she nodded. "That's perfectly fine, Leo, William can protect me."

"Right, you have William now. You don't need me by you all hours of the day," she could tell he was trying to justify abandoning a duty he gave himself, "Thank you, Mother."

"It's no bother at all," she leaned close to him, "you really like her?" He nodded, a big smile spread on his face. She watched him move his things and put them next to Nora's. Lily giggled as she spread out her bedroll. William walked up next to her and did the same.

"What are you giggling about?" he teased as he gave her cheek a kiss. She motioned over to the young ones, and he chuckled. "I see."

That night, Nora and Leo were on duty. They sat next to each other by the fire. "You know I think Ivelios is right," Nora looked over at Leo. He could see she looked worried, "The land is...bad."

He put an arm around her. "Do you feel it, too?" She nodded and laid her head on his shoulder. He didn't feel what made them uneasy, but he wished he could make it go away.

"It feels like the land wants to take a deep breath, but there's something sitting on its chest if that makes sense. It's...wanting but being denied. I've never felt anything like this before."

"I knew the land was supposed to be cursed, but I didn't think we'd feel it. I just thought nothing lived there, and the grass would be dead, that sort of thing." He rubbed her arm. "Why do you think you can feel it?"

She looked up at him. "I've always felt terrible things. When I was with the Suya, one of their elders cursed a man for beating his wife. I felt it across the camp, it was a lot more than this," she motioned to the plains around them, "but it feels similar. Hopelessness."

His eyes burned into hers. "Do you think you have magic?"

She shrugged. "Don't care if I do. Magic is trouble." He noticed how sad she seemed when she said that. She laid her head back on his shoulder, and he nodded. If she wanted to push that part of herself aside, he'd let her, for now. But he knew magic could become volatile if not used, so she wasn't completely out of the woods.

A week later, everyone was uneasy. It was around noon when the crumbling city came into view over the horizon.

"Blessed Otto," William breathed out. If Cyranar were at the height of its splendor, they had no doubt they would have seen it from miles away, but now almost every building had crumbled to the ground. Lily could almost feel the fear and agony of those who were killed by the holy blast and prayed for them.

"Gods, I can't imagine what they went through," Lily said as Artemis floated next to her.

"I imagine it was painful," he said, "but hopefully their own gods took pity on them, and their deaths were quick." He zoomed off to the head of the group with Giles while Lily tried not to imagine what it was like to die by holy fire. She reached out her hand, and William took it. She wished they were still on the same horse, but Giles insisted everyone have their own. She was sure he had his reasons, so she didn't argue.

He squeezed her hand, and she looked over at him. "This will all be over soon. Then we can get started on our life together." She nodded, desperately trying to hide the fear making her knees shake.

Slowly, the group congregated just outside the old city. Giles turned Malice to face them and wiped his sweaty brow.

"All right, according to the map, he's being held in an underground crypt in the middle of the city. Who knows what we'll run into here, so just keep your eyes open and stay alert." He pulled the map of the city out of his saddlebag. "I have a feeling our journey is almost over, and I won't lose any of you now." The black warhorse turned back to the old city and started down the little hill.

Leo stopped next to Lily. "Are you nervous?"

She nodded. "I'm always nervous when cultists and Korites are involved." She gave her little horse a kick and started after Giles, William behind her.

The closer to the middle of the city they got, the more they could smell death in the air. Lily could feel the curse on the land. No life would grow here, no one could live here peacefully, and she prayed to Otto that he could hear her and that they would get through the city unscathed. The crumbling buildings obstructed their view as they looked around the city. Lily was surprised at how stable they seemed after a thousand years of ruin. No one spoke. Even the horses were quiet as they walked through the city. It was eerily silent, and they could hear the wind blowing little rocks around their feet.

Suddenly, Giles held up a hand, and everyone stopped. "There's something around the corner." He pointed to one of the ruined buildings about fifty feet in front of them.

The horses started backing up, and Koizumi ran forward. "I'll see what it is." He moved so quickly that Lily didn't have a problem with him running off by himself. She knew he would be able to get away. They watched as he peeked around a corner before he suddenly disappeared.

A second later, he appeared next to Giles. "We should find another route. It's a—" A gasp from Nora kept Lily from hearing what it was, but as she looked up, her eyes went wide at the large, muscular monstrosity before them. Every step it took shook the ground.

"Gorgon," she whispered and started praying, "Blessed Otto," The large animal roared and covered the group in a dense green fog. Horses fled the gas as Koizumi leapt in the air above the cloud and landed behind the creature as Giles ran it down. Mal sank several arrows into the beast as it roared angrily. When Giles got close enough, the creature's long horns tried to gore him, but Malice reared on his hind legs and knocked the creature in the head with his powerful hooves. William pulled out his new bow and sank an arrow into the soft flesh behind its ear. The gorgon mewled painfully and turned, only to find Nora and Koizumi. She brought her sharp blade down on the thing's neck as the monk kicked its chest. It gave a horrible cry and collapsed to the ground. Malice sauntered over and stomped its head into the ground almost proudly.

"Father!" The sound of Leo's cry made Giles' blood go cold. Leo was still next to Lily. He hadn't joined them in the fight and saw why. Lily was atop her horse, her eyes wide with concern but she didn't move, neither did the horse.

"Lily!" William yelled and spurred his horse next to hers. He was quickly joined by Giles. Malice snorted in annoyance when he touched the other horse's nose as Giles jumped down. William quickly got to the ground and ran his hands over her leg. "No."

"She's, I couldn't," Leo was stammering, and Giles didn't blame him. He reached out and touched Lily's robe.

"Stone." Everyone gathered around and had to touch for themselves.

Nora ran her hands through her hair nervously. "Gods, what are we going to do?"

"Artemis," Giles looked down at his friend, "please tell me you can fix this."

"Please, Artemis, do something," William begged him as he laid his forehead on her leg.

The old man floated up on his carpet and touched the horse's frozen nose. "Giles, you know I can't," he said solemnly.

Leo's eyes went wide. "What? Why not? You're a mage. This is what you do!" Giles could hear how upset his son was getting and didn't blame him. His own heart was racing fast at the thought of losing her forever.

"I could help her if it wasn't a gorgon, young man," Artemis turned the carpet to face him, "There's nothing I can do."

Giles watched his son's face go white. "What?"

William shook his head and faced the mage. "No, there has to be something!" He walked over to the carpet and grabbed it. "You can't just leave her like this!"

Giles reached out and squeezed William's shoulders. "We'll try and do our best for her later, but right now, we have a job to do." He wasn't sure he believed his own words, but he needed everyone to stay sharp. William turned, letting the carpet go with a snap. Giles could see him shaking with rage or heartbreak. He wasn't sure which. The breath of a gorgon was deadly, mainly for the fact that turning their victims back to flesh was incredibly difficult, and if Artemis couldn't do it, they might have to resort to…illegal means. But he'd do it for them, for her.

Leo met his father's eyes. "William's right. We can't just leave her here."

"I'll stay and guard over her," Koizumi suddenly spoke up.

"Are you sure? It'll be dangerous." Giles didn't like the idea of splitting up, but he really didn't want to leave Lily alone, whether she was stone or not.

"Nothing will get past me," he said with a little bow to William.

Giles nodded, "All right, we'll be back this way then. Stay alert."

"I am always alert." He perched on one of the nearby broken buildings, which Giles assumed to give him a better vantage point.

"All right, let's get going."

William kissed Lily's knee and got back on his horse. "We'll be right back, Sweets, I promise." Giles pulled himself up on Malice and turned him towards the middle of town, the other horses slowly following. Leo was by his side, it had been a while since he rode there. Ever since Giles told him to guard Lily the boy had taken his duty quite seriously. "We'll find a way to save her son," he said quietly.

Leo looked over. "Do you promise?"

He nodded. "I promise." *Otto, please don't let us lose her like this.* He looked back at William. The young man was breathing hard as they rode away from his love. *Otto, please don't let them be separated like this. They just found each other,* he prayed.

Another fifteen minutes and they could hear what sounded

like a large group of people shouting, and Giles held up his hand again. "Artemis, can you see how many there are?" He pulled out a little crystal ball and cast a spell.

They watched him search the orb and sigh, "Um, all of them?"

"All of them?" Giles trotted over and looked at the orb. He could see a huge battle taking place and shook his head. "Well, we're on the right track. Unfortunately, it seems a huge army of Korites and Efrits lay between us and the crypt."

Mal groaned. "I don't think we can sneak around that."

"I agree." He sat back in the saddle and rubbed his face. "Let's head back to Koizumi and Lily. Maybe we can come up with something."

Quietly, they turned and made their way back down the road. "How are we going to get past an army?" Leo asked.

Giles shook his head. "I have no idea." He easily admitted that he wished Lily were there. Perhaps she could have asked Otto for divine intervention.

The sound of battle soon disappeared, but when they turned one last corner, Leo gasped.

"She's gone!" William cursed and spurred his horse over to Koizumi, who was on the ground with a nasty wound on his head. He jumped down and kneeled next to the monk and put his hand over the bruise, and soon Koizumi stirred.

Giles quickly dismounted Malice and helped the monk sit up. "What happened, Koizumi?"

He groaned and held his head. "Apparently, something got past me."

"Where's Lily?" William helped him to his feet.

"Those Efrits that occupy the other half of the city, they said they were taking her, and if we wanted her back, we'd come talk." He pointed at a tall building off to the southwest. As far as they knew, the bulk of the fighting was taking place to the northeast.

Giles sighed and prayed to whoever would listen. "Well,

sounds like an invitation to me." They quickly got back on their horses and started heading towards the Efrits tower.

"Sir, are you sure about this?" Nora asked, "Efrits are awfully tricky. This might do more harm than good."

"We are not the Korites they are fighting, and they have our priestess. We might be able to strike some kind of deal."

Leo fell in next to Giles. "You think we can get her back?"

"I'm hoping, son."

"We better for their sake," William said as he rode past.

After ten minutes of travel, they came up to a gate with two Efriti guards. Giles, ever the Lord, rode Malice up to them and was thankful they didn't outright attack them. "I am Lord Giles of Raventree, and I believe you have our priestess in your custody. We were told to come and claim her." Without a word, the two guards ushered the group through the gate. The building was one of the only ones left standing, but Giles could see that it was still in dire need of repair. The stonework was cracked and the lovely carvings around the doors and windows had been defaced either by time or their current owners.

Everyone dismounted, and the group walked up the winding stairs that led them into a large, open room at the top of the tower. At the back of the room, they saw a large Efrit sitting in a chair flanked by two smaller guards, and there were at least ten other Efrits milling about the room. Giles quickly saw Lily by the window, atop her horse and still stone like some kind of decoration. William gasped and ran to her. The fiery beings watched with interest but didn't stop him.

"You are not with those who worship the God of murder, are you?" The Efrit in the chair asked. There was a tinge of flame to his voice like it passed through fire when he spoke.

"No sir, we are not," Giles said. "We were told that if we wanted our priestess back, we had to speak with you," he said, motioning towards Lily.

"You were. We are willing to give her back to you, flesh and blood again if you do something for us."

"You can do that?" William asked, hope in his eyes.

The Efrit in the chair turned to him with a nod. "We can."

"We are on a mission in the old city ourselves that is rather time-sensitive," Giles said, "so we do want our priestess back whole and healthy."

"What do you ask of us that you cannot do yourselves?" William asked them. Every single Efrit in the room started laughing, making it sound like the room was on fire.

"It's not that we cannot do it ourselves, little human," the one in the chair said, "When we realized the statue was not one of the Korites, we wondered what these people were doing in our city, so we brought her here. What exactly are you doing in our city?"

Giles sighed. "We are looking for someone we heard was being held captive by cultists."

"Ah, a rescue mission. Well, if you help us push back the Kotite forces, we will give you your priestess back, restored. I have a feeling you will need her for your little mission."

"Push back?" Leo spoke up, "Are they gaining ground on you?"

"No, they are not, but we want them back farther. You can understand."

Giles nodded. "We can," he turned back to the group, and they all nodded. No one wanted to retrieve Sobrei without Lily, "we'll try and help you."

The Efrit in the chair gave a fiery smile. "Excellent. Go with Mirshesh. He'll show you to the front we want pushed back." One of the larger fiery beings stepped forward and motioned for them to follow.

William gave her knee a kiss. "Not much longer, Sweets, I promise."

Giles gave Lily one last glance and prayed she'd be all right in the viper's nest.

———

"Please protect us." Lily finished praying but quickly

found herself in a much worse position than before. She was no longer outside with her companions, she was in a stone room, surrounded by Efrits, and she could feel the heat they radiated. The room smelled of burning coal and fire. It was hard to keep control of her horse who just wanted to run away.

"What is your name, Priestess?" She turned to the voice and saw a large Efrit sitting in a chair. It was red hot from his body but wasn't melting. The Efrits around the room were surprisingly calm, so she tried not to let her fear show.

"My name is Lily, I am a Priestess of Otto. Where am I?"

"You are still in Cyranar. Please dismount and be comfortable." He motioned for her to come forward, "I feel you will be our guest for a while."

"What do you mean?" She slowly climbed down from her nervous horse, who ran away the second her feet hit the floor.

The seated Efrit motioned toward the window. "Have a look, Priestess." Slowly, she walked over and took in the sight before her. She could see how big Cyranar used to be and how glorious the city once was. Crumbled structures lay before her as far as the eye could see. The roads that were said to be paved by gold were dust now and were filled with so much debris they could barely accommodate a horse passing through.

Suddenly, her eye caught erratic movement to her left and she recognized a battle taking place. There were fiery Efriti soldiers and others laying into another large group of people.

"What's going on?"

She turned to the seated Efrit, who motioned with his hand. "Come here. This will help." She walked over and saw an orb appear in front of him. "Look here. You will see what is happening below." The closer she got, the easier it was to see the battle below. The Efrit soldiers were killing what appeared to be Korites. Why she needed to see this she didn't understand, until she saw Nora flying around the field cutting down the enemy as she moved. Lily's eyes searched the battle and saw Artemis away from the fray, casting spells at the enemy and Leo fighting valiantly next to his Lord father. William was swinging his sword with a fury she'd never seen, and enemy after enemy died before him.

"Blessed Otto," she whispered and looked up at the Efrit. "Please let me go help them."

He slowly shook his head. "No. They are fulfilling their obligation to me."

"What obligation?"

"In return for saving your life, they are helping us push back the Korites. They were smart to take the deal, a gorgon's breath is deadly in most circumstances. Thankfully we have been dealing with them for a while and knew how to counteract the gas. You will be reunited with them when the battle is over."

"Oh, Otto, no." She whipped back to the orb and watched as Koizumi easily took out one of the Korites. Ivelios was standing next to Artemis, firing arrow after arrow into the enemy soldiers. Lily's eyes were trying to take in everything about the battle when she saw a man dressed in black sneaking up behind the druid. "Oh, gods, Ivelios behind you," she whispered and wished she was there to help. Suddenly, a fiery body leapt on the man in black and speared him through the chest before diving into another group of cultists. Ivelios never turned. Lily breathed a sigh of relief and looked to those in the middle of the battle.

Giles was on Malice, cutting down the enemy with every stroke of his sword with Leo beside him. She had never seen the young man fight so furiously before and prayed he wouldn't wear himself out. Nora was still dancing from foe to foe, cutting off limbs and making them useless while Mal cleaned up behind her. There were about ten Efrits fighting alongside them, and though Lily knew nothing about battle strategy she could tell her friends were gaining ground on the cultists.

"Looks like it was a good idea asking your group to help." The Efrit got out of his red-hot throne and looked out the window. "I feel you will be reunited with them very soon."

———

When the last Korite dropped, Giles turned to the Efrit named Mirshesh. "Lily, now." He nodded his fiery head and waved his hand. Slowly, a shimmering image appeared in front of them, and Lily coalesced before their eyes.

She stumbled a bit before Leo ran up and hugged her. "Lily! Are you all right? I never thought I'd see you again."

She wrapped her arms around him and smiled. "I'm fine, a bit displaced, but okay." William ran over to her, and Leo let her go in time for him to crash into her, his arms wrapped tightly around her.

"Oh, Sweets, I thought I lost you." He kissed her head and moved down to her lips. She let him linger. Watching him in battle was heart-wrenching since she couldn't help him. She looked up at the group when William stepped back but kept an arm around her.

"Is everyone okay?" It looked like no one was injured and she said a silent prayer to Otto that her friends made it through the battle so healthy. Nora walked in front of Lily. Her eyes were searching over her like she still expected parts of her to be stone.

"What was it like?" she asked, her eyes wide with curiosity.

Lily shook her head and sighed. "I didn't feel anything, everything just… stopped. When the Efrit released me, he made me watch the battle, but he wouldn't let me join."

Giles jumped off Malice and made his way around the group to Lily. "We had to try and push back the Korite army. If we were successful, they'd fix you and it would give us a clear shot to the crypt."

Lily looked around and didn't see any Korites or Effrit. It was quiet. "Looks like you were successful."

"We were, now let's get going before they get back."

The crypt was only a hundred yards away, and they ran for it, all except Artemis, who stayed on his carpet. Mal took care of the cultist guards outside the crypt easily, and they ducked inside.

The tunnel before them was long, but thankfully, there

were lit sconces every ten feet or so, which told the group that those who had Sobrei couldn't see in the dark either.

They were halfway through when a terrible feeling made Lily shudder. "Oh my, this is bad," she whispered. The evil that radiated from deep inside the structure was almost overwhelming, and she had to catch her breath. She shuddered to think what they would find in there. Was the evil coming from the cultists or the orc they held captive? The thought that they would have to subdue something so evil made her shudder. They came to a closed door where they heard a guttural cry of pain emanate from inside, and they all knew this was it.

Nora drew her sword and quickly made her way to the front of the group. "Well, what are we waiting for?" And without knowing how many enemies were in the room she kicked open the door and ran inside.

"Nora!" Mal drew an arrow and posted by the opening as the group ran inside. There were yells echoing off the stone walls, and Lily gasped when she saw Nora surrounded by ten cultists, all wielding large swords.

"Nora!" But there was a smile on her face as she danced from foe to foe. None of them could keep up with her quick, graceful movements and Lily had a feeling she was going to be alright. Giles ran through to the middle of the room, his sword out as he charged a man in a black robe.

"Kill them, kill them all!" The cultists yelled as he thrust his hands into the air. There were several loud noises throughout the room, and Lily watched as five demons appeared, one in each corner and one ten feet behind Giles. The sound of an arrow being fired made her ear twitch, and she watched as one of Mal's arrows sank deep into the demon threatening Giles.

She turned to her left and saw one of the summoned creatures charging for her. She gasped and ran deeper into the room, away from it. But William met it head-on, and his sword flashed against its body and sank deep as it bellowed in pain. Battle like this was so fast she barely had time to think and was glad the fighting around her had distracted the demon. Yahul howled and charged into the room, leaping at a demon while Ivelios called forth vines to occupy the other ones as they wrapped tightly around their legs, toppling them over.

Lily took a moment to make sure her friends were still in fighting health when she felt an unfamiliar holy power radiating beside her. It was like nothing she ever felt, strength, pride, and power. She looked up to her right and saw an orc. He was tied to a large metal object that was suspended about five feet off the ground. She jumped a little when she realized he was staring down at her. He didn't look defeated or in pain despite being covered in bruises and wicked cuts. He looked peaceful as his eyes burned into hers.

"I knew you would come," his voice was low and tired.

"Sobrei Re'vall?" He had been, no doubt, tortured every day for years, but she could feel his power radiating from him. *How is that possible,* she thought. She knew there was no way she'd be able to call on Otto if she were in that situation. Too much pain and anguish could keep a cleric from concentrating enough. But Sobrei, it felt like there was unending power inside him. *Could it be true,* she wondered.

He nodded. "Let me loose, I can help. The lever is behind me." Lily looked, and sure enough, there was the lever on the wall, being guarded by a demon. There was no way she could take it on herself, and she called for help.

"Krag, I need you!" She heard his ax sink into something before he came running over, "I need you to take care of that demon!" She pointed at it, and the creature smiled menacingly at her.

"What priestess of water god can't take me alone? Too scared?" The demon's voice was gravelly. She barely understood it but didn't let its words get to her. It's not like it was lying. She couldn't take it on alone. Krag ran to its right, and Lily flanked it. Thankfully, the demon was more worried about the dwarf with the large ax than an unarmed priestess and engaged Krag.

Lily held her holy symbol and prayed. "I banish you in the name of Otto, the god of the sea will wash over you and cleanse your unnaturalness!" The demon didn't leave, but she could tell it was weakened as Krag's ax sank into its side, and cracks appeared throughout its red skin. The demon roared and charged, pushing the dwarf against the wall before it disappeared back to its home plane. She saw Krag still against the wall, smiling menacingly with his ax thrust in front of him a good foot.

"I'm good, Priestess!" he yelled happily as he ran to the middle of the fray and killed a cultist with one blow. Lily ran to the lever and pulled with all her might. Thankfully it wasn't rusted and moved easily under her power. The sound of clanking chains filled the air, but when she turned to see if it worked, a large red hand flew from nowhere and knocked her back against the wall. Her head hit the stone with a crack, and stars filled her vision as she fell limply to the ground. She could feel the world spinning around her as a sharp pain in her head stole her breath. A loud roar filled the air, and a second later, she felt a large, calloused hand on her cheek.

"Feel healthy, Priestess." She heard and felt that unfamiliar holy power envelop her and take the pain away. Lily opened her eyes and saw Sobrei leaning down in front of her. "Is that better?" Lily couldn't believe what she was feeling from Sobrei. He was holy, innately holy. It wasn't some campaign to keep their people in line or bully them into submission. The orcs had been telling the truth all along. Their King was a God on this plane.

"It's true," she said, putting her hands on his face, "I can't believe it."

"Believe it." He winked and helped her to her feet. Lily's eyes quickly moved to the fray. Everyone was fighting, it was chaos, but her ears picked out Ivelios yelling out in pain. She found him just as a cultist pulled his sword out of his back, and he fell limply to the ground and didn't move.

"Ivelios!" She ran into the middle of the fight, ducking from swords, and landed in a puddle of his blood. The large wound in his back was deep, and blood was seeping out in rhythm with his slowing heart. He needed a great deal of healing, or he would die. "Blessed Otto, please heal this man of his injuries. We cannot go on without him." Otto's love flowed through her, and she watched as the horrid wound slowly started to close. "Blessed Otto, I beg you to give me the power to make this man whole again so that his bright light may change the world for the better!" The world tilted around her for a moment, but she managed to stay conscious. She couldn't afford to pass out now. Ivelios groaned and turned over, and she could see the color slowly returning to his cheeks.

He opened his eyes, and she thought he looked a bit surprised. "Thank you, Lily."

They helped each other to their feet. "Are you in any pain?"

He shook his head and gave her cheek a kiss. "No, I swear I felt the light trying to take me."

"You're not going anywhere." She looked around and saw the battle was going in their favor now. There was only one cultist and two demons left, and the three enemies were surrounded by her friends, who hardly looked worn.

Sobrei pushed past the group and picked the last cultists up over his head. "You will pay for all the things you did to me!" he roared and smashed the man's head into the ground until there was nothing left.

"Oh my." Lily couldn't keep in her shock at the orc's power.

Sobrei stood straight and spit on the body, and turned to the demons. "You will follow your masters into death!" he roared, picked up the dead man's sword, and rushed the nearest demon. Lily watched as it clearly didn't stand a chance against the enraged orc as the sword flashed, and a deep cut opened on the thing's head. It quickly disappeared back to its home plane. The last demon disappeared before them, clearly scared of what Sobrei would do to him. Lily and Ivelios walked around the group, healing the various wounds they had gotten during the fight. Luckily, they all seemed to be in good health considering. Lily noticed Sobrei walking over to her and stood straight, putting on a brave face.

He dropped the sword and went down on one knee, breathing hard. "How long has it been?" She walked over and laid a hand on his shoulder, she was about to ask Otto to heal him when it just happened, no words from her at all. Holy recognizes holy, she assumed.

"Five years."

He looked up and took her hand. "I have been dreaming of a woman in white since they took me. That woman meant my freedom. The moment I saw you, I knew you were here to free me." Giles walked over to them, a little wary, but Lily could tell he wasn't going to strike.

"I think the situation has changed a bit, my Lord. The orcs were telling the truth about their King."

He was staring at Sobrei, and she knew he understood. "I fear what Max will say, but let's get to Raventree first so we can gather our bearings."

"Raventree?" Sobrei looked over at Giles.

"The Burned Hand waits for us there."

He gave a tired smile. "Do they? Then Raventree it is." Sobrei walked over to one of the dead cultists and picked up his bow. "I'll help however I can, I'm in your debt." He walked over to Giles, his hand extended. "Sobrei Re'vall."

"Lord Giles Raventree," he said as he shook his hand. "And your help is most welcome. I suppose we need to get out of here first." Artemis came zooming back on his carpet, he was missing during the fight, but Lily was too worried about getting out safely to berate the man.

"Giles, we have company."

"More cultists?"

"Just one, but he summoned friends."

As they ran down the tunnel, they could hear Malice

neighing and pitching a fit outside, and as they piled out, they saw why. A hundred feet away, a high-ranking cultist in wicked black armor was on his own horse, and he was flanked by six devils. Each was about seven feet tall, with poison dripping from their fangs.

"Lily?" he said without turning.

"Yes, Giles?"

"Start praying." He heaved himself up on Malice and, without hesitation, galloped for the cultist general. The devils ignored him and charged the group while Mal and Sobrei quickly got to higher ground where their arrows would do more good. Krag, Nora, and William met the devil's charge while lightning flew from Ivelios' fingertips at the nearest foe, but it didn't seem to do much good.

"Otto, give us strength to overcome our enemies!" Lily prayed loudly and hoped Giles could hear her.

CHAPTER 8
EXPENSIVE ESCAPE

The devils around them were different from the ones they had just faced. The barbs that pierced through their skin were just as poisonous as their bite. They were taller and more muscular and seemed to move quicker than the smaller devils. They were so powerful. Lily wondered if they would truly make it out alive. She could see Giles and Malice fighting on a hill. Giles was exchanging sword blows with the cultist general, and Malice was beating the man's horse with his powerful hooves. It was an interesting sight to behold.

Mal and Sobrei had climbed up one of the nearby buildings and were putting arrows in as many of the devils as they could, but they did little good. Leo was by her side, sword drawn protectively. Lily looked to her left and saw Ivelios had been separated from them and was surrounded by two of the red beasts, one slashed down with its razor-sharp claws, and she heard him cry out in pain.

"Ivelios!" She had to get to him, but he was a hair's breadth too far for her spells. She turned and saw Leo was busy searching for foes. "I'm sorry, Leo," she whispered and started running for Ivelios.

The half-elf's eyes went wide when he saw her coming. "Lily, no!" She heard him yell but couldn't leave him to die.

He was just in range, and she reached out. "Blessed Otto—" Her words had barely left her lips when she felt a searing pain in the bend of her neck that stopped her in her tracks. She wanted to scream, but the pain stole everything but her hearing.

"Lily!" She heard Leo as she fell to her knees. Warm, thick blood gushed from the wound. She could feel it dripping down her fingers. When she finally collapsed on the ground, she landed on her back. Staring down at her was a devil with a barbed tail. His mouth was dripping with blood. *But... he wasn't there before,* she thought slowly as an arrow burst into the creature's head. It fell forward on top of her, but it disappeared back to its home plain before it crushed her.

"Lily!" Leo dropped his sword on the ground, and she felt the young man's hands under her back. "Lily, you're going to be okay, I promise. Does anybody have a potion!" He screamed, but she barely heard him. Her eyes were getting blurry, and she thought Sobrei was leaning over her. He laid his hands on the wound, but she didn't feel the relief she so desperately wanted. Searing pain filled her body as the devil's poison was pumped throughout her body, like her blood had been replaced with thorns. She seized up painfully, but still, she couldn't scream. It was absolute agony.

"Breathe, Lily, please, breathe!" She could hear the desperation in Leo's voice but knew her body wouldn't cooperate. Her lungs didn't want to work. She never imagined breathing could be so hard to do. Everything started going numb, and she felt like she was floating. Leo leaned close, and his face came into focus. His eyes were red, and she could hear him sniffing.

"Please, Lily, don't go." He was crying, and all she wanted to do was wrap her arms around him and comfort him, but a bright light called to her as the love of Otto surrounded her, and she let it take her away.

———

"Lily!" William heard Leo's yell, and his blood went cold as the birthmark on his hip started to burn. Thankfully, it didn't distract him from the enemy in front of him. He stabbed the devil one last time, ducking from his poisonous tail, and as it disappeared back to its own plane, he saw a group of people on the ground, surrounding his love.

"Lily!" he roared, his birthmark burning and stinging now as he ran to her. Nora looked up at him. Tears were falling down her face. "Lily!" He slid the last foot to her, dropped his sword, and saw she was covered in blood.

Leo was holding her, and he was crying. "Lily!" the young boy cried, "Please don't go!"

"No, no, no." He took Lily from him and saw the awful wound on her neck. It was no longer bleeding, but her eyes were open, staring at nothing, and her lips were turning blue. "Lily." He laid his hand on her chest, but it didn't rise. "Lily, no!" He screamed and pulled her against his chest as the pain from his birthmark subsided. "No!" he roared. His heart shattered as he held his dead love, his shaking hands brushing hair from her face.

Sobrei reached out and gently put his hand on her head. "I'm sorry I couldn't help. She was a brave woman. She died well."

Leo hugged Nora. "She shouldn't have died!" he yelled. Sobrei looked up as Lord Giles began walking over. The tip of his sword was scraping in the dirt, and his horse looked near death, bleeding from various wounds, but they were alive.

"What's going on?" His tired eyes suddenly came alive as the sound of mourning hit his ears, and he kneeled next to the fallen priestess. "What happened?"

"I failed!" the boy cried unabashedly in Nora's arms. The sound from William chilled his blood. His loud, wracking sobs as he cradled his love were the sounds of true heartbreak and sorrow.

Giles slowly laid his hand on Lily's head, his eyes tearing up. "Gods." She would have looked serene if she weren't covered in her own blood. "We're going to find someone to raise her." He looked up at the group, "She needs to be in this world." He couldn't let her die like this. "I refuse to let her die here, not now."

Leo sniffed and wiped his nose on his sleeve. "Really?"

Giles nodded. "We still need her, son." *I still need her.* "We won't leave her to death."

Sobrei reached out and laid his hand on William's head. "I can raise her. I just need a few days to rest."

"I'm afraid we don't have any precious gems," Artemis said, sorrow evident in his voice as his carpet hovered an inch above the ground.

"I don't need them," Sobrei said. "Just her willingness to come back." Giles looked around him as tears fell freely down his face. Krag was the most subdued he'd ever seen the dwarf. He stood still as his eyes stared at the dead priestess. Not a hint of emotion betrayed him. Koizumi's head was lowered, his hand over his heart and Ivelios had tears down his cheek while Yahul howled mournfully to the sky. Poor Leo and Nora were crying in each other's arms. Mal had a hand on his friend's head, and William, gods, the poor man was covered in his love's blood, his tears dripping onto her face.

William sniffed as he looked up at Sobrei. "Do you promise?" He spoke through trembling lips.

"I promise," Giles could hear the conviction in the orc's voice, "you will have your mate back."

William took a breath and pressed his cheek against her forehead. "How did you know she was mine?"

Sobrei laid a hand on his back. "I, too, have made that sound. It is unmistakable." William closed his eyes and cried into her hair. Everyone knew he wouldn't be better until Lily was back.

Ivelios stepped up, tears falling down his face as he touched her hand. "She's preserved. She'll be perfect when... when you bring her back."

Giles stood and got a cloak out of the bag that was still hanging off Malice. "Good boy, you did good. I'm so proud of you," he whispered and patted his neck. He wiped his face before turning back to the group. "Wrap her in this. We'll carry her." Sobrei stood and took the cloak from him, and with William's help they wrapped Lily up tight, only her head not covered.

William sighed and kissed her forehead. "Gods, Lily, I'm so sorry I wasn't there, I'm so sorry," he whispered.

Sobrei put a hand on his shoulder. "It wasn't your fault,

young man. These things happen in battle."

William sniffed and picked her up. "I'll make sure it never happens again."

Nora sat back and brushed the tears from Leo's face. "You didn't fail her, Leo. It would have gotten any of us," she said gently.

He quickly hugged the dark-haired girl again. "I loved her," he whispered in her ear.

"We all did, Leo," she whispered in his ear, "we all did."

———

A few days later, they were out of Cyranar, camping by a stream. William had carried Lily's body most of the time. Only when he felt like he was about to collapse did he let Sobrei carry her. He said he was rested enough to raise her, but William wanted to make sure she was clean first. He didn't want her to wake in a torn robe covered in blood and tears. So, he carried her next to the stream and peeled off her ruined robe and clothes. He took one of his clean shirts and folded it a few times, and dipped it in the water.

"You'll be right as rain, my love." He washed the wound at her neck, making sure to get all the blood off her skin. It was horrible to look at. The huge fang marks stretched from her shoulder to the middle of her neck. Little bits of her armor had been embedded in her skin. It must have been agony to experience. He knew once Sobrei raised her, the wounds would heal, she might not even scar, but he knew he'd carry the memory of it the rest of his life. "I'll wash you off. Make sure you are in some comfortable clothes for when you come back, and you'll feel better." He huffed, "Of course you'll feel better, you won't hurt, you won't be dead," he sniffed, "I'll never forgive myself for letting that happen to you. I should have stayed by your side. I don't know what I was thinking."

Nora walked over, and he saw she had a brush in her hand. "Thought I'd help."

He gave her a small smile. "Thanks." She sat by Lily's

head and pulled her hair into her hands, and began brushing it.

"How are you?"

He sighed, running the wet shirt over her arms and legs. "I don't think I'll feel better until she's back. That's the only thing keeping me sane right now." She nodded, the sound of the brush in her hair the only sound. "Can I ask you something?"

"Probably not the best person to ask, but go ahead." She gave him a wink. He managed a tired chuckle. It was more than he thought he was capable of.

"Do you think I'm selfish, wanting her back? She's with Otto in his loving arms, and I want her back here, among the war and death and evil in this world. Am I selfish?"

Nora looked up, surprised at his question. "No. No, you're not selfish. You love her. Of course you want her back. What is love but being selfish anyway? That person is yours, and you are theirs, no others. That's love. You are not selfish, William. You never were." A tear fell down his cheek as he listened to Nora talk. He had no idea she was so well-spoken.

"Thank you, Nora. That makes me feel better."

"Good." They put Lily in the one dress she had in her pack, and when she was clothed, clean, and dry, Sobrei walked over to them.

"I'm ready if you are." William nodded and picked her up. The spell Ivelios put on her kept the rigor mortis away, so she molded perfectly against him as he walked back to the group. Sobrei motioned at a blanket laid out next to the fire, and William laid her on it.

"Can I touch her?"

Sobrei sat at her feet. "Yes, that's fine." William held her hand against his lips and began praying silently. Everyone gathered around and watched as Sobrei closed his eyes. One by one, they gasped as Sobrei's power filled the air. Even if they didn't understand it, they knew it was the power of a God, and he was bringing her back. Sobrei held her other hand, and Giles's eyes went wide as a light spread from Sobrei's hands to Lily.

That holy light slowly spread down her arm, over her chest, and down her legs. Everyone but William shielded their eyes from the bright holy light.

———

Lily opened her eyes and saw she was in an all-white room, and the ceiling was so far away she couldn't see it. There were people milling all around her and she knew instantly where she was, the Waiting Room. All the souls who died waited here for their Gods to come get them so they could live eternity by Their side in peace and happiness. As she was still trying to make sense of where she was when a woman wearing a long white gown walked up to her.

"Hello, welcome."

"Hello," she said slowly, still looking around.

"A little confused? It happens sometimes. You must be new," the woman said with a smile.

Lily nodded. "Yeah, new." *Am I really dead?* She wondered, hardly believing it.

"Don't worry. Your loved ones will be at peace knowing you'll be with your God soon." *William,* she thought, *Papa.* "I can't stay here."

The woman shrugged her shoulders. "Well, if you go back, be careful. Something's been trying to hitch a ride with the recently resurrected, changes them, I hear," she said and walked away. *Changes them?* Lily thought, *what did she mean by that?* She turned and heard a voice calling for her.

"Lily!" But she didn't see anyone moving towards her. "Lily over here!" A hand rose above the crowd, and she quickly made her way over to another woman with long blonde hair. She was younger by almost a decade, and her smile was brilliant. "Oh, Lily, look at you!" The woman walked up and gave Lily a hug, it was comforting, and she couldn't help but hug her back.

"Do you know me?" she asked as the woman stood back.

"I'm your mother, Layla," she said, the smile never leaving her face. Lily's jaw dropped. She had never seen what her mother looked like, but from what her father said, she wasn't lying. Beautiful with bright blue eyes and long, gorgeous blonde hair.

"Mom?"

The woman laughed and hugged her again. "I missed you so much, Lily, you and your sister." She stepped back again, "You grew up beautifully. I always knew you would."

She couldn't believe she was looking at this woman, her mother. "I, I missed you too, Mom." Layla pet Lily's face and tucked some hair behind her ear, "I don't know what to say." Lily had grown up thinking of what to say to her mother when she finally saw her, but now her mind was blank.

"You don't have to say anything, honey." Lily held her hands and just stared at her. This was her mother. She knew it. She could feel it in her heart.

"I love you so much, Mom."

She squeezed Lily's hands. "I love you too, honey. I never stopped loving you and your sister or your father. He was the love of my life, no matter how short a time that was."

"That's what he said about you. It's why he never remarried."

Layla sighed and shook her head. "He always was a stubborn man," she said with an affectionate smile. "There's some people who wish to see you."

Her eyes furled in confusion as the people around them parted, and she gasped. "Henri."

He smiled that dazzling smile of his and she ran to his already open arms. "Henri, oh, thank you, Otto." He looked healthy, no sign of the wasting sickness that took him from her. His eyes were bright, and his cheeks were no longer gaunt. He looked like the man she married all those years ago.

He chuckled as he squeezed her. "Hello, my lovely." She looked up, and he kissed her. "I see you have fallen in love again. I cannot tell you how happy that makes me," he said as he ran his hand through her hair.

She couldn't stop the laugh that came out, part nerves,

part relief. "Does it?"

"Immensely, you are meant to be loved my lovely, and William will love you like no other the rest of your life." His eyes went wide, and he looked down. "There is another who wishes to meet you." Lily wondered if it was Lavinia, but he said meet, not see. He bent down and picked up an adorable child. She watched as they shifted between looking like a boy or a girl, their hair went blonde to brown to black, and they smiled at her.

"Hi, Mama." If the dead could cry, tears would be streaming down her face as she looked upon the ever-changing child.

"Mama?" Henri smiled and handed her the child, whose arms hugged her tight around her neck.

"They found me when I arrived," Henri said, his hand on the child's back, "said they weren't supposed to go but are waiting to go back." He gently petted the child's head. She looked down at the child and their ever-changing features and kissed their cheek. This was her child, whoever they might be. She knew it in her heart.

"I love you little one."

"I love you too, Mama, I'll see you soon." They wiggled down from her arms and ran off like children do.

Her mother walked up and gave her a hug. "Little souls like that one tend to shift before a form has been settled on. But they are excited to go back."

Lily sighed and looked at both of them. "But I'm dead."

Henri chuckled. "Do you really think they wouldn't raise you? They need you, my lovely. The world needs you."

"Henri is right," her mother took her hands, "You and William will lead a blessed life, and your children will be so special. Just wait."

"Special?" *Lily Marcel, do you wish to return to the land of the living?* She heard a voice in her head say. "That was quick," she said.

"Time is different here. Hopefully, not much time has

passed on the material plane." She hugged Lily again, "Tell your father I love him, would you?"

"I will, I promise." She turned to Henri, and they hugged once more. "Are you at peace?"

"I am. You gave my life meaning, my lovely. Now go back and show the world what it means to be a beloved of Otto." He gave her one more kiss. *I do wish to return,* she thought and felt magic pulling her from Henri. "I love you, Mom."

"I love you too, honey. I'm so proud of you." She heard before everything went dark.

————

Lily opened her eyes and took in a ragged breath. As peaceful as the waiting room was, here was torture. It hurt to breathe. Her mouth was dry, and whatever wound had killed her was still healing as the pain slowly receded. She saw stars above her head and felt the warmth of a fire next to her.

"Just keep breathing, Mother, you'll be fine." She turned to the deep voice. Sobrei was holding her hand, and a bright light was fading under his hands. *In, out, in, out,* she thought until it was automatic again. When the pain finally passed, she turned her head and saw William next to her, tears falling down his face.

"William," she whispered, and he scooped her up into his lap, their arms wrapping around each other.

"Thank you, Otto, thank you, Sobrei," he cried, "I'm so sorry, my love. I should have protected you better." She squeezed him as much as she could, tears falling from her own eyes.

"It's not your fault, it's not your fault," she whispered to him. They held each other, crying from grief and relief. Giles turned from the scene and wiped the tears from his cheeks, thankful she was back. Koizumi bowed his head and placed his hand over his heart, giving silent thanks. Leo hugged Nora, who seemed to be shaking from the effort of holding back tears. But she cried happy tears and hoped he'd realize it was okay to do so. Ivelios knelt by Yahul, his head in his hands, covering his crying eyes, and Mal, Artemis, and Krag watched the scene in silent reverence.

When the couple stopped crying, Lily sat back and wiped his cheeks. "I'm here now."

He wiped the tears from her cheeks as well. "I'll never leave you like that again."

"We'll never leave each other like that." He nodded and helped her to her feet. She turned to Sobrei and held his hands. "Thank you for bringing me back." She kissed both of his hands.

"You are most welcome Priestess." He gave her forehead a kiss, and she marveled at the blessing she felt around her.

"How long has it been?"

"Two days," the orc said, "it would have been sooner, but I needed rest."

She shook her head. "No worries," she thought about her time in the waiting room, "it was the perfect amount of time." She turned as Giles walked over to her and they both wrapped their arms around each other.

His sigh was deep, and he shuddered as he gently squeezed her. "I am so sorry we couldn't protect you."

"It's all right, Giles, I'm here now. All is well."

He leaned back and gently moved some hair from her forehead. "We felt lost without you." *I felt lost.*

"I'm here now. No one will lose their way." His hand rested on her cheek, his thumb slowly moving along her skin. There was a look in his eyes she wasn't sure she had seen before on any man, a mixture of relief, happiness, and something that looked like regret.

"No, we won't lose our way," he said softly.

Leo was next to come over and hug her. "Oh, thank the gods!" He squeezed her tightly. "I missed you so much." She heard him whisper through his tears.

She made sure and squeezed him back just as hard. "I missed you too, Leo. Are you all right? Is everyone else okay?"

He stepped back and kissed her cheek. "Yeah, we're okay."

"All right out of the way." Ivelios playfully pushed him

aside with a smile and hugged Lily next. "I'm so sorry we couldn't protect you." He sounded so sad she couldn't help but feel guilty.

"Please don't fret, I'm fine. It was battle, and it was bound to happen to someone." She leaned back and held his face. "Everything's fine now."

He nodded and kissed her forehead. "You're right. We're all here and alive."

"Thank Otto," she whispered.

Nora walked over, and Lily hugged her. "I'm so glad you're alright, Mother."

"Me too, Nora." Mal came over and gave her a hug while Artemis simply gave her a knowing nod.

"All right," Giles spoke up, "let's let Lily and William rest. They've been apart too long."

They were halfway to their tent when she heard Krag behind them. "Mother?" She turned and noticed he looked rather subdued. "I want to apologize for my past behavior, I didn't realize, I shouldn't have. I was too harsh—"

She laid a hand on his shoulder, and he stopped. "You have nothing to apologize for. You were being yourself. And you were right, I don't think you've been hurt once since we left Ardenry."

He chuckled a little. "If you say so, Mother." She nodded, and he walked back to the group.

William put a hand on her shoulder. "I don't think he's said a word these last two days."

"Hopefully he feels better now." William took her hand, and they walked into a tent. The floor had a fur rug, and their bedrolls were on it.

"I don't know if you want to sleep, but I just want to lay down and hold you," his arms went around her, "and know you're safe and here."

She nodded. "That sounds wonderful." They snuggled into their bedrolls, and she scooted against him, an arm over his chest and a leg between his. "So, I take it despite my untimely demise, we walked out of that last fight unscathed."

"Mm-hmm," he laid his head on hers, "Poor Malice got beat up pretty good, but Ivelios was able to fix him right up."

"Good." She listened to his heartbeat for a few moments. "William?"

"Yes, my love?" he whispered as his hand ran up and down her arm.

"I met my mother."

He shifted a little to look down at her. "You did?"

She nodded and looked up at him. "She was as beautiful as Papa always said. She said she loved us and was so proud of who I grew into."

William smiled. "That must have been amazing for you."

"It was." She held him tighter against her, "Henri was there too."

His smile got brighter. "How was he?"

She chuckled. "Much better, back to his usual slick self. He knew about us."

His eyes went wide at that. "He did? What did he say?"

She swallowed the growing lump in her throat as she looked up at him. "That you would love me like no other."

He laughed and sighed with relief. "Glad to know he approves."

She smiled and laid back on his chest. "I met someone else as well."

He kissed her head. "Oh?"

"I met our child." His arm stilled at her words, and she heard his heartbeat speed up.

"Our child?" he whispered.

She nodded. "They said they'd see me soon."

William chuckled and hugged her. "They did, huh?"

"Mm-hmm."

She looked back up at him. The smile on his face was peaceful and excited. "I can't wait to meet them."

CHAPTER 9
RAVENTREE

The trip to Raventree would take two weeks. As they traveled, they spoke to Sobrei and learned about Dal En Val before it went to shit. He said the coup happened the night his father died. Everyone was too busy mourning to realize what was happening. Before he knew it, he was captured and taken somewhere. He assumed all his family were gone, and he was the only one left. He wasn't sure why they left him alive. Perhaps it was just another way to torture him, knowing he was the last.

Through the weeks, they learned that Sobrei was a good orc, a good male, and desperately wanted to get back to Dal En Val to right the many wrongs that had been done over the last five years. He was shocked at how quickly these new cultists popped up and ruined his city. He assumed they had to have been planning the coup for years for it to go off so smoothly. Giles told him they'd do whatever they could to get him back on his throne and wondered just how they would break the news to Max.

———

Two weeks later, the group saw Raventree in the distance. Lily swore she saw Giles' shoulders relax at the mere sight of the city and that it was safe. Lily could see the castle in the distance behind a tall gray wall of stone. People were coming and going through the gate. It was just a normal day. Until the citizens realized who traveled with them, then she assumed the town would be all a twitter with the news.

The people at the gate moved aside when they saw their Lord approaching. Some bowed, and some waved as they walked through the gate. The town inside the wall looked sturdy. Lily assumed it'd have to be, being so far from most other large towns. Stone buildings lined the brick streets, and she could smell bread in the air.

"Giles!" Lily turned and saw a woman running over to them, dark hair flying behind her.

"Siddah!" Giles jumped from Malice, and when he reached his wife, he wrapped his arms around her and picked her up. "Oh, thank the gods."

"Giles, I'm so sorry, I didn't mean any of what I said."

"No, I'm sorry, my love. I don't know why I said that forgive me." They kissed deeply, forgetting what was around them, and Lily chuckled at the display.

"Well, I guess he was worried for nothing," she whispered, and William laughed. Leo ran over and hugged his mother, who squeezed him tight and kissed his forehead. Lily could tell she was whispering to him, but not what she said. He smiled and gave her another hug as the group made their way over to them.

Giles put an arm around his wife. "Everyone who doesn't already know, this is my wife Siddah, Siddah, this is Ivelios, Nora, Mal, Lily, and William, I think you know the rest."

She smiled at them. "Welcome to Raventree. Thank you for keeping my husband safe."

William gave her a little bow. "You're most welcome, My Lady."

Giles gave his wife one more kiss on her forehead. "Follow me, I'll get you all rooms, and then we'll discuss what to do next."

———

That night everyone was washed and rested as they met with Giles and his wife in the dining room of their suite. Siddah was carrying their son, and Lily walked over to introduce herself.

"I wanted to formally introduce myself, I'm Mother Lily Marcel." She wasn't wearing her robes tonight, just a simple dress and her two necklaces, her shell, and her rings.

"It's nice to meet you, I'm Siddah. This is Giles Jr." He was a skinny boy with straight brown hair and warm brown eyes.

"Hello, Giles."

She smiled at the boy, who waved and let out a loud yell. "Because!"

Lily couldn't stop her laugh as it echoed around the room. "What?"

Siddah laughed and gave her son a kiss on the cheek. "He's still learning where to put the end of a joke."

"I see. Well done, young man."

Siddah chuckled and kissed his cheek again. "He's the light of our lives."

Everyone sat around the table while servants began putting food on their plates. "I sent Max a message, telling him that we were in Raventree, and the mission was done," *right to it* she thought and took a sip of wine. "He's going to teleport in tomorrow, along with a few other dignitaries around us that Max has been in contact with. The most tricky thing, I think, will be convincing him that Sobrei shouldn't be a captive and that we should help him get his throne back. Not just dangle him in front of Dal En Val."

"I agree," William said, "it's clear the situation has changed." He motioned to Sobrei who was on the other side of Giles.

"I am already grateful for your help in my release," he said, "if you helped me get my throne back, you would be rewarded beyond measure."

"Said like a ruler who wants his kingdom back," Artemis said, as he toasted the orc.

He chuckled. "That I do. My people have been led astray, and I want to put things right."

"Lily," Her eyes moved back to Giles, "I'd like you in the meeting with us."

Her eyes widened. "Me?" She had never been a part of a meeting like that before.

"Yes, you," he smiled, "I think you could help keep our tempers in check, especially Max. I could tell he was a bit upset that we haven't 'captured' Sobrei yet," he said with a grimace.

Lily sighed and nodded. "Then I will be there, my Lord. Hopefully, my presence will do some good."

Giles smiled. "Thank you, Mother."

William leaned close to her ear and whispered. "Mother Lily Marcel, Priestess of Otto and keeper of royal tempers." She scoffed and gave him a little nudge before he kissed her cheek. He wasn't wrong, though.

———

That night, after dinner, Nora was sitting on her bed, putting new laces in her boots. It was the fanciest room she'd ever had to herself, with a big bed, a washroom, and a dresser with clothes already in it. She was almost done with one boot when she heard a knock at the door.

"Come in!" The door opened, and she smiled as Leo walked in. "Hello, what are you doing up?" It was nearly midnight. The group had eaten well that night, filling their bellies with the best meal they'd had in months. They sat around the big fire, talking for hours afterwards. Leo had introduced her to his mother, who seemed to wholeheartedly approve of her to her delight, as she gave Nora a big hug and welcomed her to their home.

He walked over and sat on the bed across from her. "Can't sleep."

"Hmm, mind busy?" She went back to lacing her boots.

"No." He took her other boot and started lacing it. "My bed isn't comfortable."

She snickered. "Your bed isn't comfortable. How is it not comfortable?" She watched him deftly and quickly put the laces in her boot.

"It's cold."

Her eyes narrowed at that. "Cold? Is there not a fire in your hearth?"

"No there is." He handed her boot back. "But my bed is cold."

"I see," she put her boots on the floor and laid on her side facing him, "you need a warming pan?" she teased, "Cause I don't know where they are."

He smiled. "No." He lay on his side facing her. "Did you mean it that you'd stay here until I could go to the Citadel?"

"Mh-hmm," she nodded, "I did. I'm sure your Lord could find me something to do around here."

He picked at the comforter a bit. "Why?"

"Why what?" She wasn't sure where this conversation was going, but as long as he was with her, she'd indulge him.

"Why would you stay? You seem like the kind of person who isn't happy unless they're traveling around."

"I do?"

He looked up at her. "Well, I've only known you while traveling, so I guess that's why I think that. Plus, you grew up with the Suya, who are always on the move."

"Ah, well as much as I like traveling, I do want a home. Somewhere I can go every night, know where all my stuff is," they chuckled, "and greet my husband. You know when I have one."

Leo scooted a little closer to her, and she felt her cheeks blush. "I want the same."

"You want a husband, too?" she teased, and he laughed loudly.

"No!"

She scooted a little closer. "I mean no judgment. You just didn't seem the type."

He smiled widely at her. "You are unruly, Sianora," she gasped as he pulled her against him, "and I love that about you." He kissed her, and without a thought, she wrapped her arms around him.

"If your bed's cold," she kissed him again and pulled his shirt free of his pants, "you should just stay here." and kissed him again.

"It's for the best," he did the same to her shirt, "don't want to catch cold."

"Gods forbid."

CHAPTER 10
THE COUNCIL

The next day Lily walked into the council room with Sobrei at her side. The room was filled with people of high birth, and she tried not to feel small. She was just as important as everyone else here. Prince Maximilian was sitting at the head of the large table with Giles to his left. Mother Ranella, a priestess of Otto from Ardery that she knew, was also there along with another nobleman Lily didn't know. He looked a little older than Giles but more worn. His hair was almost all dark gray and his skin was leathery as if he spent a great deal of time outdoors. To her shock (which she managed to keep to herself), she saw a full-blooded elf sitting next to him. He looked young as elves went and was dressed in noblemen's clothes.

When his eyes met hers, he smiled. "Hello, Mother, I'm Kale." He stood and held out his hand, which she quickly took.

"It's nice to meet you, Kale." She made a mental note to introduce Kale and Ivelios when the meeting was over. Lily looked over at Max and could see him stiffen at the sight of the Orc God.

"Lily, this is Lord Charles from the nearby town of Marsdenport and his adopted son Kale," Giles said.

She sat next to Giles and nodded. "My Lord, it's good to meet you."

"And you, Mother." Lily didn't know much about Marsdenport, but she knew the Empire had been a rather violent presence there the last few years. Sobrei sat down next to her and bowed his head at the Lord's across the table.

"Prince Maximilian, it's a pleasure to meet you."

Lily saw the prince's lips tighten before he cleared his

throat. "And you," he said quietly. Max walked over to Lily and put his hands on her shoulders, and leaned down to her ear. "I'm grateful you're whole and healthy again, Mother. The world would be darker without you in it," he whispered in her ear.

She laid a hand on his, "Thank you, Your Highness. It was Sobrei who brought me back without the use of a focus gem." His eyes went wide for a moment before he kissed her forehead and returned to his place at the table. Lily noticed a few servants pouring wine and hoped no one would drink too much. She may not have had much experience around Nobles, but drunken anything didn't make good negotiators.

"Well, let's get down to business, shall we?" Lord Charles started, "First off, now that the true orc King is free, I want to discuss him pulling his army out of my city. We have no intention of laying our arms down any time soon or kneeling to you. We want peace, and for that to happen, you need to draw your men back." Lily had never been a part of such a gathering before and wondered if they would all talk to each other like that.

Sobrei shifted in his seat, making the wood creak under him. "I can see how my people invading your lands would be upsetting. But it was not done on my order, so they won't listen to me at the moment. But I don't condone their behavior. When I am in power again, I will withdraw all my troops from your territory. Hopefully, that will give you peace and let me get a firm foothold among my people."

"Ardenry also asks that you give back the town of Woodhollow," Ranella said, "I have spoken with their leaders, and they have no interest in being under Orcish rule. It's a human town, and they wish to give fealty to Ardenry."

Lily watched the Orc God lick his bottom lip as he cleared his throat. "Woodhollow was taken while I was a boy, and it's been part of Dal En Val for many years. Do you expect me to give up all the land we have acquired in my lifetime? I would not ask the same of you."

"So, you're not willing to concede Woodhollow?" Ranella

confirmed in a calm voice as she waved away a glass of wine.

He leaned forward and cracked his knuckles. "Not concede, no, but perhaps we can come to some sort of middle ground. They want a peaceful town. They shall have it. I will pull my troops out and let them govern themselves and if they continue to recognize Dal En Val as their mother city. They'll be left alone to do what they wish. Their taxes will still be given to Dal En Val, but my men won't occupy them. When everything settles down, I will visit with the leaders and make more concrete laws, smooth everything over."

Lily nodded. "It's hard to negotiate peace when not all the leaders of the towns are present. It will take time, but I believe we can create a peaceful world with the orcs."

Giles turned to Max. "What say you, Your Highness?"

The prince crossed his arms over his chest. "Did they tell you what I originally wanted to do with you, Sobrei?"

He nodded. "They did. It's understandable and might have worked if they wanted me back. From what I hear, a human sits on my throne now, and I believe those loyal to him were the ones who kidnapped me all those years ago. Most think I am dead and cling to the new emperor like he is their salvation. It's hard to break that kind of desperate faith." He sounded tired, and Lily could see even he doubted he would get home.

She reached over and laid her hand on his. "When they see you're alive, your faithful will rise up, Sobrei."

He gave a little chuckle and patted her hand. "Thank you, Lily. It's been much too long since I've been around someone as faithful as you. It's quite refreshing."

Max cleared his throat. "As I was saying, my goal was to get all my land back from your Empire. I've been speaking with Giles about the...new situation," he sighed and rubbed his face, "The priestess is right. Peace is possible. I'm not blind or dumb. I can tell things have changed and that I need to be more flexible. Peace for my people is what I want above all." He looked over at Giles, "What about you, Lord Raventree? What concessions would you like to put on the table?"

Giles stood and started pacing around the table. "First off, I would offer Raventree as a sanctuary to any orcs who give fealty to Sobrei. They will need somewhere safe to gather. I would also like to build Raventree up to its former glory. To do that, we will need temples, the materials to build such temples, and people to build them. We will also need high-ranking priests and priestesses to run the temples," he stopped and laid a hand on Lily's shoulder. "Lily, I want you to run Otto's temple." She jumped a little at the sudden request. She never imagined living anywhere but Ardenry. But here was her heart's desire, just freely given to her.

"Giles, my Lord, I... don't know what to say." She looked up at his smiling face.

"Say yes! I know you want your own temple. Here, you'll have a brand new one full of thankful followers." She looked around the table, and her eyes met Ranella's, who gave Lily a little nod.

"All right Giles, I accept with one stipulation."

"Name it."

"Do you need a Huntmaster?" Giles smiled and nodded his head. He gave her shoulder a little squeeze and started pacing again. "When the temples are done, I would like to establish an embassy in Raventree for any Lord of your choosing, Sobrei, and I would choose one of my own men for Dal En Val. I'd like to establish a positive relationship between Raventree and your city."

Sobrei nodded. "As would I, that is acceptable." Lily smiled. It seemed the negotiations were going to work. Peace would be possible.

————

A few hours later, everyone stood, some happy with the result of the meeting, others barely consenting. Some land was given back, and others would need more negotiating. Giles pledged Raventree's cavalry would be loyal to Sobrei if he needed them. The orc god said Raventree would be well rewarded once he took his throne back.

Lily sat back and watched the Nobles converse quietly with each other while wondering what it would be like living in Raventree. She had never lived so far away from the ocean and was already starting to miss it. Giles really caught her off guard when he said he wanted her to head the new temple. But if it was peaceful, she felt it would be a nice home as long as William and her father were there with her. She wondered if she could get him to move so far from the ocean he loved.

The doors to the council room banged open, and a little scrawny girl no more than ten with straight, raven black hair ran in.

"Mother, Mother, I found him!" She was carrying a rather large crystal ball but still managed to jump on the table and slide on her knees all the way down to Ranella. Lily giggled and shook her head, *youth,* she thought. "I knew that asshole, oops sorry, Mother, I knew he couldn't hide from me!" She said proudly as she showed Ranella the ball. This was clearly one of the little diviners that Ranella employed. She must have been something special for the priestess to bring her all the way to Raventree.

"You did well, little one," she looked up at the group, most of whom were trying to stifle chuckles. "If we're going to put Sobrei back on his throne, we need to know our enemy. I've had Isabela here look for the higher members of this new emperor's priests. All they do is —"

"Izzy, not Isabela!" the little girl interrupted grumpily.

Ranella gave her a stern look before returning to the group. "They are the ones who summon the demons that they're known for using in battle. We need to know them from the other cultists so we can get rid of them quickly. When we kill them, their summons will leave the field." She ran her hand over the orb, and everyone gasped as a picture formed on the dark red tapestry at the back of the room. "This is the man that has been doing most of the summoning. It seems like his limitations on demons are non-existent. He could very well bring the whole abyss against us."

The man seemed to be doing pushups in his room. He was muscular and lean. Lily could feel the power this man held and fought not to shudder. He did indeed have enough power to bring a horrific number of demons to a battlefield. Everyone watched as he got to his feet, and when his face was finally visible, Lily felt a shock of recognition go through her.

"I know him." Everyone turned to her and didn't bother hiding their own shock. She wondered for a moment if he wasn't a spy, but that feeling he was radiating, it was plain evil.

"How do you know him?" Ranella asked.

"His name is Dante Foss. We traveled together for a bit a decade ago, but—" she turned back to everyone, "he was a priest of Otto. He wasn't a cultist."

"Are you sure?" Giles asked.

She nodded and walked closer to the tapestry. "I'm sure, he gave me this," she held up the shell that hung from her neck, "I felt Otto in his healings and blessings. I have no doubt that he was a priest of Otto." She turned to Ranella and pointed at him. "Are you sure?"

"Isabella is never wrong." Ranella nodded.

"Izzy!" she said, still on the table as Ranella gave her the same look as before. Lily turned back to the tapestry and watched as Dante put his shirt back on and stopped. Everyone watched as he turned and seemed to stare right at Lily.

They watched as he waved his hand, and Isabella gasped, "Mother, he's spying on us."

"Can you get him to stop?" Ranella asked her. Lily was impressed at how calm she sounded.

"Gimme a sec." Lily wasn't sure what the girl was doing, so she stayed still, like a predator was hunting her. Dante took another step. There was no sound, but she could read his lips. *There you are, Love,* she shuddered, and the vision of him disappeared. "There he's gone, and he can't look in on us either."

Giles walked over to Lily and laid a hand on her shoulder. "He called you Love," he whispered.

She took a deep breath. "That was his pet name for me when we were together."

"I see. How long were you with him?"

She shook her head. "Not long." She looked over at her friend. "We traveled a bit a few years later, but I chose Henri over him, and then he decided to leave our group. I haven't seen him in almost a decade."

"Hmm, people change over the years." His voice was grim.

"True, but I don't think they change *that* much."

———

Lily found William in the stables, petting the nose of a brown mare. He looked up as her feet crunched on the hay.

"Hey, Sweets, come meet Grace." She smiled and walked over to him. Grace was a lovely horse who put her nose in Lily's hand. Clearly, she liked being petted. "Grace is Malice's sister."

Lily snorted. "No."

William laughed. "Oh yeah, same parents and everything." She petted Grace's nose and sighed. "Something wrong?"

"I have some good news and odd news."

He nodded. "Odd news first."

She huffed a breath out and leaned against the stable. "Ranella had one of her little seers look for the people in Dal En Val who summon demons. She said she found the one who summons so many it's like he holds open a portal straight to the abyss." She crossed her arms and stared at her feet, "She showed him to all of us in that meeting, and I…knew him."

His eyes turned to panic. "What? How, who is he?"

"It's Dante." She had told him everything about that disastrous trip to her sister's, including how close she and Dante had been. Had told him how she chose Henri over Dante and that he didn't stay long after that.

She looked up, and his eyes were wide. "Seriously?"

She nodded. "It was him. There was no mistaking." She looked up at the horse across the way. It was still like it was listening to her.

"Damn. Are you okay?" He put an arm around her.

"I'm incredibly confused because he was *not* a cultist when I knew him. He was anything but. I don't know what's going on, but it's clear he no longer follows Otto. He's not a spy or a plant. He *is* a cultist for this supplanted emperor. I don't understand."

He hugged her, and she laughed when Grace nudged her head a little bit. "Well, I did ask for the odd news first. That's on me."

"Yes, it is. So, the good news," she leaned back and put a hand to his cheek, "Guess who has a temple."

———

Dinner time rolled around, but Lily and William didn't want to leave their room. They stayed wrapped around each other, reveling in the good news. How she would have a temple, and he would be Giles's huntmaster. It was everything they wanted.

"So, I'm fine with living in Raventree," he kissed her cheek and down to her neck, "but are you? You're used to living in big cities. It's a big change."

"I grew up in Fairwinds. I think I can handle Raventree." She giggled, and he ran his hands up and down her bare back. "I wonder if my father would move here?"

"Maybe, what does he do?"

She snorted. "He's a fisherman."

William laughed. "Well, maybe he'd like to retire. After all, there's a little soul waiting to come down to us, and I bet he's dying for some grandchildren."

"He's practically salivating, I guarantee it." She pushed William on his back and straddled his hips. "I say when we're settled, and things seem stable enough, we go to Fairwinds so I can make that memorial for Lavinia and ask him to come live in Raventree." She laid on his chest, and his strong heartbeat made her smile.

"Sounds like a plan." He wrapped his arms around her and held her tight. "Our future sounds amazing, Sweets."

"It really does. I can't wait."

———

The next morning Lily opened their door to find little Izzy standing in the hallway. "Ranella wanted me to come get you when you woke up."

Lily nodded. "Why don't you show us where she is." William walked up and took her hand as he walked into the hallway.

"She's in the solar, but I doubt you know where that is since you've never been here." Lily chuckled. This child saw the truth and told it quite well.

The solar was on the first floor. It was bright and smelled of flowers and breakfast. Thank the gods since they skipped dinner the night before. Mother Ranella was sitting at a small table along with Giles and Siddah. Everyone's plates were covered with sausage and corn cakes, but no one was eating.

"Here she is!" Izzy yelled happily before she ran off.

Lily and William chuckled as they took chairs across from Giles and his wife. "I told him the good news." She put some sausage on William's plate while he put a spoonful of fruit on hers. Giles nodded, but she could tell he was much more subdued than the day before. "What is it?" She looked at Siddah, who looked positively pale. "Did something happen?"

Mother Ranella cleared her throat. "I've received some disturbing news from Ardenry."

Siddah reached out, and Giles took her hand. Lily knew something was really wrong. "Word has reached me that eight legions of imperial Orcs are marching on Raventree. It seems they know that Sobrei is here, and they have no intention of letting him get near Dal En Val. The two that were camping between Raventree and Salthole are thankfully circumventing us and waiting for the other legions." Lily felt the air go out of her body, and William laid a hand on her arm. No wonder no one was eating.

"So, ten legions? There was only one in Salthole, and that was six thousand. Are you telling me that sixty thousand orc warriors are bearing down on us?" She couldn't even picture what sixty thousand people looked like. From the corner of her eye, she saw William put his hand over his mouth.

Mother Ranella nodded. "I'm afraid so, along with the emperor's high priests that reside in the temple, about thirty in all. Every single one with the capability of summoning multiple demons themselves."

"Have we heard from the Citadel yet?" Giles asked. Lily couldn't help but be impressed at how calm he seemed even though every single orc in the world was bearing down on his home.

"They're sending two of their paladins, no more, unfortunately, but I feel that will be a big help." Lily could hear that priestly tone of voice she had used herself before when she knew the situation was bad and couldn't say anything to make it better.

"Just two? This could all be over if they'd send ten or more," William said.

"I agree," Ranella said, "but you know how they are. They feel the second they leave the citadel, the Shackled One will break loose. They're really quite close-fisted when it comes to the use of their dragons." Giles met Lily's eyes, and she knew just this once they were inclined to agree with the Paladins.

"When will the army get here?" Siddah asked.

Mother Ranella sighed, "A month." Giles ran his hand through his hair. It was longer than it was when they began their journey, and was starting to look a little wild.

"A month of planning, we better start then."

William leaned over and put his head in the crook of her neck. "Guess our future is going to have to wait a bit." She nodded and kissed his head.

The citizens of Raventree pulled together and fortified their town to the best of their ability. Lily could see the little kingdom was full of pride but was in desperate need of repair and new blood. She hardly saw Giles or much of the group besides William that month. The Lord was busy gathering his small army and organizing the Burned Hand Orcs with Sobrei's help. Max dealt with his legion that was already there. The King said two more legions from Ardenry could be there soon, and Giles was grateful for that. Artemis spent his time in the castle's library, researching spells that would be effective against large forces.

Mal and Nora trained with the fighters, and Lily had a feeling the girl was making a great deal of the men jealous. Ivelios spent most of his time in the nearby woods. Lily figured he wanted to be surrounded by nature as much as possible. He didn't even take a room in the castle when Giles offered it.

From their room in the castle, she could see the men doing drills together. Every day, more men showed up to fight. Some were farmers from the outlying areas, and some were men from Ardenry who weren't part of the army but wanted to fight anyway. Lily hated war but knew it was coming and hoped her army would be able to overcome the evil emperor and his army of stolen orcs.

She decided there was a lot of good she could do in this kingdom, so the first thing she did was have a few of Giles's men set up a tent for her and William outside of the castle. Every day, she would stand outside her tent and give a sermon for the people, and every day that passed, more and more showed up. She did her best to lighten their hearts and strengthen their resolve, and soon, she was doing two sermons a day. William trained with the Knights as well so every night he'd come in, she'd have a wash bin ready for him and would join him in the water. They spent every moment they could together and prayed that this battle wouldn't take them from each other.

One night after her second sermon, Lily was walking around the outside of the castle. She recognized some of it from Leo's stories. There was a small stone wall that led away from the castle. He told her it was older than the castle itself and she was amazed at the shape it was in, like it was only made a few decades ago. It must have been part of a bigger castle years ago. It was the side of the castle that faced the direction Cyranar laid, and she wondered if Raventree was as untouched from that calamity as they believed. As she walked along the wall, she saw a figure in the distance honing a sword, and she immediately recognized Leo's blonde hair. She had heard the rumors that he and Nora were sharing a bed, and she hoped they were true. They were both wonderful people who deserved each other.

"Good evening, Leo," she called out.

He looked up and smiled. "Good evening, Mother. What are you up to?"

She shrugged and sat next to him on the wall. "Just taking a walk. One can only sit around a war camp for so long before thoughts of death and battle invade the mind."

"You worried about the battle too?" Lily nodded and looked back at the castle. The sun was setting, and the sky on the horizon was pink that melted away into deep orange, to dark blue where the stars started blinking into existence.

"I thought Salthole was bad. This is going to be infinitely worse. I swear I've been shaking with nerves for days."

He nodded and looked back down at his sword. "My Lord wants me with him during the battle."

She put her hand on his back. "That's where you belong. You're his squire. You're an important asset."

"I know."

"Can I ask you a personal question?" He looked over and nodded. "Are you and Nora sleeping together?" she asked quietly, a hopeful smile on her face.

He laughed and shook his head. "Can't keep a secret around here for nothing."

Lily laughed, "Why should it be a secret? If you two love each other, it's something to embrace and celebrate."

His eyes narrowed, "I thought clergy frowned at sex before marriage."

She shook her head, "Not Otto. If two people love each other and wish to express it physically, that's their business. But he loves it when his followers fall in love and have children, more worshippers, you see." She gave him a nudge, and he laughed.

"Smart," he sighed and shrugged, "I feel my Lord might think it a distraction and tell me to stop."

Lily tsk'd and shook her head. "No, I don't think he'd do that. How do you feel about Nora?"

Leo sighed, and she could see that familiar hint of love in his eyes. "I don't want to kiss another woman for the rest of my life. She's it for me." He turned to her, "She said she'd stay here while I finish my training and come with me to the Citadel."

Lily smiled, "That sounds like a solid plan, and uh, if you ever want to get married, a big ceremony, or elope, I'm here for you." She gave him a wink.

He laughed again. "I'll remember that, thank you." He got to his feet and sheathed his sword. "I'll see you later."

"All right." She watched him walk away to the castle proper. *Please let them make it through the battle, Otto,* she prayed silently. She heard movement from the tree line and looked up as William came walking over, a few rabbits over his shoulder. "Hello."

"Hello, Sweets, what are you doing?" He put the rabbits on the ground and sat on the wall next to her.

"Walking around, ran into Leo," she leaned close and whispered even though no one else was around, "the rumors are true."

William laughed, "Good."

"What are you up to?" She tapped his foot with hers.

"Oh, thought I'd find some meat to thicken up the dinner for the soldiers. Gotta prove to Giles I'm worthy of being

Huntmaster after all." He gave her a kiss.

"You are worthy," she said against his lips.

"Thank you," he said without moving back.

———

Leo walked into the castle, Lily's words buzzing through his head. She'd marry them if they wanted. He knew Nora was it for him, but he wondered if she'd want that right now. He walked into her room but didn't see her.

"Nora?"

"In here!" She called out from the washroom. He pulled his boots off and walked in to find her in the bath.

"Hello," he purred as he pulled his shirt over his head.

She giggled. "Hello yourself." He stripped and slid into the water on top of her. Nora laughed as the water splashed out onto the floor. "Smooth."

"I thought so," he gave her a kiss. "How was your day?"

"Oh, the usual, making men jealous with my skills," they laughed, "You?"

"Fine, I spent most of it with my Lord, going over strategy. I took a break by the old wall, and Lily sat with me for a bit."

She wrapped her arms around him, and he laid his head on her chest. "That's nice."

"She told me something." Nora chuckled and kissed his head. "She told me if we wanted to elope or marry in a proper ceremony, she'd do it." He felt her go still and looked up.

She was looking down at him, her face in shock. "What?"

He smiled, "She said —"

"No, I heard you, but you want —"

He kissed her before she could finish. "I want you, Sianora, for the rest of my life. You're it, my ethereal beauty. So, if you want to marry now or later, I'm fine with that. But I want to marry you." She sat up in the water, and Leo chuckled as she got out and wrapped a towel around herself. "What are you doing?"

"Get," she started, motioning for him to get up, "out, we're going to find Lily."

Lily and William were walking back to their room when they heard footsteps running behind them. They turned and saw Nora and Leo, smiles on their faces and soaking wet.

Lily chuckled, "Something wrong?"

They stopped in front of her, breathless and dripping on the carpet. "Marry us," Nora said, her arms wrapped around Leo's arm.

Lily smiled. "As you wish. Where shall we do it?"

Leo thought for a moment. "Follow me."

Leo led them to a balcony that was in the library and looked out onto the gardens. No one was in there, and they didn't pass anyone on the way either. The stone balcony was at least four stories up, so no one on the ground could tell what they were doing. They stood next to the stone railing, holding each other's hands. The moon was half full but bright enough, they could still see by it.

"Ready?" Lily asked. They nodded, staring into each other's eyes. "Blessed Otto and special guest," she smiled at William, who gave her a wink. "We gather here under this bright moon to watch Leopold Raventree and Sianora Finch join their souls in matrimony. I've known them for a few months now, and I can feel how good they are for each other. I can see the love in their eyes and know it to be true. Leo, if you would, please tell Otto why you wish to be Sianora's husband."

He cleared his throat. "The first time I saw you, you were covered in goblin blood," they chuckled, "but you were still beautiful. I could tell you were a wildcat, but the more I got to know you, I could feel the loving woman I knew you were. I had no idea if you'd even entertain the idea of being with me. Someone who was still getting their life together, a wanna-be Knight, an orphan, but I couldn't get you out of my mind, and I thank Otto every day that I seemed to get under your skin." She smiled and kissed his hands. "We're young, but we love each other, and we're about to go up against insane odds, but I know we'll make it. I love you, Sianora, my beautiful, ethereal woman, and I will make you happy, I promise." He leaned down and kissed her cheek.

Lily looked at Nora. "Nora, if you would please tell Otto why you wish to be Leo's wife."

She nodded and looked at Leo. "I have no idea what to say," he smiled at her, "I just know that you, Leopold Raventree, see me. No one has ever seen me like you do. You make me feel alive and loved in a way I never thought I'd be. I cannot wait to see where our lives take us. I love you, Leo, with every beat of my heart, I love you, and I will love you as long as I draw breath. As long as the sun shines in the sky and mountains are covered in snow, I will love you." She got to her toes and kissed him, fast and practiced, as he held her against him. When they parted William handed Lily a beautiful obsidian bowl he snagged from the kitchen and cast a spell to fill it with water.

"Otto has heard your vows and blesses this union," she dipped her fingers in the water and ran them across Leo's forehead. "Leo, do you take Nora to be your wife, to love, protect, and provide for, to the end of your days?"

"I do." She held the bowl to his lips, and he took a drink.

"Nora," She drew her wet fingers across Nora's forehead as well, "do you take Leo to be your husband, to love, protect, and provide for, to the end of your days?"

"I do." Lily let her drink from the bowl, and William took it from her.

"We come to uncertain times, and I often think love will get us through. That the love we have for others will bring us peace and strength. I want you two to remember how you feel this night, how much you love each other, and know you will live your lives in happiness and peace. With Otto's blessing, I now pronounce you husband and wife. Leo, you may kiss your bride again." They laughed, and he picked her up and kissed her thoroughly and slowly. When they finally parted, he spun her around as she laughed.

"Congratulations, you two." Lily and William hugged them both. "Now the real question, do we tell your Lord Father about this?" They looked at each other for a moment, clearly unsure what to do.

"Your Lord Father already knows." They turned and saw Giles standing by the entryway to the balcony. He was leaning against it, his arms crossed.

"My Lord." Leo's eyes were wide as he looked at him.

"There is nary a thing that happens in my home that I don't know about. You think I wouldn't find out about you eloping?" He had a little smile on his face as he walked over and hugged him. "Congratulations, son."

Leo chuckled, "Thank you, you're not mad?"

He shook his head and stepped back, giving his face a pat. "I'm not mad. Now, your mother, she might be a little irked you left her out, but I'm sure all will be forgiven when you give her a grandchild." They laughed, and Giles hugged Nora. "Welcome to the family, daughter."

"Thank you, my Lord."

He stood straight and put a hand on Lily's shoulder. "Now I think there might be some celebratory pie in the kitchen." The couple smiled at each other and ran from the balcony, leaving the three of them alone.

"You aren't irked at *me*, are you?" Lily tried hard to hold back her smile.

He shook his head, looking out at his town. "No. You've given them something neither has had in a long time," he turned to her, "their own family. They will fight for that family and know just how precious it is."

"Well said." William walked over and patted his shoulder.

"Now," Giles cleared his throat, "wish me luck as I go tell my wife that Leo is married." They chuckled and watched him walk out of the library.

William took a step and wrapped his arms around her. "That was a good thing you did for them, Sweets."

"They belong together." He leaned down and kissed her under the half-moon, and she thanked Otto for this moment of peace.

CHAPTER 11
CALM BEFORE THE STORM

The month went by quicker than Lily anticipated and when she opened her eyes the morning of the battle, she could hardly believe it. She wanted nothing more than to wrap herself around William, make love all day, and ignore the world. But Raventree needed them today. Giles sent a note the day before that said they were to go to the armory in the morning to receive what he had made for them. She turned in bed to find William already awake. He was on his side, and his hand went to her hip.

"Today, the world changes," he said quietly.

"Hopefully, for the better."

He pulled her against him, both still naked from their activities the night before. "I just want to lay in bed with you all day."

"Let's get through today, and we'll do just that." They quickly dressed, and Lily wondered if she would see Giles that morning or any of her group that set out from Ardenry. It seemed so long ago that they left when, in actuality, it had barely been three months.

Hand in hand, they walked down the steep steps to the armory and could hear men talking and metal clanking. She looked up when she reached the bottom floor and heard her name.

"Mother, Willam, over here!" Lily turned and saw a dirty armor smith waving her over, "I have your armor ready." Lily walked over and saw an entire suit of shiny plate mail. It was impressive, but it couldn't have been for her.

"Good morning, sir."

He scoffed and waved her off with a smile. "No need to sir

me, Mother," he reached for the breast plate and held it in front of her torso. "Yep, that'll fit nicely."

"That's for me?" She couldn't believe she had to wear all that armor. She didn't think she'd be able to move.

"Right you are, Mother. Lord Giles ordered it specially."

"Oh, Sweets, it's extraordinary." William walked around it, inspecting it.

Lily sighed and shook her head. "I'm afraid I'm going to need help putting it on."

William chuckled. "Don't worry, we'll get you all strapped in."

"This one's yours." The smith pointed William to his own new suit of plate mail. It shined in the firelight, and it had a seashell stamped on the breast piece.

"William, it's amazing."

He stood staring at it, his fingers barely touching it. "With this armor, I will protect you, my love," he turned to her, "I vow no one will harm you, not while I'm alive." He turned and kissed her fiercely. "Otto will be with us."

"He will. Let's get armored up." She took her worn white robe off and hung it on a peg by the armor. William helped her into the gambeson, then the pieces of the suit. As they went on Lily expected them to be heavy and cumbersome, but it wasn't much heavier than her chain shirt. She lifted her arms and knees and was surprised at her mobility.

"I didn't think I could move so much when covered in metal."

The smith laughed. "Anyone can move in magical armor, Mother. That'll protect you if I do say so myself." Lily moved over to a tall, dirty mirror and gasped. She looked like a proper battle priest. The symbol of Otto that was engraved on the chest slowly started glowing with holy light.

"Blessed Otto, I've never worn such a thing. It's amazing," she said quietly, reaching up to touch the symbol of her God.

The smith stood behind her and smiled. "It was an honor

to make your armor, Mother." She turned and saw William had one of the smiths helping him into his armor.

"You're right, Sweets, it's so light." She watched the smith, piece by piece, cover her love in the plate mail. When he was done, her heart swelled at the sight of him. He looked like a paladin, covered in blessed armor, and she knew they'd protect each other.

"William, you're amazing."

He smiled and held her hand. They stood admiring each other when a deep, bellowing horn sounded in the air. Lily turned and saw the other men stand straight and listen.

"They're here." She heard one of the soldiers say. Her heart began racing. *It's time* she thought as she picked up her helm and started for the door. *Blessed Otto be with us,* she thought as they walked into the morning light.

———

It took them a good half hour to reach the top of the hill, where Giles told the group to meet him. He and Leo wore plate mail as well. Giles's armor was more worn but sturdy, whereas Leo's looked almost as new as hers. The young man's eyes were wide as he stared at the army now barely five miles away. Lily noticed Nora was standing next to him, holding his hand tight in new black leather armor. Krag was next to Giles, pacing and staring at the encroaching army. Ivelios was given the duty of protecting Siddah and their son. If the worst happened, he was to get them out and to Ardenry by any means. Koizumi was jumping and stretching like he usually did before a fight, and Artemis zoomed over on his carpet. Sobrei was standing with the rest of them, dressed in heavy armor and carrying a flag with his sigil on it, an orc fist with a crown above it. They were thirty-five thousand strong, plus two dragons and their riders. Less than half the number they needed.

"I cannot thank you enough for your help, all of you." He held a hand to Giles, "The use of your cavalry will be instrumental in winning Lord Raventree." They shook hands, and he turned to Lily. "I dreamed about you for five years, Mother. I knew the moment I saw your face that you would be the one to free me. I wouldn't be here if it weren't for you." He leaned down and kissed her cheek and felt a blessing.

"Thank you, Sobrei," she whispered. They all watched as he turned to the enemy army and held his flag up high.

He took a deep breath, and his voice carried across the field. "I am Sobrei Re'vall, the true ruler and true God of Dal En Val! Five years ago, those who worship that false emperor on my throne took me and proclaimed our rule was over! But I am here now, ready to take back my throne, take back my city and give the people of Dal En Val the ruler they deserve, and make sure that the human on my throne and those who worship him never hurt another living soul! If you put your arms down and recognize my sovereignty, you will be spared! Join us in giving glory to Dal En Val, the glory it truly deserves!"

Lily watched as he started glowing with his own holy power, and Leo gasped. "They're marching." She looked out at the army and realized about ten thousand of the orcs were moving toward them. But they were holding their swords out in a gesture of fealty.

"No, Leo, they're joining us." The orcs walked across the field and kneeled at the base of the hill. They were ten thousand stronger, but it still wasn't enough.

Giles sighed. "All right, Mother, let's get into position." She nodded and followed him to the back of the front flank.

Nora and Mal walked by, and she reached out, "Nora, Mal?" They stopped and turned to her. "I have a favor to ask."

CHAPTER 12
RETURN OF RE'VALL

Lily stood in her gleaming armor, looking at the enemies' army with William behind her. *So many of them,* she thought. It seemed hopeless, but it was her job to keep hope alive, and she prayed she could. As she wondered how they would all make it, a small, delicate hand slipped into hers and gave it a squeeze.

"Hello, Lily."

She turned and saw a familiar face framed by bright golden hair. "Hello, Golden One," she said with a smile.

"It's been a while since I've seen battle. Especially one so large."

Lily turned back to the approaching army. "Do we have a chance?"

Mirvana smiled at her. "There is always hope, Lily. You know that." She took a step and gracefully turned into a gargantuan golden dragon. "May the Gods be with you, friend."

"And with you, Mirvana." With that, she leapt into the air and flew back to her paladin.

"You failed to mention you were friends with a dragon, Sweets." She could hear the tease in his voice, and it helped her relax.

"I'll tell you the story when the battle's over. I promise." She felt him kiss the back of her head and knew it was time. Lily took a breath and raised her arms to the sky. "Blessed Otto, we battle to bring peace to the world, as backwards as that sounds. We ask for your blessing that this day goes in our favor. A false emperor sits on Sobrei's throne," her voice slowly rose above the din as she prayed, "This army must be defeated for him to be returned to his rightful place. Bless my soldiers with strength so they may stand strong. Bless them with courage so nothing they fight will turn their hearts!" The soldiers around her began banging on their shields. Apparently, it was how they psyched themselves up for battle, and Lily let herself get caught up in it. "Otto, bless my men to victory!" she yelled, and the men around her cheered.

"Otto!" They echoed her three times before the two dragons roared into the air and took off. She could hear the Burned Hand chanting, "Re'vall!" as they began marching towards the enemy. As soldiers moved past her, she turned and saw Giles riding up, the sigil of Raventree emblazoned on his chest with Leo at his side.

"May Otto bless you, my Lord."

"May he bless all of us, Mother. I hope to see you on the other side." Malice trotted after the soldiers, and Lily watched as Giles stood in front of his cavalry.

"Mother?" She looked up at Leo, "I know we'll win because you're here." Even though she was literally shaking in her boots, she managed to smile at him.

"Thank you for your confidence. Best go join your Lord Father." He nodded and quickly joined Giles at his side. As she stood at the top of the hill, the armies anxious for battle, she felt the peaceful presence of William behind her, ever stalwart, ever loving.

"William?"

"Yes, my love?"

"Marry me."

He put a hand on her armored shoulder and unsheathed his sword. "In every life we live, I will marry you." She quickly wiped a tear away so no one would see it.

———

Lily had never been part of a battle like this. She thought the fights she had been in with her group were bad enough, but when the enemy army finally reached hers, the sound was deafening. Metal on metal clashed together, and she felt her teeth chatter from the impact. Arrows came next, some sank into the ground while others found their targets. Men yelled out and fell to the ground around her, so she did the only thing she knew to do. She ran through the injured soldiers, making sure they wouldn't bleed to death, William behind her the whole way. He could heal a little as well, so she was glad for more than one reason that he was there. There were so many it was all she could do for them. She kneeled and pulled an arrow out of a soldier's leg, who screamed as his blood poured onto the ground.

"Blessed Otto, heal this man so he won't die of his wounds." She watched the blood stop, and his skin barely knit. If he moved much, it would rip open, and her healing would be undone.

The soldier sat up, he was breathing hard, and Lily saw his eyes go wide. "Mother, look out!" She turned and saw a large devil running straight for them. William roared and met the devil head-on. Her hands started shaking as she reached for the dagger on her belt. "Take my sword, Mother, please!" The soldier begged, but she couldn't. She knew it was too heavy. William slashed down, and a huge gash opened on the devil's leg. "I banish you in the name of Otto!" she yelled and put her hand on her glowing symbol. The devil laughed deeply but kept coming. Lily licked her lips and stood her ground, "You have no power here, beast!" It swatted William aside and lunged for her, but Lily stood her ground as the devil disappeared a mere inch away from her. She caught her breath and ran to William, but he seemed more concerned for her.

"Are you all right?" His eyes ran over her, but she was fine.

She shook her head and helped him to his feet. "He didn't touch me." They looked up and saw several devils around them stop fighting when their comrade disappeared. One pointed at Lily and said something in Abyssal before a few started running back to the enemies' army, but others started running straight for her.

Lily's eyes widened, and she held up her seashell. "Shit.

Otto, banish these monsters back to the abyss!" William stood in front of her, his sword sank deep into one of the devils, and it disappeared. Another devil, once again, disappeared when they would have overrun her. She had never felt such power and thanked Otto for the help as she started healing the soldiers. William stood straight, breathing hard when his eyes went wide. "Lily, run!" he yelled, and she turned as a devil with a great sword swung the wicked weapon at her. There was no time to move. Everything happened so fast, as the great sword hit her breastplate and shattered. Time seemed to slow down. She watched the formidable weapon break apart against her and looked up at the devil. Confusion flashed on its face, and Lily reached out and touched him.

"Begone!" Before he could react, he disappeared, leaving Lily standing alone, her outstretched hand touching the air. William ran up to her and turned her around, again his eyes searching for where she was hurt.

"Blessed Otto, what was that?" His voice was frantic.

"It broke. Its weapon broke as it hit me." She still couldn't believe it herself. William pulled her into a hug and kissed her forehead.

"Thank you, Otto."

———

The battle was chaos, orcs, devils, and humans clashing around her. She ducked from swords and felt dizzy when they managed to hit her armor, but more of them shattered in the wielder's hands. She had to remember to ask the smith what exactly he made this armor from if swords simply broke when they hit her. Her eyes spied a man about fifty feet away with an arrow in his leg, still fending off an Imperial orc while he lay exposed on the ground.

Lily held out her hand. "Otto, give me the power to help him!" Lightning streaked from her hand and hit the orc, who flew ten feet away and didn't move. The soldier dropped his sword as Lily ran over. "You'll be all right." She pulled the arrow out with a sharp yank, and he yelled and hit the ground with his fists. "Blessed Otto help me to keep his blood from soaking the ground." She prayed and felt Otto's love flow through her and knew he wouldn't die from this wound.

He picked up her hand and laid a kiss on her skin. "Thank you, Mother, thank you."

"You're welcome." She looked up and saw William engaged with a single devil. He was glorious against the huge beast, matching every move with incredible speed, but Lily could see he needed help, and she started running over. "Otto, give my beloved strength!" She prayed and watched as the devil tried to rush him, but William didn't move as their swords clashed together. Her love was too strong, and she watched him sink his sword into the creature's head, and it disappeared.

William turned and started running for her when an arrow miraculously found a space between his armor and sank into his back. He yelled out and fell to his knees. Lily screamed his name as she ran for him, but a rushing orc slammed into her, and she found herself flying away from him straight into a nearby melee.

She landed on her back, the wind knocked out of her, and as she struggled for air, another orc aimed his sword right at her. She managed to roll out of the way and pulled her dagger free. The movement kickstarted her lungs and she breathed in a ragged breath. She was surrounded by humans and orcs fighting to the death, pushing, flailing, and throwing. Her eyes could barely take it all in. She got to her feet and tried to run, but more orcs blocked her path. All the humans around her were hurting, yelling out in pain for whatever god they worshiped to help them. She raised her arms. "Otto, I beg you, help us!" she screamed into the air.

William watched helpless as Lily was knocked into a group of men and orcs and disappeared in the fray.

"Lily!" he yelled, but the pain from the arrow was stealing his strength. He couldn't move and watched as the melee got bigger. "Otto, I beg you, please help her!" He prayed, it was the only thing he could do. Suddenly, a huge pillar of bright light filled his vision, and he cried out as he covered his eyes. The sound of yelling filled the air, then suddenly stopped. He opened his eyes and saw Lily forty feet away, surrounded by dead orcs. The humans around her looked amazed and quickly left to find more foes. "Lily!" he yelled, and her head snapped to him.

"William!" She ran around the dead bodies. There had to be at least fifty of them. When she reached him, she grabbed the arrow. "Take a deep breath." He did when he breathed out, she pulled it out. He screamed, but the pain was gone in an instant as she healed him. He turned and grabbed her arms.

"I thought you were dead. I saw you disappear into the fight. You were gone!"

He looked up and saw she had a bad cut on her forehead. "I'm here now." He laid his hand over the cut and healed her what little he could. "Thank you." She helped him up to his feet. "We have more to do."

He nodded and followed her as she ran back into battle.

———

Nora and Mal took orc after orc out of the fight, working their way towards the priests of the false emperor. The battle had raged for so long that there was only one left, and Nora was glad it was the one Lily wanted. He was surrounded by the demons he had summoned and didn't look the least bit worried that she and Mal were coming straight for him.

"Is that the one Mother wants?" Mal asked. Nora spun and sliced her sword into the nearest orc, and his arm went flying about ten feet away.

The orc dropped to his knees in agony, and Nora calmly walked to Mal. "Yeah, that's the one." They approached the circle of devils, and Nora pointed her sword at the human in the middle. "You're a wanted man, Dante!" Nora wasn't sure why Lily wanted him, but she wouldn't argue. She'd give Lily this man or die trying.

He laughed. "Am I?" He raised his arms, and half the

circle engaged Nora and her friend. She had no trouble dancing around them, slicing into their red skin and watching their dark blood puddle underneath her while Mal sank arrow after arrow into them.

When they were finally gone, the hunters turned back to Dante. He didn't really look impressive to Nora, but knew power when she saw it. "Well, aren't you two just a pair of tornadoes?" Dante mocked them and pulled out a sword. "If I'm wanted, does that mean you can't kill me?"

"Alive is better, but I'm sure Lily could work around that," Mal said.

Nora watched the priest's eyes widen. "Lily? She's here?" he asked as he lowered his sword.

"Yes, she's here, and she's asked us to bring you to her."

"Has she?" He dropped his sword and raised his hands above his head. "Well, why don't we head that way now?"

Nora looked at Mal. He looked as confused as she felt. "Just like that?" she asked. Dante nodded with a little smirk, keeping his hands up. Nora shrugged her shoulders and started for him when Koizumi suddenly appeared behind the priest and hit Dante in the back with a sickening crunch that made the man crumble to the ground. "Koizumi gods, why did you do that?" Nora ran over and saw Dante was still alive but completely unconscious.

"I didn't trust him not to try anything."

Mal walked over and flung the unconscious man over his shoulder. "Let's put him somewhere safe."

———

The battle raged for hours, and the Raventree army, along with the Burned Hand and what troops Ardenry could spare, was enough to keep Raventree safe. But as the sun set, it was clear it was not enough to put Sobrei back on his throne. They could not advance towards Dal En Val, and when the last of the orcish army fled, Sobrei stood next to Giles. A little hurt, but he didn't seem to notice as they watched the two dragons make sure the Imperial orcs weren't going to backtrack.

"I thank you for your help, Giles, but I'm afraid it wasn't enough."

Giles sighed and nodded his head. "I know, I'm sorry."

"Don't be sorry, my friend. We did what we could, and your home is safe. I was foolish to think I would win my throne back after one battle. But I pray that my people will soon realize that I'm back and will rally around me."

"You're welcome to stay here until that time comes."

"Thank you, Giles."

Leo came walking up, his bloody sword hanging down at his side. "Did we win?" He looked exhausted and hopeful that the battle was finally over.

"In a way, son, but we didn't see the victory we needed."

He sighed and dropped his sword. "Then what was the point of all this?" Giles understood why Leo was so distraught. War without the desired outcome was rarely a happy thing.

"They needed to know we are still a threat and that their rightful king is alive. They'll come around soon enough, son."

"Leo!" He turned and saw Nora running up to him, breaking away from Mal, who was carrying some cultist priest over his shoulder.

"Nora!"

"Leo, you're okay!" She smiled as she jumped and wrapped her arms and legs around him, "I couldn't find you. I was afraid," He leaned back and held her face, it was streaked with dirt and blood, but he didn't hesitate as he pressed his lips on hers. Giles smiled and motioned for Sobrei to follow him.

"Let's go see if Lily needs any help."

CHAPTER 13
NEW DANTE

Lily and William helped each other out of their armor in their tent. They were both covered in bruises that they weren't aware of and knew the next day they'd hardly be able to move, but it was better than being dead. They sat on the bed and drank the water they desperately needed.

"What was that light?" he finally asked.

She knew what he was talking about. "It was a smaller version of holy fire aimed at the orcs. I could only do that once, so I figured it was time."

He laid a hand on her back. "I had no idea you were so powerful, Sweets," he kissed her forehead. "You are worthy of this temple Giles wants to build for you."

She gave him a little smile. "Thank you."

The tent flap moved, and she watched Nora step inside. "That man you wanted us to spare is tied up in one of the empty tents. Did you want to speak with him now?"

"I did, yes, thank you, Nora." She nodded and turned to William, "Will you come with me?"

He leaned over and kissed her cheek. "Wild orcs couldn't drag me away from you." She smiled and took his hand as they walked out of the tent.

"Hey, Lily?" They turned as Nora walked out of their tent, "Be careful around that guy. He's a real nasty piece of work."

"He didn't used to be." She sighed and walked over to the tent where Dante had been interned.

———

The full moon was bright, and a cool spring breeze was blowing through the air, making all the tents flap in unison. As

Lily and William walked to the edge of the camp, she passed by many of the soldiers who fought in the battle. A great number of them stopped and waved at her, and she managed to smile in return. A few that she remembered healing on the field kneeled where they were and laid their hands over their hearts.

She had never been so moved in her life and stopped in front of them. "You needn't kneel to me, gentleman."

"We saw how the demons just vanished at your touch, how their weapons broke upon you. Otto truly lives in you, Mother," one man said.

"It was Otto that banished them, not me. Thank Him for your lives." One of them took her hand and gave it a kiss before she walked away. She had never felt so loved or appreciated, it would have brought tears to her eyes, but she felt they shouldn't see her cry.

"They're right, though, Otto may work through you, but he feels you're special enough to do so." She patted William's hand, unable to find the words.

They saw Giles and Sobrei in the distance. The two sovereigns looked tired and disappointed as they headed their way.

"Lily, do you need help with anything?" Giles asked.

She shook her head. "No, I was just going to speak with Dante."

He sighed and laid a hand on her shoulder. "All right, well, we'll be around if you need anything."

He shook William's hand. "Thank you, my Lord," he said. Lily gave him a little bow, and Sobrei touched her cheek before they walked towards the extra tent they had set up for Dante.

Mal was standing guard outside of the tent and nodded as they walked up. "He's tied up good, Lily. He shouldn't give you any trouble."

"Thank you, Mal." She turned to William, "I just need a few minutes." She put her hand on his chest and could feel his heart beating wildly under her fingertips.

"Are you sure?"

She nodded. "He's tied up, it'll be fine."

He kissed her forehead. "If you say so. Mal and I will be right here if you need us." She nodded, and both Mal and William started pacing outside, letting her walk in alone.

It was dark. A single lamp in the corner was the only light, and she had to let her eyes adjust. When she finally saw Dante, he was indeed tied to a chair in the middle of the empty tent. His head was down, his chin resting on his chest, still unconscious from the fight. He was still wearing the dark red robes of his status that marked him as a high priest of this human emperor. She didn't see what happened to him. In fact, she hadn't seen him at all during the battle but was glad Nora and Mal managed to spare him.

He looked older than he did the day she said goodbye to him all those years ago, but he was even more fit. Dante was always muscular, but after taking care of himself, she could tell he was bigger in the shoulders. There always seemed to be a perpetual beard on his face when they traveled. But now, he was clean-shaven, and his salt and pepper hair was neatly cut. As she looked at him, she could feel how unnatural he was. Just being near him made the hair on her arm stand on end. Something evil lived in his heart, and she had to know how it got there.

Lily reached out and gently touched his head, healing him just enough so he would wake. She didn't want him at full strength in case he got free. She had no doubt that he could easily kill her.

He took a deep breath in and cleared his throat. "I knew it would be you," he mumbled and lifted his head. The light blue eyes she once had fallen in love with now filled her with dread and chilled her blood as they slowly looked over her body. She could practically feel his hands groping and rubbing on her skin.

"Stop that," she suddenly barked out.

Dante smiled. "What? I'm not allowed to appreciate your beauty?"

"No, you're not."

He gave a chuckle but didn't take his eyes off her. "You're even more beautiful than the day you chose that piece of shit over me." Lily sighed and crossed her arms over her stomach. He was trying to bait her, but she wouldn't let him.

"What happened to you, Dante? You left Salthole intending to find a temple, and then I find you a priest of this false emperor. Summoning demon after demon from the abyss? That's not who you were." She leaned down and got face to face with him. "What happened to you to make you this way? Just tell me."

He smiled a slimy kind of smile and tilted his head. "Oh, if you insist." Suddenly, his arms flew up, and the ropes fell to the ground. He moved much quicker than a wounded man should as he dragged Lily close and covered her mouth with his hand. Her eyes were wide with fear as she tried to push against him, but he was so strong, like an unmovable wall. *He was supposed to be tied up*, she thought as she felt his hand move around her waist and take her dagger out of her belt. "Nice, clean. I bet you've never used it on a person." He whispered and pressed the tip to her throat. "Well, there's always a first time for everything." She felt the tip flick quickly on her neck before a thin line of blood trickled down and stained her shirt. "If I let you go, will you scream?" He put the knife in one of his pockets, but she still didn't feel safe. But neither did she feel satisfied. She had to know. She felt it was a piece of a puzzle she might be able to solve. She quickly nodded, and he slowly moved his hand, and good to her word, she kept silent. But he kept his arms around her tight enough that it wasn't a loving embrace. She kept pushing back against him, but it did no good. His eyes still roamed around her as he leaned forward and smelled her hair. "Gods, I'd forgotten how intoxicating you are," he whispered. "You really are the most beautiful woman in creation." He sounded like he meant it, but his words didn't move her.

"Stop it," she snapped at him. "Tell me what happened."

His eyes darkened as he dipped his head and smiled at

her. "I'll admit that while I was with you, I was happy. I couldn't imagine a better life. But after Lavinia, when you couldn't bring yourself to be with me when you chose that—"

"Don't say another disparaging word about Henri." She hissed at him, and he stopped.

"You chose *him*. I was forced to find a new life. That new life was dangerous. The town I ended up in was dangerous, and one day we were attacked by the orcs." His eyes roamed over her once again, "And I was killed." He said it like it was no big deal and Lily's jaw dropped from a combination of shock and disbelief.

"Killed? When, how?"

"Eight years ago," He pulled her even closer. It was getting hard to breathe from the pressure. "I didn't really see who it was. I just knew I was dead. When I heard the call to come back, I quickly accepted. Some random priest of Alar had made his way to town and was helping in the aftermath, raising who he could. When I woke, I felt different. My thoughts drifted to you, as they often did, but you weren't important anymore. The only thing that mattered was that I had to go to Dal En Val and there I would find where I belonged. My life was now for the Shackled One and his bidding."

Lily gasped and pushed back against him, though it did little good. "The Shackled One? I don't understand, I thought you worshiped that false emperor in Dal En Val?" *How could this once loving man worship the Shackled one?* She thought it couldn't be possible.

Dante chuckled. "I do." He quickly reached out and pulled her face to his, his fingers clawing into her cheeks. He was so close she could feel his warm breath on her cheek. "They are the same," he whispered as he nuzzled her cheek.

Lily's eyes widened in shock as his words echoed in her mind, *'They are the same.'* "The seal," she whispered.

He pulled his head back. "Has been breached, you know this. He is slowly leaking out of his prison right under those pathetic paladins and empowering our Emperor." Lily was right. The Shackled One was making a bid for power in her lifetime. She felt her knees start to buckle, but she didn't dare show weakness now. She stared at Dante as he spoke. It didn't sound rehearsed, like he'd been waiting to tell her these things, and she could hear the truth in his words.

"Worshiping him, doing his bidding, gave me more power than I ever got from Otto."

She couldn't believe she was hearing this from him. "I never thought you could be an evil man, Dante, but then again, you're not you, are you?" She pitied the man he once was, that he was stuck in this body. She could mourn the priest who saved her life, who loved her enough to let her go, but this man in front of her was not that man.

"Well, I wouldn't say that," He held her chin between his fingers, "I have been wanting more power recently but hadn't figured out how to get it, and I think I know what's been holding me back."

She jerked away from him, his arms falling away from her. "Enough about power. Power isn't everything. Besides, you're going to be executed soon, so you wouldn't get to enjoy this 'new power' anyway."

He stayed put but smiled. "Don't you want to know what's holding me back?"

"No." She turned to the tent flap, "Ma—" His hand was clamped tightly over her mouth. His fingers dug into her cheeks as his other arm pulled her back against him, that wicked strength making her unable to escape.

"Uh-uh-uh, I'll not have you bring that orc in here, not yet. It's been so long since I laid eyes on you that I realize I'd forgotten how beautiful you are. The second I saw you spying on me, I remembered how much I love you. *That's* what I've been needing. A good woman by my side." She had to get to Sobrei and tell him who was really sitting on his throne. She twisted in his arms, his fingernails cutting into her face. She screamed, but with her mouth covered, it didn't do much.

"I know it's been a long time, Love," She closed her eyes tight at the sound of his favorite term of endearment, "but seeing you brought everything back." His arm held her tight against his chest. She tried kicking back but hit nothing. "Your beauty, your kindness and love." She felt his lips against her ear as he spoke softly. "I can't wait to sheathe myself into you. We never got to do that, did we." She screamed again and threw her head back and connected with his nose. Bones crunched, and she felt warm blood running down her back, but he didn't let go.

"Come back to Dal En Val with me, and together, we could rule the church. We'd have everything we've ever wanted because He will give it to us, I promise Love." The hand around her waist moved up as he groped her chest. She thrashed as much as she could, but the more she moved, the harder he squeezed. His hand stopped. "But it won't work, not unless you change too." He turned her around to face him, his nose was broken, and blood was pouring down his face. She could feel blood dripping down her own cheeks from his fingernails. He smiled so sincerely that it made her blood go cold. "I changed when I died, you see. When I bring you back, you'll be changed, too, and we'll be together forever, Love." She gasped and again tried to pull herself away from him. There was only one thing she could think to do, but she had never cast a spell without speaking and hoped Otto would hear her. She stopped struggling and laid her hands on his chest, closing her eyes in concentration.

He chuckled low. "That's it, I'll make it painless, I promise." She felt a hand go to the back of her neck, and she prayed, *Blessed Otto, please help me from this deranged man!* Her shell began to glow, and he gasped a second before they were surrounded by holy light.

William paced outside the tent with Mal. The smell of fire and death filled his nose, and he tried to ignore it. It was going to take months to erase the battle from the fields of Raventree, but he'd help how he could.

"So, who is that guy?" Mal asked, pointing back to the tent with a thumb.

"An old friend of hers," he crossed his arms over his chest, "she hadn't seen him in a long time."

Mal's eyes went wide. "She was friends with someone like that?"

He shook his head. "She said he wasn't like that when she knew him."

"Damn, wonder what happened." He pulled out an arrow and started twirling it between his fingers.

William shrugged and sighed. "No idea, I think that's why she wants to talk to him, figure out what happened."

"Well, it doesn't matter what he says. They're going to execute him anyway."

"True. But I think she just wants to know why he changed, not try and save him." It didn't make any sense to him either. People changed over the years, but to completely flip your personality, your god, it made no sense. He could hear men screaming in pain nearby, whether from injury or losing a friend, he couldn't tell. Those cries sounded the same to him, and he wished there was something he could do for them.

"You two fair okay during the battle?"

Mal nodded. "Oh yeah, well-oiled machine we are."

William tried to hide his smile. "Did she tell you they eloped?"

Mal's eyes went wide as his head jerked towards him. "What!" William laughed. "She did not!"

"Well, next time you see her, you should congratulate her."

The orc sat still for a moment. "Nora's married." He chuckled, "Guess my work's done."

William laughed, "That was your job, making sure she got married?"

He smiled, "No, making sure she found somewhere safe.

The married thing is an unexpected bonus."

"True." William turned to watch the sun set behind the trees as the birthmark on his hip began burning. He gasped and laid a hand over it.

Mal looked up at the noise. "You all right? Still hurt from the battle?

"No, I'm fine, I don't," Lily filled his mind, and he remembered what happened the last time his mark hurt. "Oh shit." He took one step towards the tent as Lily burst from inside. Her face was bloody, and she looked terrified. "Lily!" He opened his arms, and she ran into them. "Mal, get him!" The orc ran inside, and William looked down at her. She was breathing hard, and there were bruises and bloody fingernail marks on her cheeks. The front and back of her shirt were covered in blood, but he wasn't sure it was all hers. "Blessed Otto, please heal your most beloved servant," he prayed, and the bruises faded. "What the hell happened?"

Mal walked out of the tent, he looked pissed. "Coward teleported away."

William cursed and pressed Lily against him. "Let's go find Sobrei." She nodded and they started for his large tent, Mal behind them, his weapon drawn just in case. People stared at them as they made their way through the war camp. Where they were once smiling and giving her thanks, their eyes filled with worry.

William threw open the tent flaps. Sobrei, Giles, and a few of the other Lords were around a table looking at a huge map.

Giles looked up first and ran over to them. "What the hell, are you okay?" He gently touched her cheeks, and she hugged him. "What happened?" Sobrei moved over and laid his hand on the back of her head and healed her. The marks slowly faded from her skin, though the dripping blood remained.

"He got loose," she said, "The ropes just...fell away."

"Blessed Otto," William whispered, and she turned back into his arms. Even though she was safe, she couldn't stop shaking.

William kissed her forehead, and the feel of his lips calmed her heart. "Here, sit down." He walked her to a nearby chair and she sat as he kneeled in front of her, holding her hands.

Mal walked in, still looking pissed off. "He was tied down. I did it myself. I don't know how he got loose." He ran a hand over his face. "The knot was still done when I went inside. It was still tight."

"Where is he?" Giles asked, his tone impatient.

"He teleported away. I didn't even get a chance to hit him." Mal's shoulders sank as he walked from the tent.

"Who are they talking about?" Kale asked, his once gleaming armor still covered in gore.

"One of the priests of the false emperor," William said, "she wanted to question him."

Giles kneeled to her side, his hand resting on the arm of the chair. "Are you all right?"

She took a deep breath and nodded. "I'm all right." She looked up at the orc god. "Sobrei." She held out a hand, and he walked over and held it, his other hand going to her cheek. "That man on your throne, he worships The Shackled One. He's not just some random human they supplanted there." She watched as his eyes grew wide as his hand slid off her cheek, and she swore his green skin turned ashen. Sobrei put a hand on Giles' shoulder, and he turned to everyone else.

"Please excuse us." Everyone looked at each other for a moment then left the tent. The orc turned back to her. "Are...are you sure?" She never thought she'd hear fear come from such a powerful being.

"Yes, positive."

Sobrei sat on the ground. He sounded like the wind got knocked out of him. "That's who these Imperial cultists worship, The Shackled One." His breath shuddered out, "They must have found out." His voice was barely above a whisper.

"Found what out? Who?" William looked between the two of them, and she put her arms around him and pulled him close.

Sobrei sat forward, his head hanging down. "My throne, it is a direct line to our divinity. My family has used it for so long that we're now born with our innate divine abilities, and the throne strengthens us. But if someone else sat on the throne, someone who didn't worship us, they would grow strong with the power of their own God."

Lily squeezed her eyes shut. "The seal, it all makes sense now. They had to get rid of the cup so the throne could release him in a controlled manner, where *they* wanted him to go."

"What?" Giles looked between them.

Sobrei got to his feet and started pacing around the tent. "The Shackled One is making a bid for my throne. With that pretender of an Emperor, right now, it's helping him escape that prison under the Citadel, bit by bit. But if the right person were to sit on my throne, The Shackled One would immediately be in our world. Whole and powerful." William cursed and hugged Lily tighter.

"What kind of person would be the right one?" Giles asked.

Sobrei paced. "It's hard to say, a high-ranking priest, or gods forbid, someone who shared blood with him."

Lily looked over at him, horrified at the revelation. "Is that possible?"

Sobrei sighed heavily, "I would put nothing past him."

Giles sat back on the ground, his mind flying with the news. "Is there a way to cut that power off from the throne?"

Sobrei leaned against the table, Lily noticed he didn't want to look at them. "It's said if all our line dies, the connection dies."

"That's why they kept you alive," Giles stood and walked over to him, "They didn't want to risk the power not being in the throne."

Sobrei nodded. "I'm sorry I didn't tell you. I had hoped to keep some things to myself. But it seems that's not possible. Kill me, and it'll keep him from coming back."

"No," Lily got to her feet and laid a hand on his arm,

"Absolutely not. We will not sacrifice you like that. There has to be another way."

He laid his hand over hers. "I'm sure there is. We just can't see it yet. But I would gladly give my life to keep that abomination of a god off this world."

She reached up and put a hand on his cheek. "You shouldn't have to die for the world to live." She could feel his divine nature flowing around her, powerful and pure. There was no way she'd let him sacrifice himself like that.

He sighed and laid his hand over hers. "My wonderful, faithful friend. I shouldn't, but it may come to that." His hand slid off hers as he began pacing again.

Giles shook his head and got to his feet. "That information doesn't leave this tent," everyone agreed, and he took a step over to Lily and put a hand on her cheek. "I'm sorry we lost him."

"Don't be, we were woefully unprepared."

"For a lot of things, I fear." He sighed and started for the tent flap. "Rest, Raventree is safe and is waiting excitedly for its new temple and priestess to give us hope." She nodded, and he left the three of them, his shoulders a little lower.

Sobrei turned to follow. "I am glad you're staying. Raventree needs you." He left the two of them together, and William got to his feet and hugged her again.

"I can't believe this," he whispered.

"Me either. I knew. I just knew we'd have to contend with him in my lifetime. I wish I was wrong."

"What do we do now?"

She kissed his head and held him tight. "Live as much as we can while we still can."

CHAPTER 14
THE TRUTH COMES OUT

Lily sat in bed in the castle, unable to sleep. "Sweets," William whispered and sat up, "You haven't been up all night, have you?" The sun was starting to stream in through the curtains. She had been watching it slowly light the room for the last hour or so. Her mind was too busy with what Dante had told her about his death and resurrection.

"I think I need to thank Sobrei for more than just bringing me back."

"Do you?" He pulled her against him and started petting her head. She hoped it would help her relax. Her eyes were dry, and she could feel her limbs shaking from exhaustion. But she was herself. There was nothing else she could sense that she had been changed when she was brought back over a month ago. She was her usual self. But Dante, clearly something evil was in him, it made sense yet didn't.

Lily licked her lips and tried to gather her thoughts. "When I was in the Waiting Room, there was a spirit there. She welcomed me and told me I was going to be a little disoriented, but I'd be okay. I told her I had to go back, and she said if I did, to be careful because something has been trying to hitch a ride back with the recently raised. I forgot all about it until Dante said when he was brought back, he changed."

"Changed?" His hand kept running down her hair, and she could feel her body giving into sleep.

"He told me he died when the town he was in was attacked by orcs, and a priest of Alar brought him back. He said when he came back, he was different, changed. *That's* why he worships the Shackled One now. Something came back with him, changed him so completely he's no longer himself."

The hand on her head stilled. "You mean, something corrupted his soul so completely that he forsworn Otto and worships the most evil god the world has ever known?"

She nodded. His heartbeat was lulling her to sleep at last. "I think something is really wrong in the afterlife."

"I agree." He laid his head on hers and listened as she finally fell asleep. He said a silent prayer to Otto that Lily came back whole and unmolested. He thought back to the last person he had to search for, a young man who was also recently raised from the dead. His family said his personality flipped. He was no longer loving but filled with spite and hate, but they wanted him back. He found the young man in Ardenry, trying to force himself on a young woman. He fought back, and William was forced to kill him. He wrote what he found and sent a letter to the family, but he wondered just how widespread this was, how many people had been changed. More importantly, could they stop it before it became an epidemic?

CHAPTER 15
HOME AGAIN

Artemis was kind enough to teleport her and William to Fairwinds two days later. She felt strong enough to visit and to mourn her sister once again. They had to wait for the mage to have some time, so it was just after sunset when they appeared in front of her childhood home. The smell of the sea surrounded them, and Lily sighed happily. The lights were on in the house, so she knew her father was home. There were still flowers under the windows, and she smiled, wondering if anything had changed.

"Have you ever been to Fairwinds?" Her fingers laced with his as they walked to the front door.

"A few times," He looked around, "never for long, just to catch one boat from another."

"Well, I can't wait to show you around and show you off."

He chuckled and gave her cheek a kiss. "Did you want to get married while we're here?"

She nodded. "I'd like my father to be there and Father Wayman to do the ceremony."

"Maybe when we're done here, we can go visit my mom. Give her the good news."

Lily chuckled. "I'd like that." She knocked on the door and felt her heart in her throat when she heard footsteps coming to the door. It opened and she saw her father and her heart burst with love. "Papa!" He looked the same, straight-backed and proud, with streaks of grey in his hair.

"Lily!" She leaped into his arms, and he held her tight. "Oh, blessed Otto, you're all right!" It felt like his arms were shaking as he hugged her. He sniffed and when she leaned back and saw his eyes were tearing up, she expected that.

"Of course I am, I missed you so much, Papa."

"I missed you too. Come in, come in." He tried to sweep her inside, but she stopped him.

"Wait, Papa, there's someone I want you to meet." She took his hand and motioned to William. "Papa, this is—"

"Aunt Lily!" She stopped at the words she'd never heard before and saw a young boy standing behind her father. He looked to be around ten and had dark hair and familiar green eyes.

"Aunt?" She looked at her father and there was a look on his face she didn't understand, a mix of apprehension and joy.

The young boy ran over and hugged her. "I'm so glad you're here, Aunt Lily. My papa really needs you!" She hugged him back. Far be it from her to deny a child a hug, even if he was confused.

"Your papa?" She looked up at Etienne. "What did he mean by 'Aunt'?"

The boy looked up with a smile and started pulling her inside. "They told me you were my 'Aunt,' come on, Papa Rysden's in here." She stepped inside and had never been more confused in her life. She turned back to William, who shrugged. He was just as confused.

Etienne turned to him, still standing on the porch. "You might as well come in." He stepped aside and he walked in and held out his hand.

"Thank you, I'm William Voltain."

Etienne shook his hand. "Etienne Vale." William turned and saw Lily frozen in the doorway of a bedroom.

———

"My Papa's in here, please help him!" The boy begged and opened the door to her childhood bedroom.

"I'll see what I can do, but—" The first thing she saw was a man laying on her sister's bed. He had a wound on his side and could smell his blood. He looked near death, pale as a sheet, and his breathing was uneven. The woman next to him had a baby in her lap and her back to the door. She could only assume she was the boy's mother.

"Mama, Aunt Lily's here. She's going to help Papa Rysden."

The woman started to turn as Lily spoke. "Son, I'm not—" but the words caught in Lily's throat as she saw her own face staring back at her.

"Lily." It had been ten years since she heard her own voice and felt her knees weaken.

"Lavinia." She let go of the boy's hand, who ran over to his mother. Lavinia handed the baby to the boy, and they stared at each other for a moment before they ran into each other's arms. "I thought you were dead!" They said at the same time, hugging each other tightly as tears ran down their cheeks.

William and Etienne stood in the doorway, watching the embrace. "Lily thought her sister was dead. She said she felt her die," he said quietly.

"Same with Lavinia. She cast a spell, and we saw her being carried by an orc, covered in blood." He ran his hand over his mouth, "It was the worst thing I've ever seen."

William nodded. "It was an awful time. She was only gone a few days, thankfully." William's ear twitched when he heard another baby cry, and Etienne walked back to another room and came back with a baby girl. She looked to be around a year old, as did the one in the room. Twins.

———

The sisters took a step back and held each other's faces. "You're blonde," Lily chuckled through the tears. The last time she saw her sister, her hair had been dyed black.

"I am," she laughed back. "Not for lack of trying, I assure you." They both chuckled tearfully, and Lily wiped her cheeks. "Lily, I'm so sorry I hurt you. I was in a bad place, and I didn't know how to deal with my trauma. I was broken and hurting." The words fell from her mouth. "I didn't mean to hurt you like I did, but I couldn't control myself. I let the rage of what happened to me take over, and I regret everything I ever did to you. But I'm better now. Rysden helped me find myself, him and Kaythen."

Lily hugged her again. "It's okay, I forgive you, I hope you forgive me." While she didn't physically hurt her sister, the things she said, she had wished for years she didn't say them.

"I do, I do." They cried and stayed still, their arms around each other for a little while longer. Lily knew her sister was different, but she wouldn't let that stop her from having some kind of relationship with her, not now. Not after she felt her die, and the thought of being alone crushed her heart more than anything.

When they were able to steady themselves, Lily looked at the man in the bed. "Who's that?" Lavinia sniffed and took the baby from her older boy. "Matter of fact, who are all these children?" She said with a chuckle.

Lavinia put her hand on the older boy's head. "This is Kaythen, he's ten. Kaythen, this is your Aunt Lily."

"It's nice to meet you, Kaythen." She opened her arms, and he settled in them. She had a nephew. For the last ten years, she was an aunt and didn't even know it.

"It's nice to meet you too." He stepped back and Lavinia walked close with the baby boy.

"This is Davaros. We call him Davi. He's a year old, and" she pointed behind Lily, who looked to see her father holding a baby girl the same age, "that is Desdemona. We call her Desi."

"Twins?" Lily gasped and looked between the two of them. The girl, Desi, waved her little hand at them, and Etienne walked in and handed her the little girl. "Blessed Otto." The little girl hugged her, and she gave her a kiss on her head. Davi leaned forward out of Lavinia's arms, and she passed him to Lily, who held both of them. She kissed Davi's head and reveled in their little hugs. "Oh, Lavinia, you're so blessed," she said, trying to speak around the tears.

She gave a little smile. "We truly are."

Kaythen pulled gently on her sleeve, and she looked down at him. "Can you help Papa Rysden?" She remembered him saying something to that effect when he pulled her into the room. She looked over at the bed and saw the symbol of the Shackled One around the man's neck and sighed. "Help him, Auntie, he can't die," Kaythen begged.

Davi leaned back and reached for Lavinia. "Hep hep!" The little baby babbled as Lavinia took him.

"I did hope you'd show up before," Lavinia sniffed and bit her lip. She always did that when she wanted to keep from crying. "But I thought you were dead, so I steeled myself to watch him die from his wounds."

She handed Kaythen his sister and sat next to the man. "What happened?" Her voice was quiet. Healing a follower of the Shackled One was something she never thought she'd do.

"A cursed wound, my healing doesn't work, and no one at the temple is strong enough."

"Not even Wayman could heal him?" Her eyes went wide in shock. If Wayman couldn't heal him, she wasn't sure she could either.

"Father Wayman died six months ago, I'm afraid." She heard their father say from the doorway.

"Oh no." Her heart broke at the news of her mentor. She hoped it was peaceful. "How did it happen?"

"In his sleep, thank Otto," her father said, "Leif is the head priest now," he said with a small smile.

"Leif, really?" That news lifted her heart a bit. She'd miss Wayman but knew he had lived a long, blessed life and was grateful to have been taught by him.

Etienne nodded. "They've been here for a week," he said as he and William walked further into the room, "He's just getting worse." She turned back to Rysden. His eyes were closed, and she could tell he wouldn't last much longer. His heart was slow, and his breathing uneven.

"Who is he to you?" she asked Lavinia, her eyes studying

him with the scrutiny of a healer.

"My husband," she whispered. "My children's papa, the love of my life." Rysden took a deep breath and moaned in pain but didn't wake.

Kaythen crawled onto the bed and lay across Rysden's chest. "Please help him, Aunt Lily." Lily nodded and closed her eyes. She laid her hand on his chest and cast the strongest healing spell she knew and a sleep spell so he'd continue healing after the blood loss. She removed the bandages, and everyone saw the wound was now closed and his breathing became normal.

"Thank you, Lily." Lavinia put her hand on her sister's shoulder.

She nodded and got to her feet. "He needs to sleep. He's lost a lot of blood, but I'm sure you know that."

Kaythen crawled off the bed and hugged her again. "Thank you, Aunt Lily."

She wrapped her arms around the boy. "You're welcome, Kaythen."

Lavinia stepped up and laid a hand on her son's back. "Why don't we go into the living room and let your papa rest."

"Okay." He turned and picked up his sister and followed the women into the living room, leaving Etienne and William in the room.

"Surprise," Etienne said with a smirk as he turned to William.

He chuckled. "Lily and I are getting married, surprise." Etienne laughed and patted his shoulder as he turned and followed the group into the living room.

———

Half an hour later, dinner was ready. Kaythen had the roast beef on a plate and was cutting it up. "Like this grandpa?" he called out.

Etienne walked over and nodded. "Yep, just like that." Lavinia was sitting on the couch, watching Kaythen with a smile on her face as Davi wiggled around in her arms.

She leaned over to Lily. "Papa is absolutely in love with these children," she laughed. "I think he's been lonely." Lily sat next to her, Desi on her lap, her little hands playing with the rings on her necklace.

"He has been, I'm glad he finally has grandchildren."

Lavinia reached out and put a hand on her arm. "You and Henri didn't have children?" She shook her head, not surprised she knew about Henri. She assumed their Papa told her. "I'm so sorry."

"It's okay. William and I will have children." She looked over at him. He was tickling Desi's chin, who was giggling like a maniac.

"You've moved on?"

She nodded and turned to him. "William and I are getting married." He looked up and gave her a wink. She turned back to her sister. "Will you stand up with me?"

Lavinia smiled in a way she had forgotten she could. "I would be honored."

Lily looked down at Desi and kissed her head. "These little sweeties can come too."

"I've never been to a wedding." Kaythen sounded excited at the prospect as he set some plates out for everyone.

"It'll be a small affair, but I'm glad you'll be there."

"Dinner's ready." Etienne clapped his hands once, and William took Desi from Lily and walked over to the table and put her in one of the two highchairs.

"There ya go, little missy." She squealed and started banging on the little table in front of her. Lavinia put Davi in the other one and he laughed as he watched his sister. Lily sat next to Desi, and Lavinia sat next to Davi while Etienne sat next to Lily and William, and Kaythen took the chairs across from them.

"Lily, would you bless this meal?" She smiled and held out her hands, her father taking one, and she took Desi's, who promptly started chewing on her fingers. She looked up at Kaythen, who was staring at his mother.

"Is that okay, Lavinia?" She asked her.

Lavinia nodded and looked at her son. "Kaythen, it's okay." He nodded and took William's hand and his mother's.

"Blessed Otto, please bless this meal that we never thought would happen but are grateful for. Thank you for Desi and Davi, and Kaythen, I hope to get to know them. Thank you for letting Lavinia trust our father enough with her family, and thank you for granting me the power to help their father. Thank you for family this day, in your glorious name." A blessing sank into everyone at the table. Etienne and William smiled, Desi and Davi sat still, Lily assumed they had never felt such a thing, and Kaythen looked wide-eyed at his mother.

"Mama?" He sounded scared.

"It's all right, Kaythen, it won't hurt you," she said. He nodded but still looked nervous.

"I'm sorry if that frightened you Kaythen, but know a blessing given in love will never hurt anyone." He nodded, and she could tell he had calmed down. His shoulders weren't as tense, and he smiled at his siblings. Etienne put some potatoes on the babies' highchair plates, and both of them quickly put their hands in them and brought them to their mouths.

"Oh goodness." Lavinia seemed shocked at how messy they ate, but Etienne laughed.

"They love my mashed potatoes." They passed food around, and when everyone's plate was full, Lily looked around the table as they ate and talked and couldn't believe this was happening. She was having dinner with her sister and her children, her niece and nephews, her father and her betrothed. She felt tears in her eyes as she looked at them. *Thank you, Otto.*

———

When dinner was over, everyone moved to the living room. "I'm going to check on Rysden." Lavinia handed Davi to Etienne and disappeared into the room.

"Well, what shall we do?" He asked Davi, who smiled and put his hands on his grandpa's face.

"How about a song?" William looked between them.

"Oh yeah!" Kaythen smiled and hopped in his chair. William chuckled and cleared his throat.

"Hold on tight to your roots, in the garden where your family tree takes root, it's the branches that sustain you, guiding you through the storms that you'll go through."

Lily smiled. She had never heard him sing before. He had a lovely tenor, strong and sure.

"We're bound by a common thread in our bloodline, we're connected through the highs and the lows. We'll stick together. That's how it goes."

Desi and Davi turned to listen to him, bouncing in Lily and Etienne's lap, their little arms flailing in the air.

"We'll weather the storms, we'll face the sun, we'll keep on dancing till the day is done."

He stood and held out his hand to Lily, who giggled and got to her feet, Desi still in her arms. He slid an arm around her waist and started dancing around with them.

"Our roots run deep. Our love is strong in our bloodline, where we belong. In our bloodline, we're forever intertwined."

Desi laughed and put her hands on his cheeks, but he didn't miss a beat.

"Through the laughter and the tears, in every heartbeat's rhyme, we'll walk this path together, side by side, In our bloodline, where love will always reside."

He gave Desi's little hands kisses then kissed Lily's cheek. "I had no idea you could sing," she said as they sat back down.

"Lily, you're marrying a man and didn't know he could sing?" Lavinia said as she walked back into the room, satisfied with how Rysden was doing. "How long have you known him?" She crossed her arms over her stomach as she stopped behind her.

She looked over at him. "Um," he made a cringing face, "three months?"

"Lily!" She gasped, trying not to laugh.

She looked back at her. "Lavinia!" she teased, and the two sisters laughed. "When you know, you know." She looked at William, and he gave her a wink. Desi and Davi laid their heads on their prospective cuddler's chest and yawned.

"I think it's time for bed." Lavinia took Davi from her father and ran her hands through his golden hair.

"I have an idea." Lily looked over at her sister, and she smiled.

———

The twins laid on their backs in the backyard, the stars shining bright above them. Davi was sleeping on Lavinia, and Desi was sleeping on Lily. She was in baby heaven.

"This was a good idea," Lavinia said quietly.

"It was. So, how did Rysden get hurt?"

Lavinia looked down at the baby and gave his head a kiss. "The group I was with, they were assembling items that were to be used in some kind of ritual. It wasn't until later I learned what that ritual was. Another priest of the Shackled One met up with me and said he and a few other high-ranking priests had plans for Kaythen."

Her heart leapt at that, and an instinct she didn't know she had flared with anger. "What?"

Lavinia nodded. "They wanted to put the soul of the Shackled One in him. They wanted to take him to Dal En Val." Lily gasped and snuggled Desi closer. Sobrei's words rang through her mind. With the perfect vessel, he would be back, and they thought her nephew was that person? "When I heard that, I snapped. I know He gives me His power, and I know I owe him a lot, but...I didn't want...I don't want to lose my sweet boy. So, we dropped the children off here and tracked them down and killed them. But Rysden was hit by a curse before we left, and I couldn't heal him. I brought him here hoping someone could heal him, but it was clear you were his only hope, and before I sent you a message, I felt it," She turned and looked at her, "I felt you die."

"I felt you die as well. I think I felt other things over the years too," she said, thinking back to that horrible feeling that plagued her when they reached Shaldoon ten years ago, "but when I felt you die, it hurt, it physically hurt."

Lavinia nodded. "It did, like something was ripped out of me. My hope for Rysden died with you. So, when I saw you walk in earlier...." she almost looked ashamed, "it was the first time I thanked Otto for anything."

"Vinia," she reached out and took her hand, "you don't have to feel bad about that. Your love was dying. It makes people do crazy things."

Lavinia chuckled. "It does. I'll always be grateful to you for that."

"I did it for the children. They don't deserve to lose their father like that."

"They don't." She squeezed Lily's hand and let it go.

"Can I ask you something?" Lavinia nodded. They had been apart so long. Lily wasn't surprised there were a million questions between them. "Earlier, you said you lost yourself in rage and pain. What rage, what happened?"

She sighed, and Lily saw the determination in her eyes to finally tell her the truth. "When I left home, I was guided by my God to find a priest who could teach me to worship Him properly. I found that priest outside of Buckland, Tanri, was his son." Her eyebrows went up at that. She remembered the young man who clearly loved her sister and always wondered how Tanri came to be there. "My former master taught me well for two years. Then one night, he tried to rape me," Lily gasped and squeezed her sister's hand, "but the Shackled One saw how worthy I was and gave me the power to kill him before he could. I didn't know how to process what happened to me, and I acted out in the worst way."

"Gods, Lavinia, I'm so sorry that happened to you."

She shook her head and sighed. "It's all right, Lily, you didn't know, and I didn't tell you. I should have. Perhaps things would have turned out differently if I had. But Rysden and Kaythen helped me crawl out of that pit I was in. I feel a lot better now."

"Good, I'll be forever grateful to him for that alone. Where is Tanri?" She remembered the young man seemed to act more like a servant than lord of the manor when she visited. Perhaps he left after she married Rysden."Is he dead?"

"Hmm, sort of."

"Sort of?" Lavinia took her hand back and waved it. An instant later, Tanri appeared, see-through and ethereal. He was smiling at Lily.

"What..." She didn't know what to say. He looked like a specter.

"I realized my feelings for Tanri way too late, so I asked Him to give me the power to keep him. This is the result." She watched him look over at Lavinia for a moment, then back at her, the same smile on his face. "He says he wants to thank you for being the only one who encouraged him to love me."

"Oh, well, you're welcome. I'm sorry you died."

He again looked at Lavinia, then back to her. "He says it's all right. If this is how he gets to spend eternity with me and Kaythen, he'll gladly do it."

"Kaythen?"

"Tanri is Kaythen's father." Lily's eyes went wide as she looked at him and could see the familiar ears and nose of the little boy.

"Oh, I'm so...I'm."

Lavinia smiled. "It's all right. You don't have to say anything." Even after all these years, they still had more in common than they realized.

"So, Desi is Rysden's?"

Lavinia nodded. "Yes. Kaythen was so excited he just knew she'd be a girl. He was practically drooling for a little sister," she giggled. Lily swallowed hard and looked over at Davi sleeping peacefully on Lavinia.

"And Davi isn't your blood?"

Lavinia's head snapped over to her. "What? Of course, he is, don't be ridiculous." But Lily gave her that look that told her she knew the truth. "Davi is mine. I love him. He and Desi were born on the same day...how did you know?" she whispered.

She reached over and gently touched his cheek. "He has dimples." Lavinia's eyes narrowed in confusion. "Dimples are only passed on from parents who have dimples. You don't have them, and Rysden doesn't have them either."

Lavinia sighed. "You were always too smart for your own good."

She chuckled. "Where did you find him?"

She kissed her son's head, and he made a little noise but didn't wake. "His mother was either a sorceress or a dragon. Either way, she crash-landed on our front lawn the day I went into labor with Desi. She shifted into a human form, and Rysden brought her inside, and she was...wasn't going to make it, and she told us, 'Don't let my son die,' so we didn't. Rysden cut him out of her before she took her last breath. He was chubby and crying, and he had a little golden tuft of hair, and I fell in love with him in that moment. I told Rysden I was going to keep him. There would be no arguing with me about it. He teased me, saying I was about to have a baby, and I wanted to add another?" They both chuckled, "I told him they'd be twins, no one else but us would ever know, and they'd grow up together. Desi came that night, bloody and screaming into the world. Davi started crying then, and I knew Rysden was thinking, 'What am I getting into.'" She smiled at the memory. "I told him to bring me Davi, and he put him on the bed next to me. I wrapped Desi in a blanket, still attached to me, and laid her next to him, and they both stopped crying. It was like they knew, they were both safe and would be loved."

Lily sniffed, and a tear rolled down her face. "Vinia," she sighed, "I want to know them. I want them to know me."

She nodded. "I'm sure we can work something out."

But Kaythen, she was worried about him, that he was in danger. "About Kaythen, and what they wanted with him,"

Lavinia shook her head. "They're all dead. It was only a few of them that wanted to do that, and they're gone, so he should be safe."

"Until someone else gets that in their head, why him?" Lavinia sighed and was quiet for a long while. Lily wasn't going to push her. She had to tell her in her own time.

"Somehow, they found out that Rysden wasn't his father," she whispered and gave Davi's head another kiss. "Remember I said Tanri was dying, and I asked Him for the power to keep him?" Lily nodded. "He granted my wish that night, but in return, I had to bear him a child. Tanri is his father, but He…He made it possible."

"Oh, gods," she whispered, but Lavinia didn't elaborate. Lily understood the implications. "I will do whatever you need to keep him safe."

"Even though you know who his father is?" She looked over at her sister, tears in her eyes.

"He is *my* nephew. I will protect him with my life." She stared at her sister, her own face looking back, and could tell there was something else she wasn't telling her. But she didn't care because she would do anything for her nephew. No matter who he was related to.

"Thank you." Lily nodded. Lavinia cleared her throat, "Can I ask *you* something?" Lily nodded again. "That priest that came with you when you visited, his name was Dante, yes?"

She sighed and rolled her eyes. "Yes."

"I knew that it was him," Lavinia scoffed, "I never liked him. He annoyed me, but now that he's in Dal En Val, worshiping my god, he's insufferable. He's insisting every worshiper come to the orc city. We're delaying until we absolutely have to. I don't want to raise the children there." Lily told her what happened in Raventree, and she rolled her eyes. "Bastard. I'm glad you're alright, but I haven't heard anything about beings attaching themselves to the recently revived but I'll do some digging. If I find anything out, I'll let you know."

"Thank you."

Lavinia looked up at the sky. "William seems like a good man. I'm glad you're happy."

"I am."

She scoffed. "Three months, really?" Lily struggled to hold in her laughter.

———

William and Kaythen helped Etienne with the dishes while Lily and Lavinia visited outside.

"So, William, tell me about yourself," Etienne asked.

"Let's see, I'm originally from Raventree. My parents bought a farm about a week from the Citadel when I was five, so I grew up there. Six years ago, I started working for Lily and Henri, finding people who had been kidnapped. It was fulfilling work, and I seemed to have a knack for it. A few months ago, I got a missive from Prince Max about joining this expedition to find Sobrei Re'vall, in which we were successful."

Etienne dropped a plate in the water, and it splashed onto Kaythen, who laughed. "You found him? Where was he?"

"Cultists had him in Cyranar."

"Whoa," Kaythen looked enthralled, "I want to go there, it sounds like it has lots of hidden treasure."

William smiled at him. "I'm sure there is. Currently, Efrits hold the city, so you'd have to get past them."

His smile disappeared. "Efrits? I've never seen one before."

"That's probably for the best young man." William dried his hands and threw the little towel to Kaythen, who caught it as he jumped in the air. "Anyway, I'm going to be the Huntmaster for Lord Raventree, and Lily is going to run her own temple."

Etienne smiled as he sat down in a chair by the fire. "Her own temple. I knew she'd have one, one day."

William sat on the couch, and Kaythen sat on the rug in front of the fire. "I know we haven't known each other long, but

I love your daughter, and I will make her happy the rest of her life."

He nodded. "Good to know. I imagine you've been through a lot together in the brief time you've known her. I know traveling creates tight bonds and lifelong friendships. I'm glad she met you."

He smiled and Etienne noticed for the first time he looked apprehensive. "She was kind of hoping you'd move to Raventree with us."

He laughed. "A fisherman in a landlocked country, I don't know what I'd do with myself."

"I said as much. But hopefully, when we have children, you'll change your mind."

The corner of his mouth tilted up as he looked at Kaythen. "More grandchildren, could Otto bless me more."

———

Rysden opened his eyes and was surprised at how well he felt. It didn't hurt to breathe, and he didn't smell blood anymore. The room was bright. It must have been daytime. The last thing he remembered was the babies crying at night.

"Papa!" He turned just as Kaythen hugged him. "You're all better!" He hugged the boy and saw Lavinia sitting next to the bed, smiling.

"Hello, my love," she said, tears in her eyes.

"How?" He was amazed and kissed Kaythen's head. "I thought I was dead." There were footsteps, and he looked at the door and saw who could only be her sister walking in, Davi on her hip. "Lily." She slowly walked over. He could tell she was being cautious. "You're alive."

She nodded. "I am. Kaythen begged me to heal you, so I did. How do you feel?" Davi reached out for him, so she sat him on the bed, and the baby crawled up and laid on Rysden's chest.

"Perfect." He kissed Davi's head. "Thank you." She nodded. Tiny, unsteady, slapping feet walked into the room, and Lily moved aside as Desi walked in, her little arms reaching up.

"Da-da-da-da!" She screeched, Lily laughed and picked her up and put her on the bed with her siblings.

"My little darling, you're walking!" Rysden kissed her cheeks, "I'm so proud of you." But Desi continued to babble, not listening to him.

"Do you feel well enough to eat?" Lavinia asked him.

He nodded. "I feel like I was never hurt."

"Good, we have a busy day ahead of us." He looked at her, his eyebrows up as the sisters smiled at each other.

———

That afternoon, Lily was wearing a lovely peach dress that her friend Miri had found. She had baby's breath in her hair and delicate white slippers on her feet.

"One more thing." Miri handed her a box, "William got you a present."

"Oh, he didn't have to do that." She opened it and saw a lovely silver bracelet with blue and silver stones on it. "It's gorgeous." Miri helped her put it on.

"I'm sure he said the same of your gift." Lily snickered. She had given her father a dagger to give him, their initials engraved on it. It was more decorative than utilitarian, but it would look good on his side. Etienne walked into Miri's room. He had on a cream-colored tunic, and his hair was pulled back from his face.

"You look lovely."

"Thank you, Papa." She got to her feet, and he held out his arm.

"Ready?"

"Ready." She slipped her arm through his, and the three of them walked from the store down to the park.

———

Under the big shady tree in the middle of the park, everyone was gathered, waiting for Lily, Miri, and Etienne. William was standing by the priest who would marry them. His name was Leif, and he and Lily grew up together and wouldn't let anyone else perform the ceremony. Lavinia was standing across from him in a blue dress. Her husband was feeling better and standing nearby holding Desi while Kaythen was holding Davi. The babies were enthralled by the huge tree and how the wind made the leaves make noise. William could tell there were a few people who were surprised that Lavinia and her family were there, but no one said anything rude to them.

William looked up and saw Lily standing with Etienne down the makeshift aisle. She looked radiant in a peach colored dress, and saw Miri had given her his gift. He was proudly wearing his dagger on his side as well. Miri walked down first and stood next to Lavinia. William clasped his hands together and watched Lily and her father walk towards him. His heart was thundering, but he couldn't stop smiling.

———

Lily felt like she was floating down to William. The smile on his face was pure delight. He looked handsome in his dark green tunic, and she could see her gifted dagger at his side. Her father walked her up to him and gave her cheek a kiss before standing off to the side.

She stood in front of William and took his hands. "Hi," she whispered.

"Hey, Sweets." Her smile got bigger as he called her that.

Leif stepped up before them. "I welcome you all here as we come to witness Lily Marcel and William Voltain join their souls in holy matrimony. I have known Lily my whole life and I am honored beyond measure that I get to marry her, to her soul mate. William, I've known two days," people chuckled, "but he's blessed beyond measure, and I know he will give her a good life. That together, they will create a life blessed by Otto." He looked at William, "If you would, please tell Otto why you wish to be Lily's husband."

He gave a little nod and gave her hands a squeeze. "Sweets, from the moment I met you, I loved you. I wasn't sure I should, but try telling a young person 'wait' when they're in love," people chuckled, "I knew you were a worthy woman, funding people to find the lost, and I was honored to meet you. But when I saw you in that dining hall, that dark green dress making your eyes shine, I later told Max I felt like I had been hit by a carriage." She smiled at that. "We have been through some tough times the last few months, but also some good and even great times, and I can't wait to experience what else life has in store for us. I will provide, protect, and love you and whoever else comes along," he gently touched her stomach, "for the rest of my life, and every life after, this I vow." She squeezed his hands as a tear fell from her eye.

Leif turned to her. "Lily," she looked over at her friend, "you know what to do," he said with a wink.

She laughed and wiped her tears away. "William, the first time I saw you, you radiated such peace I couldn't believe it. I soon learned your heart was kind as I told you things I've never told anyone. I could feel my soul calling to yours like we'd known each other forever. We braved horrors that no one should and lived. We fought against Dal En Val, and though we didn't get the victory we needed, we won peace for our new home. I love you, William, more than I ever thought I could love a person, and I cannot wait to start our lives in Raventree. I will love you with my entire being for the rest of my life. I will protect you and provide for you the best way I know how, this I vow." Leif smiled and stood between them, the white shell already filled with blessed water.

"William, do you promise to love, cherish, and protect Lily for the rest of your life?"

"I do." Leif held up the shell, and he took a drink.

Leif turned to Lily. "Lily, do you promise to love, cherish, and protect William for the rest of your life?"

"I do." She drank deep of the blessed water.

Leif put the shell aside and stood behind them. "Otto brings us together for a reason. Clearly, these two were meant to be. It just took a bit to get here." They smiled at him. "I want you to remember this day, who is here celebrating with you, and know they love you as you love them. And whenever things get hard, never forget the love you feel for each other this day. In Otto's name, I pronounce you husband and wife. Lily, kiss that man and kiss him good!" Everyone laughed as she wrapped her arms around him, and they kissed without a care in the world.

———

That night, the family was sitting around a fire in the backyard, resting from the day. The newlyweds held hands as they spoke quietly to each other. Etienne was watching his family, a proud smile on his face.

"We need to get back home," Rysden said, taking Lavinia's hand.

"I know." She looked up at Lily, William was whispering in her ear, and she was giggling. "Tomorrow." She bent down and picked up two rocks. "Lily?" She looked up from William, a smile on her face. "Can I talk to you?"

"Sure." She stood, and they walked into the house and sat at the kitchen table. "You're leaving." It wasn't a question.

"Tomorrow. We need to get back home and make sure Kaythen stays safe."

"I understand." Lavinia held the rocks she took from the garden and held them in the palm of her hand. Lily watched as she cast a spell on them. Something like fire blazed around them and then disappeared.

"Whenever you want to see me, just hold this in your hand and squeeze. I'll feel the other heat up. Same with mine." She took a piece of paper from the living room and cut her finger with a dagger.

"What are you doing?" But she didn't answer as she drew a rune on the paper with her blood.

"This will get you into our house in Ardenry. Number twelve on Oakenwald, just put it against the door, and it will open for you. That's where we'll meet. That's where we'll take our children to know each other."

She gently took the paper, not wanting to disturb the rune. "Really?"

Lavinia nodded. "I don't know how long we can do this, but we'll try."

"We will."

———

Two weeks later, after visiting with her father and William's mother, they teleported back to Raventree and walked to their room in the castle.

Lily was exhausted but didn't care. "Well, I guess we better start on this blessed life we're supposed to have."

She teased as he picked her up and laid her on the bed. "I know just how to start."

EPILOGUE

4 years later:

Lily stood at the newly finished temple door and held up her shell. "Blessed Otto, I consecrate this temple and this land in your name. May it stand the test of time and bring the citizens of Raventree peace and happiness in challenging times." She felt the blessing fill the temple and turned to the people of Raventree. "The temple is now complete!" She threw her hands in the air in triumph, and the people cheered as they started filling in to look around.

All the seashells that made up the dais were imported from Fairwinds. The light pink marble floor was specially picked out from the quarry outside of Salthole. It was the only temple for Otto in the world that had that marble. Lily smiled at how the people awed at her temple as she walked down the steps to the courtyard. Giles had set up a little party to celebrate the milestone, and almost every citizen of Raventree, human and orc alike, had come to pay their respects. She walked up to Giles as he stood next to a big table covered in food. They watched happily as the people admired the lovely building and began praying to Otto. Children were running around playing, it was a peaceful sight.

"This was a good idea," Giles said with a smile.

Lily chuckled. "Yes, it was. It's a shame Leo and Nora couldn't be here."

"Well, they're having fun at the Citadel, I imagine. Dragons for him and weapons for her," he said with a smile. Lily knew Giles missed his adopted son and his wife, but there was no way he could tell him to stay home when Leo's dream was to become a dragon rider. Since they had been there for six months, she assumed they were letting him train.

Sobrei walked up and shook Giles's hand. "You've done good, my friend."

"The workers did an excellent job, with Lily's input, of course." Giles rarely took credit for much. He was entirely too humble to be a Lord, but he pulled it off well. Sobrei leaned down and gave Lily a hug. She always felt his holy power when he was close, and over the years, more of his people had come to Raventree, making his power grow little by little.

"Your temple will be the pride of Raventree Lily," he said affectionately.

"Not my temple, it's Otto's, but yes, it is rather wonderful, isn't it?" She couldn't help but smile, the temple was complete, and tomorrow, she would do her first sermon inside.

"Mommy!" She turned to the sound of her oldest son Foster and picked him up before he ran into her legs. Lily giggled and twirled them around as he squealed happily. He was going to be a tall man there was no doubt. Four years old, and he was taller than all the other children his age.

"Hello, my boy, how are you?" she asked in between cheek kisses.

"Mommy, you gots a letter!"

"I do?" She had no idea who would write to her, but when she saw William, he did indeed have a letter in his hand. "Is that for me?" she asked as he walked up and kissed her cheek.

"It is Sweets. It's from Mother Ranella." Lily put Foster on his feet, who quickly climbed up into Sobrei's arms. The orc god proceeded to toss the little boy in the air, filling the air with Foster's happy laughter.

"Where's Christopher?" Lily asked as she broke the wax seal with a satisfying snap before she unfolded the paper.

"Your father's got him. He's having fun with the baby chickens." Lily looked over at the little petting zoo one of the farmers had set up next to the temple and smiled. Her rollie polly boy was laughing as the fluffy chicks hopped around him. He had just turned two but still hadn't shed his baby fat, making him look younger than he was. "The temple is a wonder, Sweets, I think Otto favors you." But she didn't hear her husband. Her attention was stolen by what was in the letter, which she read over and over. She didn't want to misunderstand. She almost didn't want to believe it. "What's it say?"

Lily folded it back up and put it in her pocket. "Apparently, the church in Ardenry wants me to be the new Pontiff for Otto." Both William and Giles gasped at the news. Being Pontiff was like being Otto's voice on the prime. It was an incredible honor, but she wasn't sure if she wanted it.

"Lily, that's incredible!" the smile on Giles's face was happy and proud.

"Sweets," William smiled a little, "that's... I'm so proud of you!" He hugged her and kissed her cheek again.

"William, I don't know if I want it." His face dropped in shock. Every priest should want this honor, so she understood his confusion.

"You don't?"

She shook her head. "I need to think about it."

Giles laid a hand on her shoulder. "Good, you think about it. Maybe you could just visit and talk to them about it."

She nodded. "That's a good idea, Giles, I think I'll do that."

"Well, whatever you do, Lily, you will bring peace and enlightenment to the people." Sobrei gave her a smile.

She felt William give her arm a little squeeze. "We'll go wherever you go, Sweets. Don't let us hold you back."

She smiled and held his hand. "You would never hold me back, William. You're my husband and father to my two wonderful, miracle children. My life is complete with you no matter what I do." She silently prayed to Otto for the strength to be able to turn Him down, she just couldn't leave Raventree, not anymore.

Karen Thrower was born in Tulsa, OK, and still resides there with her husband, daughter, and cat. She graduated from The University of Tulsa with a BA in Deaf Education in 2005. She is a member of Oklahoma Science Fiction Writers and has served in several capacities, such as President, VP, and is currently Facebook Wizard. She has been published in various genres since 2018 and was included in the bestselling anthology 'Secret Stairs: A Tribute to Urban Legend' in 2019.

www.ingramcontent.com/pod-product-compliance
Lightning Source LLC
Chambersburg PA
CBHW021518240626
47154CB00002B/690